LONER LIFE
◆ IN ANOTHER WORLD ◆

Loner Life in Another World (Light Novel) Vol. 3
© 2020 Shoji Goji
Illustrations by Saku Enomaru
First published in Japan in 2020 by OVERLAP Inc., Ltd., Tokyo.
English translation rights arranged with OVERLAP Inc., Ltd., Tokyo.

Seven Seas press and purchase enquiries can be sent to
Marketing Manager Lianne Sentar at press@gomanga.com.
Information regarding the distribution and purchase of
digital editions is available from Digital Manager CK Russell
at digital@gomanga.com.

Seven Seas and the Seven Seas logo are trademarks of
Seven Seas Entertainment. All rights reserved.

Follow Seven Seas Entertainment online at
sevenseasentertainment.com.

TRANSLATION: Eric Margolis
ADAPTATION: Veles Svitlychny
COVER DESIGN: Kris Aubin
LOGO DESIGN: George Panella
INTERIOR LAYOUT & DESIGN: Clay Gardner
COPY EDITOR: Meg van Huygen
PROOFREADER: Jehanne Bell
LIGHT NOVEL EDITOR: Kelly Quinn Chiu
PREPRESS TECHNICIAN: Jules Valera
PRODUCTION MANAGER: Lissa Pattillo
EDITOR-IN-CHIEF: Julie Davis
ASSOCIATE PUBLISHER: Adam Arnold
PUBLISHER: Jason DeAngelis

ISBN: 978-1-64827-457-2
Printed in Canada
First Printing: October 2022
10 9 8 7 6 5 4 3 2 1

LONER LIFE
◆ IN ANOTHER WORLD ◆

NOVEL

3

**TELEPORTATION MAGIC
FOR THE CRYING GIRL**

WRITTEN BY
◆
Shoji Goji

ILLUSTRATED BY
◆
Saku Enomaru

Airship

*Seven Seas
Entertainment*

CHARACTERS

CLASS REP

Leader of the student council for Haruka's class. Has known Haruka since elementary school.

HARUKA

A high school student summoned to another world. The only member of his class not to receive a cheat skill from God.

ANGELICA

The former emperor of the Ultimate Dungeon. Haruka used "Servitude" on her. Also known as Miss Armor Rep.

VICE REP A

One of Haruka's classmates. A cool beauty prone to glaring at guys when they do something stupid.

VICE REP B

One of Haruka's classmates. Widely beloved as the most popular girl in the class. Fierce on the battlefield.

VICE REP C

One of Haruka's classmates. An excitable tiny animal who longs to grow up into an adult. She's like a class mascot.

QUEEN BEE

One of Haruka's classmates. Leader of a group of four fashion-obsessed girls. Former model.

STORY

Haruka, a loner, was summoned to a fantasy world along with the rest of his class. Even after defeating a plot by the math genius Tanaka to acquire all his classmates' cheat skills and reuniting with his classmates, Haruka felt like the girls still mocked him too often. In order to find an item to raise his sex appeal, he set off for the Ultimate Dungeon, but he got caught in a trap and fell to the lowest floor. He threw himself into battle against the final secret boss, the dungeon emperor, and despite being completely overpowered, he managed to eke out a victory thanks to his Servitude skill.

With the help of the enslaved Dungeon Emperor, Angelica, Haruka managed to escape from the dungeon. However, he didn't notice that the skeleton monster he enslaved had transformed into a beautiful blonde, blue-eyed girl. Angelica learned to speak, and they began to learn about each other and deepen their bond.

FANTASY WORLD TELEPORTATION. Teleportation magic. If I could get books from back home, maybe I'd be able to figure out how it worked, but those bookstores were totally out of reach now.

To Teleport perfectly, I would have to figure out my current coordinates, right? But where in the world am I?

If I just concentrated on a vague location and used Teleport like they did in fantasy stories, I'd probably die. More likely, I would dissolve into nothingness. *I can't focus at an atomic level!*

Nonetheless, Teleport was still a magical ability. I could wrap myself in magical power, reinforce it, and shift my position forward, but that was the best I could manage. Giving it my all, I could barely move. Even so, I didn't always move in one piece, and the human body did not take kindly to teleporting in parts. I did have Revival, but that didn't lessen the pain. Plus, I got the feeling that Revival wouldn't bring me back from the dead.

Sometimes my Magic Entanglement skill activated Teleport on its own, so I started getting used to it, but not enough to feel in control. I was still a long way off from being able to calculate the coordinates of my destination in my head.

The tomato-like fruits were important, but I had to focus on calculations. At the very least, I could now deliver objects where I wanted them to go without moving. There was no online book delivery, so why did it feel like I was setting up my own delivery service?

It's not like I could make it in time, either way.

An insurmountable distance. At least I could establish the coordinates. Her ring let me do that.

I wanted to get close enough to minimize the margin of error. In the meantime, I did some mental math: I would need to transport a particular quantity of tomatoes to manufacture my own ketchup.

I wanted chili peppers for chili sauce, too. Wild tomatoes came from South America originally, so couldn't there be a plant that tasted like chilis around here somewhere, too? As much as I wanted peppers, though, I also wanted to ensure I had enough time to perfect my teleportation calculations. But time was the one thing I didn't have. Finally, I had to determine how much space I would compress.

"Damn, why does it have to happen that fast?" I said, "It took me by surprise. Is teleportation seriously just another form of compressing distances?! That's all it is?!"

I was just chasing after another girl in the end. So, why did I go through so much misfortune and anguish looking for my missing sex appeal?

This time, I had to do my best not to make the girl cry. If she did, my precious sex appeal would plummet even further!

LONER LIFE
◆IN ANOTHER WORLD◆

DAY 39
NIGHT

Apparently, there's an enormous gap in my popularity among my friends vs the outside world?

**INTERLUDE:
OMUI GUILD**

AFTER MANY DAYS constantly on the go, I was exhausted. Guild work had never tired me out this much before. But I supposed we should be thankful for all the business. It was the first time I was this busy, and I beamed with pride.

Yet again, that boy was the reason for all of us at the guild working overtime. The merchants had lined up to put in their spellstone orders first thing in the morning.

More and more merchants spent bigger and bigger mountains of cash to buy our spellstones. Merchant guilds that previously wouldn't have deigned to travel here even if Duke Omui got on his knees and begged now groveled to get their trade permits. The guild bustled, and the whole town reaped the massive profits.

Up until now, all guild members had to risk their lives hunting down monsters in the forest, thinning out the monsters emerging from the dungeon. Despite that, there were never enough adventurers for the amount of work. With only a few merchants visiting town at any time, there was hardly any reward for those who put their lives on the line.

But now, at last, we could compensate those adventurers—their poor equipment never matched their true might. We had lost so many lives already, but now that we could supply proper equipment, more adventurers would survive and more would sign up. My heart ached when I thought of the many lives lost before today.

The guild master didn't have a choice before. He commanded us to defeat monsters, protect the people, and defend the town. No matter how dangerous the job, he had to give the orders. He couldn't just give up.

Duke Omui sent out as many soldiers as he could spare to protect the town, even deploying his personal guard. He sent aid to the guild even when it cost him dearly. Yet, there were never enough soldiers. We didn't have enough of anything. There was no way to have enough resources when you were up against the massive dark forest and the ancient Ultimate Dungeon.

More people lost their lives than were protected,

so we had to do our best to provide recompense. Back then, there was only tragedy and despair in our domain's future. My eyes welled up with tears when I thought of how hope had finally arrived in Omui.

It was one boy who banished all our misery and brought such profit and prosperity to our city. As a mere level 9, he defeated a fierce group of Mega Greenwolves, rescuing Ofter and his party. Then, despite being unable to join the guild due to his low level, he exchanged a mountain of spellstones. He even saved Duke Omui from danger. He was the savior of our city.

That unknown, black-haired lad never spoke. Then, the largest monster rampage in history erupted, the worst ever known. It was led by no less than a powerful orc king. We had no chance of defeating them. Our town and its surrounding villages would've all been destroyed if not for that black-haired youth and his companions. They all had black hair and black eyes, and they all had high levels with unbelievably strange and powerful skills.

Although they likely had nothing to do with this kingdom, much less our little city, they were willing to put their lives on the line to protect us. Later, we found out they were only sixteen years old. No one would fault them for running away at that age. In fact, as much as we wanted to yell at them to run for their lives, we had no choice but to bow our heads and ask for their aid.

We waited for the hellish onslaught of death, but no monsters appeared.

The black-haired boy got to them first. We didn't have a single casualty—that single boy massacred every last monster. He didn't even bother looting their weapons or spellstones. Then, he decided not to tell anyone about it. Instead of boasting, he kept completely quiet. Before anyone realized, he had single-handedly eliminated the most dangerous monster rampage of all time, without even a scratch to show for it.

That's why we were so busy.

I could hardly recognize any of the adventurers anymore with their fancy new equipment. The old gear was trash by comparison. They were all clad head to toe in rare, top-of-the-line equipment sought by the most discerning adventurers.

It was hard to believe for a guild that used to be so poor. Thinking about how many of our dead companions we could have saved with our current equipment was enough to make anyone weep bitter tears. It was impossible not to imagine it—not grieve for them.

The person who gave us these weapons and equipment was none other than that same lad. He apparently looted this gear from a horde of level 58 Frogmen from the labyrinth and gave them to the guild as thanks.

Lost in the Ultimate Dungeon with no one to help, yet he obliterated the monsters of the dungeon by himself. He climbed up a hundred floors, alone.

He donated tons of spellstones to the guild, saved the lives of countless adventurers with his potions, freely given, and he provided our poor town with clubs so even the weakest had a hope of defending themselves. He single-handedly transformed our town—that lone, raven-haired boy.

No one had a chance to praise him, to uplift him, to give our thanks. He didn't even get paid, yet he saved us all.

We only knew his group by their appearance—black hair and black eyes. When he donated the Frogmen's tridents to our city, Duke Omui broke down into tears. Each tear signified a life of those lost, the soldiers who could've been saved with those weapons. He wept with gratitude for the boy who nobody really knew.

I was no different. I thanked him and tried to tell him that we couldn't accept such a large quantity of high-grade weapons, but he pushed them on us and vanished, leaving me bowing my head in thanks over and over again.

I would never forget what Duke Omui said next.

"All of a sudden, our dying, hopeless town has become a place of joy. For a people who have known nothing but sorrow, it is the first miracle we have ever known."

As he spoke those words, tears flowed freely down his cheeks. The whole town broke out in tearful smiles and laughter.

That boy had saved all of us without any praise, thanks, or reward. A black-haired boy named Haruka.

Due to his cursed skills, he had yet to reach level 20, leaving him unable to form a party. Even after fighting so much and slaying so many monsters, he was still under level 20! He couldn't wield proper weapons or equipment either, so he was reduced to fighting with a wooden branch, without a party, and burdened with his awful skills.

Rather than reward him for his goodness, we did nothing. He was still unable to become an adventurer, and he still fought alone.

He saved our town, our entire domain. That boy gave us hope for a new and brighter future.

It may have been impossible to fully repay him, but that didn't mean that we could just leave him in such a state. *No, of course not!* But how were we supposed to reward someone who didn't seek titles or status, and was entirely self-sufficient? I had no idea what we even *could* do for him.

He always complained about not having money, but that was because his money was spent giving life to Omui. He had endless reserves of wealth, weapons, equipment, even medicine...and it made our city rich. What could I do for a boy who wielded a humble wooden stick, wore a leather bag and the clothes of a commoner, and fought entirely alone?

No matter how busy things got, or how much work I had, I couldn't stop thinking of him.

Everyone in Omui was rewarded with happiness, yet that boy received nothing, remained cursed, and fought alone. The thought of the boy with black hair, laughing with his black eyes, haunted me.

Suddenly I'm a criminal for having too many pheromones.

WHEN I LEFT MY ROOM, all the other doors were ajar, and through them, I saw...people glaring at me.

"Uh, good morning? What's up?" I said.

Hang on, what was up with all this glowering? D-don't tell me this hotel provides wake-up glare service?! I don't wanna know how much that costs every month! Who the hell put that in the lodging contract?

"Good morning! Last night sure was fun!"

All the doors slammed shut in unison. Did they hear us last night?

I had set up a sound-proof barrier around the scene of the crime. Besides, Miss Armor Rep didn't even make much noise, just a tiny bit. *My god, her voice...*

Unless—could it be? Don't tell me the girls peeped in my room with Presence Sense!

21

They couldn't have seen or heard what was going on, but they could still figure out what was happening, like watching shadow puppets. *This is a serious invasion of privacy!*

And I was an innocent minor, no less! Even though I had Jupiter Eye, I always did the decent thing and avoided looking at them in the bath and everything!

Yes, despite immense temptation and anguish, I managed to resist. *I swear!*

We did both leave from the same room, so there was no use hiding it. I wasn't really trying to be discreet in the first place, but my classmates' reaction put me in a tight spot.

At least for now, Miss Armor Rep had no desire to be released from my Servitude skill. Since she was still technically my slave, she couldn't be called my girlfriend, either. *I sound seriously pathetic.*

Maybe that didn't necessarily disqualify her from being my girlfriend! She did say, "I like you," after all. It was pretty much in a whisper, but she said it!

Plus, the status conditions in this world never really reflected reality. I was still a NEET, a shut-in, and a loner, and she was still the former dungeon emperor. I shouldn't have been able to use Servitude in the first place!

It almost felt like she became my mistress or something. Sure, I haven't had a girlfriend yet, but I ended up getting a mistress first! *How the hell did that happen?* Still, it seemed like she wanted to stay with me forever. *Lifelong service for a NEET?*

I couldn't really remember what we talked about. Conversation with her was an uphill battle to begin with—it kind of collapsed from the start, eroded by the tidal wave of urges that motivated this teenager to engage in more *physical* forms of communication. Our conversations never lasted long. There was nothing I could really do to explain the situation.

I suspected being together forever made anything acceptable, but the situation cost me a lot in terms of reputation.

More specifically, it was going to tank my sex appeal! The girls whispering, "She's not even his *girlfriend*," were fatal wounds, beating me while I was already down!

To be fair—they were right, I did have fun. I had no objection to that statement, absolutely none whatsoever. I had a freaking amazing time! But my classmates treated me like a pariah because of it.

The sharp, judgmental looks were making Miss Armor Rep self-conscious, too. Was this bullying?

It was pretty baffling that they would dare to bully the all-powerful emperor of the Ultimate Dungeon. I'd never heard of someone beating the crap out of their bullies yet

still getting bullied. Maybe in this world, the real victims of bullying were invincible warriors? I guess they were kind of like nerds...and I definitely bullied *them*.

There was an oppressive atmosphere hanging like storm clouds over our class in the dining hall. At least it was time for breakfast. *Yes, the solution to all my problems!* When I whipped up a fried fish meal, all the girls seemed to lose the ability to glare at me instantaneously.

It was fried fish with soy sauce and white rice, after all. Back on Earth, folks said that young people in Japan didn't care for rice anymore, but my classmates were clearly an exception as they shoveled heaps of sticky rice into their mouths. If I tried to take it away, I'd probably lose a hand. I reckoned that next time they'd start clamoring for miso soup.

Thanks to all the profits from the dungeon expedition, my classmates' pockets were heavy with coins, and I raked in ridiculous profits from the meals I cooked every day. I had bought tons of ingredients, locally sourced and hella cheap, so I had plenty of stock. Thanks to Holding magic, I could effortlessly make food for large groups, so I was totally ripping them off.

"I was thinking about going back to the dungeon," I told Miss Armor Rep. "Wanna come? You can stay if you want. I know you were the emperor, so it probably brings back bad memories, not to mention all the stairs involved."

Unexpectedly, she did want to go. I would've thought she'd want to steer clear of that darkness. I wanted to test something out in the labyrinth. If it went badly, at the very least I could make sure Miss Armor Rep got back safely.

When we reached the dungeon, Miss Armor Rep glared at the entrance. Or maybe there was a hint of pride in that look. Did seeing her old domain please her or something?

"Well, I put in a lot of work converting the entrance into a smooth, modern ramp, so it's, like, way more welcoming, y'know? Really ties the space together, right? I mean that grandiose stairwell was just intimidating, yeah?"

Huh? Miss Armor Rep seemed displeased. She was giving me a dirty look, so I guess I shouldn't have started renovations without consulting her. I didn't see anything wrong with just overhauling the first floor. I mean, there were literally a hundred more.

We went down the first thirty floors with not a monster in sight. Using Presence Sensing, I detected nothing further down.

"Didn't my classmates say there were still monsters left between the 30th and 46th floors? Where'd they go?"

Miss Armor Rep nodded.

I couldn't feel anything down below. Did someone defeat them?

I figured some adventurers must've stopped by to make some money. I didn't really care. I just wanted the treasure chests.

I found a hidden chamber on the 30th floor, but the treasure chest only had a "Profession Medal: Job Enhancement." Hey, we were both unemployed! How would a NEET get enhanced, anyway?! Would I become even more bored and lazy? *Oh, well, onward and downward.*

There was another hidden room on the 36th floor. The hidden rooms remained almost entirely undisturbed. Treasure chests existed outside of these hidden rooms, but they only held consumables like potions or money, never anything rare or unique.

That's why I beelined for the secrets. As usual, the one on the 36th floor wasn't locked or trapped.

Inside: "Demon Ring: Enslaves demons (up to 3)."

They're already all dead! I thought.

Considering the intended dungeon route, I was definitely supposed to get this ring to enslave the Demon Swordsmaster! It was obvious foreshadowing—but it was way too late for that! If I was meant to find this, then I shouldn't have gotten dropped to the bottom floor!

Even though the progression would've made sense if I did the floors in order, sending me down that pitfall totally broke all the event flags. It would have made perfect sense to enslave the Swordsmaster and acquire his Heavenly Sword of Gathering Clouds without fighting. Instead, I bludgeoned the Swordsmaster to death and stole his sword. Finding the Demon Ring now was pointless! A waste!

I was leaning against slotting it into my gear, unsure if it would ever have any use. On the other hand, I had six slots remaining in my Ring of the Destitute, having only fused the Trap Ring ("Automatically deactivates traps") in one slot. If it ended up being a waste of space, I could just take the Demon Ring out again. In any case, I was likely to forget it even existed, so for the time being I decided to slot it in.

Thus far, I hadn't found a suitable offering for the insatiable goddess, Miss Armor Rep. If we didn't find anything good, I'd have to buy her something when we got back to town.

On the 41st floor we found a shield.

"Bladed Shield: Attack bonus (small). Defense bonus (small). Magic defense (small). Shield Bash +ATT."

ATT is short for Attack, I guess?

If it instead meant +ATTENTION, I definitely didn't need more of that. I had to sell this junk ASAP.

The effects seemed good, but they were all "small." Did an attack boost to Shield Bash mean that the shield could do piercing damage? There was a sort of blade attached to the bottom tip of the shield, but was it for defense or offense? *I'm definitely selling this one,* I decided.

On the 45th floor, we found the "Shirt of Temptation: Seduction bonus (large)." Yeah, that one was no good. That wouldn't help my sex appeal in the long run. It was as sleazy as a skill like Mesmerize. All I needed was a little pheromone ring to make me more appealing, not something as criminally perverse as this thing.

Right? There's no way this shirt wouldn't make me look like a creep.

Maybe it would've boosted my popularity, but I had to seal it away forever. Not that I really wanted to use it in the first place. Plus, wouldn't the effect end as soon as I took off the shirt? That would cause problems, although I could surely come up with some bedroom roleplay scenarios to get around it!

I couldn't use it, but I couldn't sell it either. I had no choice but to seal it away.

"Not even any monsters to fight," I said. "What do you want to do? Check out the 100th floor? Kind of like a homecoming, yeah?"

Miss Armor Rep didn't sound interested. I supposed a place cloaked in eternal darkness wouldn't feel particularly nostalgic for her, either. Maybe she wouldn't mind if I converted it into an underground bathhouse?

It didn't feel like ordinary darkness down there—it was more like the total oblivion of death. I couldn't feel the presence of life, not a single breath. It would be best for everyone if that darkness disappeared.

I didn't find any good loot in the dungeon, but at least I could pawn all the junk. Besides the Shirt of Temptation, that is. The medal and the shield were fine, if I wasn't unemployed, and I could wield weapons besides my stick and the Heavenly Sword would've scored a great haul, but alas.

We didn't find anything for Miss Armor Rep either, so I had to buy her something nice when we got back. It was probably a bit past lunch. How did anyone keep track of time down here, anyway?

We killed some time ambling through the town, buying everyday necessities and miscellaneous things for Miss

Armor Rep. We checked in at the Adventurers' Guild and heard that adventurers and soldiers had indeed finished off the rest of the monsters in the dungeon over the last couple days. No wonder there wasn't anything besides the secret treasure rooms. Fine with me. It made our trip easy.

Since we were already there, I decided to ask for intel about other dungeons. Normally they would only tell other adventurers, but they made an exception for me. Maybe the gift of fruitcake changed their minds. Besides, I made sure not to ask the tight-lipped Receptionist Rep. She would probably find out later and get annoyed, but for now, the adventurers looked pleased with their cake. Yikes, I saw her lurking in the back!

Miss Armor Rep and I had a pleasant shopping trip, cheerfully peeking into stores that caught her eye. Throwing money around was probably much better for her health than being cooped up alone in the dungeon. At this rate, she was going to buy up the entire town, but at least she was healthy and safe.

After some more shopping, we went back to the inn.

Since all my classmates were there, I asked if anyone was interested in buying the Profession Medal or the Bladed Shield. The items were, surprisingly, in demand.

The medal in particular was a hot commodity, as the job enhancement it offered was supposedly an extremely rare effect. Whatever, I definitely didn't want to boost my unemployed status.

"Then let's do an auction," I announced, "Let's start with a minimum price of one thousand eles, who's in?" I did the shield first.

"Three thousand!"

"Five thousand!"

"No, six thousand!"

"Hey, I'll do nine!"

"Ten!"

"How about twelve thousand!"

"I'll do...fifteen!"

"No, twenty!"

"Twenty-one thousand, twenty-one thousand!"

Even the girls who didn't use shields couldn't help getting in on the action. Vice Rep A definitely used dual swords.

"One hundred five thousand, how about it?"

"I'll do one hundred ten thousand!"

"One twenty!"

"One twenty-five!"

"One forty!"

"One fifty...one fifty-five!"

"Two hundred!"

Caught up in the frenzy of the auction, the price surged ever higher. Strangely, the nerds were quiet. They loved weapons like this, so why weren't they jumping in? They seemed to be grinding their teeth furiously, but restraining themselves from giving any bids?

The price went to 250,000, 260, 280, 290...

"Three—three hundred thousand!"

"What?!"

In the end, one of the twin telephone pole girls won the auction. She wielded a giant shield, so it made sense. It suited her, but 320,000 ele for a shield was absurd . The twin telephone pole girls pooled together their money to win the auction. I decided to toss in some potions as freebies.

Then for the medal, the nerds went all out from the start and won. Even though the starting bid was a thousand ele again, they bid one million ele right off. No one could beat it, and they won just like that.

They must've spent all their money combined. There was no doubt why—they were going to give it to the Guardian to max out his forcefields and protect their heads. I'd have to figure out a new way to burn their hair off.

LONER LIFE
◆IN ANOTHER WORLD◆

Your Presence Detection going up by three without even fighting is definitely abnormal.

EMERGENCY GIRLS' MEETING, commence!

The girls piled into the bath for the emergency meeting. We surrounded Angelica and began interrogating her in earnest.

"What did you say to him?! You actually said something?!" everyone shouted.

"If he did anything to you, we'll destroy him!"

She looked troubled at first, but then smiled radiantly. Her beauty was so overwhelming, it was almost terrifying to behold. When her perfect features broke into a smile, we were all entranced.

There was just one thing that we were dying to ask: How did she even manage to communicate with that king of incomprehensible ranting? How was it even possible? And then...did something happen? *Tell us, tell us!*

"I s-said...th-thank you."

Apparently, she hugged him tightly as she said it. It was a pure, honest expression of her feelings. But she chose to say it to Haruka-kun when he was totally unprepared, naked in the hot tub in his cave.

"So action *was* necessary! I knew words wouldn't work!" I shouted.

Even Haruka-kun couldn't turn that situation into a joke. Seeing the body of a girl as dazzling as Angelica's standing before him, he was like a deer in the headlights. She overcame his senses. She could express how she truly felt, and he could respond in kind.

As she wept and expressed her thanks, as she told him she wanted to be with him forever, he gently stroked her head. *So he* is *capable of kindness.*

"That's so adorable!" Vice Rep C said.

Angelica blushed under our questioning as she recounted what happened next. Apparently, it was unbelievably amazing. Haruka-kun was apparently...the dominant sort.

"That's almost...sexy?"

We pried every last detail from her, the bath getting steamy with the descriptions.

I mean, she was alone for so long—alone for an eternity. Unlike that so-called Loner who kept insisting that he was a mere background NPC, she had been truly isolated, alone in that darkness. No wonder she seemed thrilled just to talk to us.

As we listened with rapt attention, she told us everything, even the smallest possible detail. Everyone flushed bright red and sank deeper into the baths. We collapsed when we got back to our rooms, rose up in excitement and collapsed all over again. Only a dungeon emperor could describe *that* in such titillating detail, using sound effects and metaphors, and when she lacked the words, hand gestures. We definitely got TMI, swooning from the heat of the story more than the bathwater.

Her phrasing was clumsy, but she was oozing with joy. She seemed to melt away as she remembered last night, closing her eyes in rapture as she spoke. Her dreamy expression was so enticing, and her gestures left nothing to the imagination as they conveyed her raw, vivid sensations.

It was too much. Too much, way too much, every time we uncovered our faces, she overwhelmed us again. We all came back for more, even as she blew us to bits. Heaps of maiden corpses lay strewn about. *Is this a dungeon emperor's true power?!*

It was extreme, to say the least. But she seemed like she wanted to talk about it.

At least she was finally happy.

Before, she only waited for an end to her sorrow. Then, all at once, her misery crumbled, her destiny was trampled, all reason was torn asunder, and she was dragged out of that dark place and given a joyful new lease on life.

That's why Angelica was so beautiful—her happiness flowed out of her with every word, every gesture...and we were all drowning in it.

We practically drowned, dizzy from the steam and the heat. *If you catch my meaning.*

We returned to our rooms, shocked by the climax of the girls meeting. All of us, pure-hearted maidens, swooned over the many explicit details...Haruka-kun was too much! He made a formerly undead immortal dungeon emperor feel like she was going to die!

"But she said it was good, right?" Vice Rep B said.

"That's what she said..." I responded.

"That's nasty!" added Vice Rep A.

"She felt like she was going to die! As an immortal!" yelled one of the mean girls.

In spite of it all, Angelica was obviously happy. And she seemed just as pleased that she could talk with us all now.

Having exhausted her endless emotions, Angelica went off to Haruka-kun's room with that same bewitching smile on her face. Everyone's Presence Detection was bound to level up tonight, no matter how careful they were. My Presence Detection had already gone up three levels!

"Angelica sure seemed happy." I said, still blushing.

"I mean, how could she not be after all that? Of course, she is!" said a girl from the Athletics club.

"She said they were entwined...is that how it works?"

"Of course! That was entwining! Entwining!"

"Her smile was so lovely, happiness just poured out of it."

"Yes, it was pouring out...along with a lot of other things!"

"She said she felt like she was flying? Flying?! Did he use flying magic on her?"

"She's supposed to be a monster, right? That's why he used Servitude."

"That's hardcore!"

Well, she definitely wasn't his girlfriend. But she *was* madly in love with him, willing to follow him to the death, and didn't mind dying for him out of sheer gratitude.

She loved and respected Haruka-kun for his kindness: his absurd kindness that led to a willingness to throw his life away in order to help others without even a second thought. That's why she stayed with him, that's why she wanted to follow him. She may have been a monster, but she had the heart of a human, and he protected that heart, saved it. That's why she wanted to stay with him.

In fact, she went so far as to say, with a beatific smile, that she would be happy if every last one of us married Haruka-kun so we could become even closer. No one knew what to say to that.

"Well, I guess polygamy is totally normal in this world," said Vice Rep B.

Where did she learn *that*? We were in the same party, so I had never really seen her outside of our group...but apparently polygamy was normal.

"Angelica wants him to have a harem of twenty wives with her at the bottom of the pile, just to get close to us? Is that supposed to be normal?!" Vice Rep A said.

However fantastical this world was, there was no way in hell that polygamy like that was normal. But no one at the time could bear to burst her bubble and wipe away that innocent, joyful look in her eyes.

Hang on, why was everyone staring at me now?!

THE GUILD was so busy, we had a labor shortage. I was sure the duke felt just as overwhelmed.

Yet the guild master and the duke were still holding daily council. No matter how hectic every day was, they still made time to meet every night.

Assigning personnel throughout the town and its surrounding land, management of public works that were unaffordable until now, drastic increases in workloads and labor shortages—there was no limit to the projects they needed to discuss.

They couldn't possibly cover everything in these meetings. They needed to prioritize the most important work or nothing would ever get done.

And everything was in constant flux. New projects appeared every time the black-haired boy visited, and with every new project, all the old plans had to be revised. Drawing up new plans, only to see them crumble like a house of cards. Somehow, those two always ended up discussing what to do about that boy.

And so the pointless discussions began:

"Now we come to the matter of the boy who saved our town," said the duke.

"The lad who ushered in a new era of happiness for this town?" asked Guild Master Hakiess.

"None other, that very lad who has brought about a golden age in Omui."

"The boy we couldn't hope to compensate for his many deeds?"

"Indeed, is it right that the boy should go unrewarded for his efforts?"

"He has risked his own life for the happiness of others!"

"Now, let us take a step back and recognize how preposterous this conversation is! There's no such boy. It's simply not possible!" the duke intoned.

"Indeed, I've seen that black-haired lad skulking around my offices literally every single day. He is nothing like the boy we described."

"Surely, if the boy was as pure hearted and selfless as all that, he would've been killed by monsters long ago. The only black-haired lad I know is a vicious slayer of monsters. All alone, yet he exterminated them without breaking a sweat."

Hakiess added, "To be honest, I don't think he was ever in any danger. Only the monsters became endangered."

"Is it wrong to say he saved us all? He massacred those monsters for his own reasons, but it happened to bring us peace."

"What possible debt could we owe him? He slew the monsters that menaced us without a permit. The spellstones are more than enough reward for his efforts."

"Indeed, to imagine that he selflessly ushered in a golden age is the height of absurdity, is it not? He has profited greatly from his monster slaying. He controls practically all the wealth in this town."

"Precisely! He has flooded the town with spellstones, weapons, and rare mushrooms, and he buys up the inventories of all the local shops, yet he remains wealthy beyond anyone's wildest dreams."

"Of course, we are grateful to him, that much should be self-evident," said the duke. "But those are merely the consequences of his massacring every last monster."

The duke and guild master were born out here in this frontier town, so they were used to this sort of existence.

But I had never before experienced a town filled with such kind, warm and generous people before.

When my family was destitute and at wit's end, the people of Omui welcomed us without question. They helped complete strangers as if they were family. No other town was like that.

In other places, even in the royal capital, those reduced to poverty receive no help or are exploited further. There's no shortage of selfish people who will deceive and extort them, squeezing every last drop out of the unfortunate souls.

Indeed, this town received a new lease on life because of the goodness of the people here.

That boy merely reflected that goodness back onto the town.

He was welcomed with open arms, and because of that, the town profited. Being here, he slew the monsters, and brought peace to the town. That was what really happened.

The boy brought joy to this town without meaning to. He isn't as compassionate as some believed.

If he and his comrades had encountered another town, one where the townspeople tried to swindle them, it would've been utterly destroyed. That sort of town would have vanished from the face of this world.

If Omui had tried to bargain too hard with that boy, he would've gone elsewhere and brought his profits with him.

But this was an honest town that appraised goods fairly. Even if the shops were desperate to make a profit, they bought goods at their true value. Not just the shops, but the guild and the duke too.

That's the real reason this town flourished. That's why he protected this town.

The boy is neither a blessing nor a curse.

We went to help him in the Ultimate Dungeon, so he thanked us by gifting the weapons he collected. People here treated him well and he returned the favor.

He didn't spare a single thought for compensation, adulation, rewards, fame, or really anything at all.

That boy couldn't even remember our town's name! No matter how much effort we spent thanking him, he still didn't recall the name of the guild master or the duke!

The way he saw it, some old men did him a favor, and he paid them back. That was all. To him, this was just a nice town filled with nice folks.

He did as he pleased and it happened to make the people around him happy. It was as simple as that.

They assumed too much about him. He did what he wanted to make himself happy, and it happened to make others happy. No matter the misfortunes he and others faced, he only sought to become happy himself. It just so happened that in a town like this, what made him happy brought joy to others as well. If this wasn't the case, the people around him would surely not be so joyous.

He deserved neither harsh judgment nor bountiful praise. There was nothing wrong with the way he acted, but there wasn't anything noble about it, either. Simply put, if he was truly miserable, he wouldn't have been able to make those around him happy.

That's why this whole meeting was a waste of time. *Be done with it and get back to the real work!*

I think it's gonna require some money to check out the neighborhood and do some fantasy world sightseeing.

*L*ET'S CONSIDER *our core principles: what ideals should we hold, what actions will we take, and what results do we desire?* I needed guiding principles that unified intent, action, and consequence.

No matter how I looked at it, the biggest problem was my lack of cash. If I didn't do something, I wouldn't even be able to stay at the inn. So money was my number one priority, definitely.

"So, I'm thinking about visiting another dungeon, y'know? Dungeons are easy money, and who doesn't like a bit of sightseeing?" I said. "Fantastical labyrinths—realms of adventure and romance! Where dreams and profits are made! And let's not forget the most important factor: loads of money!"

"Aren't you a little too eager?" said the Class Rep. "Besides, you listed money twice."

"Dungeons aren't your personal piggy bank to crack open!" Vice Rep A said, giving me a sharp look.

"Like, aren't all dungeons filled with deadly monsters, where we have to fight tooth and nail to survive?" the Queen Bee said, her eyebrow twitching with irritation.

"Seriously, who ever heard of taking the scenic route through a labyrinth of death traps?!" the nerds screamed.

Why did everyone have an issue with my proposal? *Could I be wrong about dungeons?*

"Well, I figured that the monster population will steadily decrease after we enter, y'know?" I said, nodding at Miss Armor Rep. "Besides, it's not like I didn't work hard in the Ultimate Dungeon! I had to climb so many stairs!"

Besides, since Miss Armor Rep had only recently escaped that dungeon, I thought it would be a good idea to show her more of the world. For that matter, I hadn't seen anything besides this town and the forest, either.

"Dungeons are, like, so freaking dangerous!" one of the mean girls said.

"More like the dungeons are in danger," said Nerd A.

"Oda-kun, don't you have anything useful to add?!"

"How about, 'Dungeons, run for your lives!'"

"Okay, just shut up!"

"Why are you so mean?!"

It was important to broaden my horizons. There weren't even any travelogues to read about the surrounding region. In fact, there was nothing to read at all! *Doesn't a travelogue about the uncanny frontiers of a fantasy world sound awesome?*

"So, are we going to stomp and yomp through the wilderness and find more dungeons or what?" I asked.

"What the hell's yomping?! You just want to stomp dungeons into dust, admit it," said the Class Rep. "You realize you'll just fall down another pitfall again, right? Instead of stomping anywhere, you're just going to fall on your ass. Another tragic fall suffered by a clueless teenage boy."

"Stop acting like dungeoneering's just a casual romp!"

To be fair, I did plummet down that labyrinth. But I crawled back up, step by step, you know? That dungeon had too many damn steps!

"Well, y'know, I don't mean any kind of serious expedition. Just some wandering at your own pace, letting our whims guide us to the nearest dungeon, making some cash, and coming back, yeah?"

"Just a casual stroll to make some cash, and return?!" chorused my classmates.

"I'm pretty sure the last time we went to a dungeon… we all literally almost died!" the Class Rep said.

"Kakizaki-kun, don't you guys have anything to say?" one of the twin telephone poles demanded.

"I'm famished, dudes! Let's eat already!" he shouted.

"Like we keep telling you bros, don't worry about Haruka-kun. He's hopeless, dude," added another meathead.

"Never mind, I shouldn't have asked."

Obviously, the meatheads were meatheads for a reason.

"That's so unchill!"

"Why would you even ask the meat-nerds their thoughts? You'd have a more intelligent conversation if you strolled right into a dungeon and asked the monsters how safe it was," I said. "They're not nearly so stupid-looking, y'know? Goblins are much better conversation-alists, am I right?"

"You're treating the nerds and the jocks as the same group, now?!" everyone yelled.

What could I say? They both struggled to survive by the skin of their teeth. When the nerds found themselves in life-or-death situations, they basically acted just like the meatheads. *Why's everyone giving me dirty looks?* I didn't say any of that out loud, did I? I was starting to get scared, so I tried to keep my mouth shut.

After a pause, I explained. "The nerds spilled the beans when I was torturing them the other day. There are a ton of dungeons all over the place," I said. "Besides, it's not like there are really any monsters left in the forest, right?"

"That may be true," Class Rep said. "So, after exterminating all the monsters of the forest, you now want to wipe the rest of the dungeons off the face of the earth?" She paused before resuming, "Hey, why are you casually bragging about torturing Oda-kun and his friends?!"

There was nothing to be gained from further discussion. Every time I got my next payment for all the spellstones I sold to the Adventurers' Guild, it got confiscated right away. All I had was my measly 50,000 ele per diem allowance. Miss Armor Rep, the Goddess of Greed, was starting to get upset about the lack of pocket money.

"Well, maybe *torture* is the wrong word," I said. "I haven't even burned all their hair off yet. It was more, y'know, normal. They just kind of told me while I lightly scorched their scalps. I didn't even give them any proper burns or anything!"

"You're the one who called it torture!" my classmates shouted.

"Besides, having a conversation while setting someone's head on fire is not normal!" the Queen Bee insisted.

It's not like they really got burned. Thanks to that stupid Profession Medal I sold them, the Guardian's forcefield skills saved their scalps. Lobbing sixteen consecutive meteors at their heads wasn't nearly enough to burn them. Those cheat skills were so unfair. They should be apologizing to me, the NEET, for having so many unfair advantages!

"It's settled, then. We'll finish breakfast, then go downstream to the next town and tour the new dungeon," I suggested. "How about it?"

There were apparently numerous small villages further downstream, and the closest dungeon was in that area. Since it was our first time there, it'd be like a nice little tour of the neighborhood.

"A tour of the neighborhood?! It's not like you're shopping for real estate!"

"Can someone explain how a dungeon is any different? Why can't I tour it like a condo?" I asked.

"Whether or not we go on a tour, you're just planning on conquering all of the floors yourself, aren't you?"

"And the dungeon is not for sale! You're just going to try to steal it from the monsters," Fish Girl said. "Wait, wouldn't that normally be a good thing?!"

Apparently, my classmates had little interest in either neighborhood tours *or* real estate. But we couldn't keep going like this, letting our debts pile up at the inn until I got a fresh payment from the guild, then spending it all on our bills. *What kind of light novel is this? Drowning in Debt in Another World?*

And let's not forget about the Goddess of Greed! I did make the general store lady sell her a low-cut dress, but still. Dresses and lingerie weren't cheap. Sexy but expensive! Naturally, I bought them in every color, but that cost me everything I had!

As a teenage boy, it's not like I had a choice. At least I made sure to get my money's worth last night.

Think about it! I was a high school sophomore summoned to a fantasy world. Up until now, the only sexy dresses I'd ever seen were worn by hostesses on TV. How could I say no to a virgin-killer dress? The kind that unzipped all the way down the back, and even when on left nothing to the imagination. I had to buy it. It was my prerogative as a teen boy! Those dresses were wonderful, not to mention what was under them!

"Conveniently, it's supposed to be a new and pretty weak dungeon. Wouldn't it be just perfect to convert the tenth to twentieth floors into a nice underground mansion? It's so close to town, too!"

"I knew you just wanted to move into the dungeon! Convenient, my ass. That's what you wanted from the very start!"

If I excavated it to a hundred floors, like the Ultimate Dungeon, I could make an enormous bathhouse... though on the other hand, walking up a hundred floors still felt excessive. I would definitely get too cold leaving the bath.

"But it's so spacious and in such a great location. You'll really love it! It's a great price for ten floors! My only concerns are about the neighborhood and the floor plan, y'know?"

"We're talking about a dungeon, not a condo! There's no such thing as an affordable dungeon, Haruka-kun!"

"And what do you mean, 'floor plan?' I've never heard of a dungeon map that listed three beds, two baths!"

"And how could a ten-story house be a reasonable size?"

It was a spacious underground residence close to town, situated right next to a quaint village. Not to mention the scenic nature features and the view! To be fair, everything around here was surrounded by nature, but even so.

"Stop muttering all your thoughts out loud!"

In fact, I was already formulating plans to start a business in there. *Just imagine, an underground shopping mall with an expansive bookstore!* If the dungeon was already like that, I'd raid it in a second!

We'd never know for sure unless we checked it out, so I thought we shouldn't waste any more time. The Ultimate

Dungeon was a good starter dungeon, but it was a bit *too* spacious for my tastes.

Not to mention the lower floors were full of holes and the whole thing could collapse at any moment. Oh no, now Miss Armor Rep was glaring at me!

LONER LIFE
◆ IN ANOTHER WORLD ◆

When your descriptions are that detailed, I think it's gonna cause problems. It keeps popping back into my head...

I STARTED RUNNING FASTER than the eye could process, leaving behind afterimages courtesy of my Dash and Super-Speed skills. Thanks to level ups, I was way faster than I used to be, but something still felt off. For some inexplicable reason, even though I wasn't paying any attention to my high-speed movement skills, I somehow wasn't falling over or crashing into anything.

Well, I still avoided making drastic movements, so it wasn't exactly convenient, and it was definitely useless in battle. There was certainly an awkwardness to being the only person in a fantasy world to constantly faceplant.

"Looks like I'm going to get there soon even without flying. Not that I'm complaining. I didn't enjoy the crash landings."

It was a nice day. Waves of grass undulated in the fresh breeze. For once, no carriages were under attack. The usual thieves and highway bandits were nowhere to be seen; everything was peaceful and calm today.

In the meeting, my classmates eventually conceded that both in terms of gaining more experience and securing the safety of the city, investigating the dungeon was the right move after all. That meant that the plan for today was a short neighborhood tour and preliminary inspection. After checking things out, we'd split up into parties and divvy up all the nearby dungeons between us.

Since I couldn't officially join a party, it'd be just the two of us. I would be alone with Miss Armor Rep...but I really had no intention of doing anything weird! She gave me a firm warning: no afternoon delights...probably.

I felt the pinpricks of her glare. *I swear, I'll keep my mind out of the gutter!* That's why I led the way. If I followed behind, various...features would distract me. Even the meat-nerds acknowledged that they couldn't stay composed around her insanely curvaceous figure. Besides, if I gave her the wrong kind of look, she'd shred me to bits with her sharp glare.

The brief glimpses of her hips shifting beneath her crimson cloak...*no, I'm not looking at anything!* I was just...reminiscing.

Miss Armor Rep had become fast friends with the other girls and started getting invited to the girls-only meetings. She went to the baths with them, and she was starting to get better at talking, too.

She also wanted to cook with me, but she had no experience in the kitchen, so things didn't go smoothly.

Some girls were natural cooks, but it seemed like Miss Armor Rep was not one of them. Maybe getting job-based advantages in combat skills came with penalties to crafting. That meant all the combat specialists in my class were doomed. Some of the girls tried to practice cooking, but the most they could manage was frying fish and making salads.

In that case, learning to cook would be an uphill battle for Miss Armor Rep, since she was basically a combat legend. I didn't really understand the mechanics of jobs and skills in this world, so that was my best guess.

I did want to teach her, but the penalty to crafting skills made it pretty much impossible.

At least she enjoyed talking. Surrounded by the girls, she relished these easygoing days of laughter and sunshine. It made sense. She was trapped all alone in eternal darkness until recently. She deserved some rest and relaxation—so long as she stayed out of the kitchen!

The rest of the class tried their best to get back on

their feet, to smile and laugh. Even I recognized that they plastered on smiles to hold back tears, trying so hard that their teeth chattered.

"Everyone..." said Miss Armor Rep, "Their families... ache. Sad, painful."

Made sense to me; they all got sucked into a world of chaos out of the blue. The situation had only started to settle down recently. Everyone was starting to feel homesick now.

"W-we talked so much," Miss Armor Rep said. "I listened so much."

I had no idea what Miss Armor Rep, with her halting, clumsy speech, could be talking about with the other girls. When I asked, she simply told me it was a secret between girls. In any case, so long as she was happy, whatever she talked about was surely fine.

"They say...they say they don't know—this land. They came from far away."

As we stumbled through conversation, Miss Armor Rep tried with all her might to keep the conversation light. Of course, I was glad that she was enjoying herself, but I wish Miss Armor Rep would spare me the detailed descriptions of all the girls bathing together. I had trouble walking, given all my vivid teenaged imaginings. Particularly, the figure of a certain Miss B formed clearly in my mind.

Fields sprawled by the river and beyond them a handful of buildings clustered together. A few more structures were scattered around. It seemed likely this was a village. Obviously, a village of farmers, judging by the surrounding fields.

"Oh, it looks like a village, right?" I said. "Well, more of a hamlet than a village. A farming hamlet?"

There was no entry fee. A short wooden fence surrounded the hamlet, no wall or gates. Even the shoddy fence had holes in it here and there. This place was utterly defenseless, totally vulnerable to monsters!

Hmm, this is strange. Should I call out to someone? There should at least be a guard or something, right? There was no one around.

Where was the standard village greeter NPC? Though I'd be pretty worried if that was all someone did for a living.

"Uh, hello?" I called out. "Anybody home? I wanted to ask if there were any nice dungeons nearby!"

I tried asking a villager loitering by the fence. He didn't have the signature leather bag of Villager A, but he did look like a typical villager. *Maybe a typical farmer?*

"Eh? Hullo there. Don't know 'bout any nice dungeons, but there's a dungeon downstream on the right. You an adventuresome type, lad?"

So it wasn't a *nice* dungeon. I'm glad I asked a local first. They would be the ones to know. Getting information on the ground was absolutely essential.

"Well, I'm kind of like an adventurer, if you were to generalize, as in I came here from around the area where there's an Adventurers' Guild, if you catch my drift?"

"Much appreciated, boy. We was wondering when someone from that guild would come 'round here. It ain't much of a dungeon, but we're mighty close to it and we're a mere hamlet. Gives us the spooks."

What's so spooky? The surrounding area was totally serene. Were they scared the river would flood?

Maybe something had gotten lost in translation? He probably spoke some sort of quasi-European language and the words were getting jumbled. The surrounding lands were definitely a flood plain—the whole area was liable to go underwater in heavy rains. The soil must have been extremely fertile, but still, that flood risk was nothing to sneeze at.

"Uh...well, I'll go inspect the dungeon all the same, thanks."

It wasn't a great piece of land according to the farmer, but since I came all the way here, it would be a shame not to take a look for myself. I could always build some levees to prevent water damage. Time for a proper real estate inspection.

Alas, it was a bit—no, it was *tragically*—far from an ideal dream home.

"It's just a hole in the ground. Can you really call this a dungeon?"

It was a dump, to put it mildly. The entrance was cramped and dark, and it looked like a limestone cave inside. This was no good at all. I didn't even need to inspect the floor plan, there was no point in renovating a space like this.

I wasn't sure whether to blame the river or something else, but it was clammy and dismal—not a suitable residence at all.

"Do you still want to go in?" I asked Miss Armor Rep.

I couldn't read her expression. Monsters weren't a concern so much as the damp. It was uncomfortable and probably unhealthy.

Honestly, I'm ready to pass.

"Right, you can tell from the entrance, it's no good. This isn't what we're looking for. This is way worse than my forest cavern; even though it's not as bad as the first floor of the Ultimate Dungeon, it's still pretty awful, right?"

Even if I expanded the entrance, the interior was so cramped, it'd be wasted effort. It was just long, narrow, and dull. I doubted I could even flatten the floor. The air was stagnant, too. Not even a hint of elegance. What a crappy dungeon!

"I don't need a dungeon like this. You can wreak havoc on it. We can always come back tomorrow and collect spellstones and treasure chests, y'know?"

Miss Armor Rep didn't seem to get it, but nodded when I suggested wrecking the dungeon. If the ex-emperor of dungeons was okay with it, the current dungeon king should have no objections.

There was no point even exploring it. We dealt with it like the famous Siege of Takamatsu, diverting the river and flooding the whole place. The humidity was stifling.

Afterward, we had a relaxing barbecue by the river. Miss Armor Rep may have been armor clad, but enjoying a barbecue with a lovely girl fulfilled one of my teenaged fantasies.

"All done—it's hot!"

Miss Armor Rep nodded cheerfully.

I handed her the grilled meat skewers. She gobbled them up with a smile. With her helmet removed to eat, she became a proper beautiful girl.

Maybe she wanted to talk now that the helmet was out of the way, but she seemed pretty focused on eating.

Although it was still unclear how many years she had been a seventeen-year-old girl, she was drop-dead gorgeous. I had no complaints!

We'd flooded the dungeon two hours ago, and I wondered if the monsters were done drowning. Surely the demons and liches had drowned by now. Come to think of it, I had never heard of drowned skeletons before.

As we enjoyed the barbecue, I vaguely felt presences in the dungeon getting snuffed out one by one, like candles in a rainstorm. The monsters were dying.

I'd deal with that after lunch. Next up, I grilled some fish!

Miss Armor Rep finally stopped glowering so she could focus on enjoying her grilled meat. I'd worry about the dungeon later. It seemed so damp in there.

From what I could sense, the dungeon king wasn't a fish or an amphibian. In the off chance it was a reptile, would it revive itself when the waters drained away? Would the dungeon resurrect, too? *That would suck.*

LONER LIFE
◆ IN ANOTHER WORLD ◆

I was too scared to admit it was actually my fault.

WHEN WE GATHERED to discuss the different dungeons we all explored, the incident came to light. Normally listening to Haruka-kun was a trial in itself, and this was bound to be a long story, so we postponed his explanation.

It was only appropriate that the guy who spouted incomprehensible nonsense would give his report last. As expected, his report delivered.

"The river was full of fish and the barbecue was delicious, but the place had a Humidity Discomfort Level Max, so I kind of let it drown, y'know?"

From what I could surmise, he destroyed the dungeon he was supposed to explore. Rather, he flooded it.

He was one hundred percent responsible for flooding

it, but he made it sound like it had happened naturally. *Was it really an accident?*

He definitely caused the flood on purpose, and because he was confident that he could go open up the treasure chests tomorrow, he left without even checking to see what had really happened.

"You drained the water and left?!" we shouted.

"Uh, yeah? I still have to go back tomorrow, y'know. There are probably some aquatic monsters left, and I doubt the undead can even drown. To be honest, I'm not looking forward to dealing with swimming ghosts."

Since the place didn't live up to Haruka-kun's idea of a nice dungeon property close to town, he decided to divert a river and drown the dungeon and its king. So why did he spend half his report talking about a barbecue?

The other half of his report was all about the humidity and the risks of mold and water damage. It seemed like Haruka-kun could only think of the dungeon in terms of architecture and construction.

We could all see that Haruka-kun's complete lack of common sense was the real problem.

He rambled on and on about the problems with the location and architectural foundation of the dungeon. He was coming at this from entirely the wrong angle.

He didn't even bother to find out what kind of monster the dungeon king was. He just flooded the whole place because it was too damp for his liking.

All of us, knowing Haruka-kun as well as we did, exclaimed, "I knew you'd do that!" No one was surprised in the least.

Of course he massacred another dungeon. That's exactly something Haruka-kun would do.

"Can dungeons even die from flooding?" Vice Rep A added.

"I wasn't expecting him to defeat a dungeon like *that*!"

"Wouldn't flooding a building take a ridiculous amount of effort?" Oda-kun asked.

"Why'd the dungeon king build a dungeon so close to the river?" Chika-chan said.

"The king definitely didn't expect a flash flood!" said Fukunuki-san.

Haruka-kun didn't even enter the dungeon because he claimed it was too humid! I really wanted to ask him why he decided to flood the place preemptively, but I knew deep down that it was pointless.

"Well, building on a flood plain like that, it's only natural that it would get flooded," Haruka-kun insisted. "No matter how lucky you are, water will just seep in, y'know?"

The criminal confessed without the tiniest ounce of remorse.

Unbelievable, I thought.

"This wasn't bad luck. You did it yourself!" Vice Rep A said.

"You're giving luck a bad reputation!"

Haruka-kun was the only person leaving matters up to luck! He flooded the dungeon because it was too musty and hoped that was enough to kill all the monsters!

Instead of wasting time trying to wring any common sense out of Haruka-kun, I had to figure out a way to explain his crimes to the Adventurers' Guild. To do that, I needed to come up with some sort of rational excuse. After all, whenever Haruka-kun made a mess, I was the one who had to explain what happened.

I *really* wanted to lecture him. Technically, he wasn't an adventurer, and thus technically wasn't allowed to enter dungeons in the first place. But he didn't even *try* this time. Did that somehow exonerate him?

Angelica was making some sort of "Can you believe this guy?" gesture, but she was clearly an accomplice!

Not so long ago, she had melted our hearts with her claims that she would follow Haruka-kun to the ends of the earth, but now she acted like she didn't even know him! She must've gotten used to delegating responsibility as a dungeon emperor, so she merely expected him to handle everything. But when you stopped to think about it, hadn't she abandoned her post as dungeon emperor? It was clearly irresponsible.

Then she joined Haruka-kun in destroying her own dungeon, and helped him bring down another one today. Angelica acted innocent, but she was just as guilty as he was!

We had croquettes for dinner. All the girls flipped out and stuffed themselves with flaky, fluffy, piping hot croquettes. Everyone totally forgot about lecturing him. They forgot themselves altogether and ate until their stomachs hurt.

It was dangerous. *Potatoes are the true weakness of teenage girls!*

"That was amazing. My stomach aches, but that was amazing!"

Apparently, he got the potatoes from the hamlet downstream. He bought all the potatoes they had. Potatoes were their specialty, but since the farmers in other hamlets didn't really eat potatoes, they had trouble finding buyers. As a result, the villagers were thrilled when Haruka-kun bought out their stock.

"Look at the value tourism brings!" Haruka-kun said. "Trade is also important! I never would have managed this without visiting that rural hamlet! Even the great Marco Polo himself would've been impressed by my potato discovery!"

As he fried more croquettes, he talked up the hamlet, and in his excitement over croquettes and farms, he completely forgot about the dungeon.

Destroying the dungeon was truly incidental in his mind. He cared more about the potatoes than anything else he'd done. His first priority was telling everyone about the barbecue, and his second, potatoes. Somewhere in the middle of his rambling, he mentioned that the dungeon drowned in passing.

I tried getting a confession out of his accomplice, Angelica, but all she could say was "The scenery was pretty—it was my first barbecue. It was delicious—I tried cooking the meat myself—the weather was nice, and the cold river felt nice."

She was obviously pleased. She must've thought of the trip as a picnic date. *Good for them, I guess?*

In the end, the only things I understood were that the dungeon was too humid and the local village had a lot of potatoes. *How nice for him. It sounds like it was a real lovely day for sightseeing,* I thought bitterly.

His partner in crime certainly enjoyed their outing together. She beamed whenever she talked about it.

Oh, and the dungeon flooded, of course.

I supposed it would be fine. The Adventurers' Guild would have to accept what happened, right? The duke would *probably* understand.

Our meeting concluded. Haruka-kun's dungeon report was light on lectures and heavy on potatoes. This time, the furious Valkyries of scolding had their mouths too full of croquettes to harangue. *Potatoes are the true enemy of teenage girls!*

Another croquette, please?

LONER LIFE
◆IN ANOTHER WORLD◆

Everyone is pushing me around!

THE DOWNSTREAM HAMLET DUNGEON

WHAT A WONDERFUL, radiant morning—helped in no small part by a *very* pleasant night. I had high hopes for the day...dashed immediately by the events that followed. I forgot that we were going back to that soggy dungeon.

To be precise, it wasn't just unpleasant. It maxed out my discomfort index. *It's just so humid!* The dungeon was a sopping, musty, splashing *dump*. Drowning in dirty looks was bad enough, but drowning in dank air emanating from wet dungeon walls was a thousand times worse!

"This dungeon doesn't even have proper drainage or ventilation, never mind basic amenities like a dehumidifier! I want to give the dungeon king a piece of my mind! Though it's probably dead already."

There was probably nothing left of it besides its spell-stone by now, which meant that I couldn't register my many *violent* complaints.

The Ultimate Dungeon was way too big for a home, but at least it followed solid construction principles. The face of the dungeon emperor was even better made. *Not to mention that body—*

I coughed conspicuously and said, "I wasn't thinking anything! There's no need to draw your sword! Someone could get hurt with that! I mean, I suppose we're in a dungeon, so maybe you should draw your sword. But wait, the monsters are all converted to spellstones by now, so there's really no need for violence!"

Miss Armor Rep glared at me.

The floor and the stairs were slippery from the damp and there wasn't even a banister to steady myself on! How could they forget such a basic architectural feature? This dungeon displayed a real lack of hospitality for any invaders, there wasn't even a "SLIPPERY WHEN WET" sign.

"This place sucks; it's unsafe and uncomfortable! No wonder this dungeon is so unpopular. It completely lacks safety features for adventurers. Everyone must've spread the word about how dangerous it is, and now no one bothers to come here! Not even the local villagers bothered! That's how bad it is! I hate this place!"

I grumbled the whole time I walked down the stairs, but Miss Glare was silent, even if her glowering spoke volumes.

We collected any spellstones we found, but they all looked cheap. Still, I was destitute ever since Class Rep started confiscating my paychecks to pay for room and board. I needed every ele I could get!

If I didn't find something worthwhile in the treasure chests here, I'd be in the red from yesterday's potato splurge. But it's not like I could've passed up those hot potato deals—we needed them.

My boots squelched through the muddy dungeon tunnels—I couldn't even afford to get them cleaned. I wanted to at least collect enough spellstones to offset my potato investment. Granted, I'd already made an insane profit selling off surplus sweet potatoes...but money just disappeared so easily, y'know?

Honestly, I didn't even want to come back to this damp hellhole, but I got bullied into it.

Even worse, my classmates warned me that lewdness was strictly prohibited inside the dungeon! Everyone kept telling me what to do!

"I hate all this cold and wet squelching! I can think of way better wet and wild activities to...I'm not doing anything! These are idle thoughts—not even thoughts!

I mean, there's all sorts of fun uses for lotion in the company of a beautiful girl but...no, I swear I'm on my best behavior! Let's just keep going!"

This stairwell is cramped, can't you please put your sword away?

What if I got pneumonia or some sort of fungal infection and died at the tender age of sixteen, all because I was forced to spelunk in a mildewy dungeon? Well, I did have Revival, but even so, I didn't want to catch any diseases in my sweet youth.

We finally reached the fifth floor. *This really sucks.* If we were going back up, I would've been able to enjoy the view of a certain curvaceous adventurer, but there was nothing fun about going deeper into this dungeon. Looking at the top of her helmet didn't excite me at all. Not that anything would've made this dungeon any less miserable, but even so.

"It seems like there's something lurking on the next floor. What should we do? Collapse the ceiling onto it?"

"W-won't work...g-g-ghosts?" Miss Armor Rep said, shaking her head. *G-g-ghosts? So what, an attack would just go through the ghost?* As if my spirits could get any lower.

Great. I had to spar with a floating ghost on a slippery floor, without even a safety rail to stay upright. *Worst case scenario.* Sure, I had my special boots and Airwalk, but that was hard to control. Just when I was starting to worry, I saw a flash of platinum armor, a silvery thread stabbing straight through the specter and sending it to the hereafter.

A low-level ghost in a low-level dungeon was less than nothing compared to a despotic former emperor. This felt like a common case of workplace harassment to me.

I was so unmotivated in all this humidity. Why couldn't I just go home? This was a terrible piece of real estate; even the hidden rooms and their treasure chests were garbage. That ghost wasn't even scary!

In the secret chamber on the fifth floor, we found a "Freeze Sword: Ice Attribute (small). Power +10%. Speed +10%."

10% was a pitiful boost. This sword was totally unworthy of a dungeon emperor.

"Pass. Even the girls won't want this, right?"

Miss Armor Rep nodded.

Still, it might fetch a pretty penny at the armory. Even then, it was probably too expensive for the average person to buy—they tended to go for cheaper self-defense options. I wanted to find better equipment, but I also wanted money, so I supposed it was fine if I could pawn it.

This still didn't make the dungeon worthwhile, though.

"Can't this at least be the Legendary Sword of Something or Other? I guess I've already got the Heavenly Sword of Gathering Clouds, so I doubt that I'll be able to find a sword more epic than that. Still, at least let me find some sort of weapon I could get hyped about, something that sparks my imagination! There's nothing exciting about, like, 'You found a divine sword lying on the ground.' Why can't I find a weapon that's all, 'Only the chosen one can pull this sword from the stone!' or something?"

Considering our equipment, we weren't likely to find better weapons or armor, but I still wanted to find some gear with unique skills attached. The Ice attribute was fine, but I didn't want "small" effects! Besides, I would rather have found something with a Fire attribute. Ever since those dweebs improved their force field skills, I had hoped to find something with a "Scalp Scorching (large)" effect.

A level 6 phantom floated around the sixth floor. Wasn't that basically the same as the ghost we just faced?

It was just a floating, translucent white figure. *It's literally identical!* It didn't even look humanoid, so what kind of spirit was it? Miss Armor Rep drew her rapier and struck an elegant battle stance, then unleashed a furious stream of slashes, thrusts, and counterattacks, obliterating the phantom faster than my eyes could follow. I had the same thought earlier, but since when could physical attacks harm spirits?! Was it actually not immune to physical damage?

Besides, when would I get a chance to do anything at all? I could've totally extended my Wooden Staff until it was six feet long and heroically flown over with Airwalk or something. By the time it occurred to me, Miss Armor Rep had already finished slaying the phantom. Maybe I was her hireling, destined to follow behind her and collect spellstones. I mean, I hadn't had the chance to do anything yet.

In conclusion, that's all I'm good for in this dungeon. In the hidden room on the seventh floor, we found another spellstone and a treasure chest. Inside, I found another trash-tier weapon: "Thunder Spear: Lightning Attribute (small). Power +10%. Speed +10%."

Well, it'd definitely sell enough to cover the cost of more sexy outfits. *Yeah, I wasn't done shopping!* The virgin-killer dress that zipped down the back was great, but we passed up a V-neck dress with a neckline that plunged all the way to the bellybutton. *Truly amazing.*

Miss Armor Rep's figure was so perfect that even super-revealing clothing looked classy on her. Still, I got way too excited about it and she ended up yelling at me about it. *Not my fault,* I thought. I was just a simple teenage boy burdened with Super Horny and Alpha Male skills that kept leveling up. *I deny all accusations!*

The ninth floor had another secret treasure room and a normal treasure chest in the hallway. The hallway chest had a worthless HP potion, but the hidden chest contained "Spike Armor: Defense Boost (small) + ATT." As soon as I showed it to Miss Armor Rep she recoiled in disgust.

It was creepy armor covered in spikes from helm to boot. It was the perfect look for an evil villain or dungeon boss, yet it made her distraught just looking at it.

As I suspected, she wanted something more glamorous.

Well, if she did put it on, in all its spiky glory, she would be the picture of a sinister final boss of an RPG. It probably offered good protection too, but it seemed like she hated it.

We found another lone treasure chest in the hall containing "Earrings: Decorative (B-class)." This wasn't even real equipment, but it would have to do as an offering for the insatiable Miss Armor Rep.

The earrings were inset with pale blue stones, so they matched her blue dress with the slit, and they'd still look great when she took the dress off! *Yeah, I want her to wear that blue dress tonight. I'm definitely going to do my best!* The slit on that dress went all the way up to her hips!

Of course earrings suited her. Despite her being such a beauty, she had to spend such a long time as a skeleton without anything nice to wear. There was nothing wrong with treating her to some finer things until she felt better.

We started to find better spellstones as we went deeper, at least judging by their size and luster. They still seemed to be F-class stones, but that was because those had a stupidly big range, going from F1 to F10 with plus and minus variants of each rank, making for 30 total ranks. It was overkill! How was I supposed to have any clue how to appraise them?

On top of that, the price of spellstones was starting to plummet. Even an F10+ spellstone would likely only bring in around five million ele now, half of what it used to be.

Spellstone value had apparently skyrocketed before due to a supply shortage, but now the guild was trying to stabilize the supply to keep the whole spellstone market from crashing. It wasn't so easy to sell them anymore, so equipment was a better bet.

Even if I made a ton of money, I was bound to blow it all on sexy outfits. *Too bad dungeon treasure chests don't carry any sexy clothes, unless...* I decided if I found any, I'd set up a campsite immediately!

LONER LIFE
IN ANOTHER WORLD

Why did everyone make the villagers wait so long?

WE FINALLY REACHED the 12th floor. Even if we got a few items and spellstones, we certainly didn't get any training or experience. In the Ultimate Dungeon, the monsters were too strong to fight directly, but in this dungeon they died pretty much immediately.

It figured that a dungeon as poorly constructed as this was bound to have worthless monsters and low-quality spellstones.

At least there were plentiful treasure chests, even if they didn't have anything worthwhile. That Ultimate Dungeon really was something special. The dungeon emperor was especially notable since she turned out to be such a babe. Though she was just a pile of rattling bones back then.

Without a doubt, she was the greatest treasure of the Ultimate Dungeon. In that way, I was grateful that I ended up in this world. I made sure to express the full extent of my gratitude every night.

"This is so boring. None of these monsters are anywhere near your level, and they can't even reach me before you strike them down. Do you think you could do me a huge favor and let a few go, so that I have something to do?"

She shook her head vigorously.

If I considered the situation from an outside perspective, I was nothing more than the lowly squire to a glorious knight in gleaming platinum armor! I was totally a background character! It wouldn't surprise me in the least if I got the title of Manservant.

That would piss me off so much. I'm already stuck with titles like Loner, NEET, and Shut-in!

I had nothing else to do but think about this stuff. There were practically no monsters left in this dump. They were bound to go extinct at any moment. We were surrounded by spellstones because these stupid monsters didn't know how to swim, or at least they couldn't handle the floodwaters.

"I sense something on the 13th floor—any clue what it is?" I asked. "There's not a lot of them, but they're moving around a lot, y'know?"

"D-demon s-si-ze..."

Demon size? What does that mean? I had to admit, it was so cute when someone so pretty had trouble saying something. I wanted to just take her and...*never mind! She's glaring at me again!*

Did she mean demon sidekicks, demon psychics, or just very large demons?

"Yeah, we'd be in trouble facing off against demon thighs. They'd crush my skull like a grape!"

She started miming some sort of action, swinging her arms around. Whirling around like demon...flies?!

I figured that I wouldn't get it until I saw them myself, so we went downstairs, and they turned out to be level 13 demon *scythes*. And here I was, worried that they were demon spies or something.

Hang on. They were flying demon scythes. They looked like the kind of scythes the grim reaper would carry. Nerds in junior high would've totally thought they were epic.

Three scythes whirled around and zoomed toward us. Yeah, flying scythes were total nerd-bait. In fact, if a bunch of nerds showed up here, they'd totally try to steal the flying scythes for themselves!

They skimmed through the air, whirling in some sort of spiral attack pattern, dark blades glimmering. Three blades, but they were only level 13, so that wasn't too bad.

I couldn't resist, my inner loser nerd wanted to keep them forever!

"Um, Servitude?"

They clattered to the ground. That seemed to work. Suddenly, I remembered that I recently acquired the Demon Ring, so that's why they froze in place and dropped, totally helpless. *Are they waiting for orders?*

"Uh, fly," I said, my voice uncertain.

Oh shit, they actually flew! Three black and silver halberd-style death scythes leapt up into the air. *This is awesome! It's so cool that I don't even feel any shame about being an edgy nerd.*

I commanded them without speaking. With a simple thought, they began to whirl around me. They followed my every whim, so maybe I really could use them. Although I needed to level them up first.

I'll figure it out as I go, I thought. They would level up naturally as I experimented with them. If only I had a fourth scythe, then I could reap every nerd at the same time. Pity.

I messed with the demon scythes for a while. I could control each of them independently without any trouble. Maybe that was one of the benefits of Supreme Thinking.

This was so badass, though it made me look even more villainous than usual. I already dressed in all black, and if

I imbued my clothes with the Spike Armor, adventurers would definitely mistake me for a dungeon monster and attack on sight.

We entered a passage with a higher ceiling, so I could finally give these scythes a whirl, slaying the evil spirits that lurked within. *What's the difference between my Servitude skill and the control I got from the Demon Ring?*

My Servitude skill didn't seem to compel those I enslaved to follow my commands, but the Demon Ring certainly did. So why did the mean girls follow me around like creepers when I first used Servitude?

Apropos of nothing, I realized that I hadn't encountered a mirror since coming to this world, but my eyes apparently changed color at times. I was told that they turned *golden*, so I was a golden-eyed, black-cloaked, scythe-wielding edgelord dork! *That's so cringey.* It was probably good for my mental health that I couldn't see what I looked like!

But now I could finally mow down some monsters myself in this dungeon. The scythes even had an auto-pilot function—I could make a garden with these bad boys! Right now, they were mincing up some brown worm-like monsters. When I got a chance, I could probably clear-cut some trees in the forest. These scythes were awesome. *I'm glad I came here.* I got potatoes and landscaping tools!

As I was having a grand time commanding my giant whirling death scythes with my mind, we continued further down. As soon as I thought there wasn't enough room in this claustrophobic dungeon for my scythes, they transformed. The long, wicked blade folded up, turning them into spears. Both convenient and very fun.

But there were still almost no monsters to fight. On the 16th floor, the monsters were all already reduced to spellstones when we got there, even in the hidden room.

The treasure chest contained: "Counter Shield: Reflects impact and magic damage up to a certain threshold. Defense +20%."

I decided to sell this one to my classmates. They got the first offer to buy higher-grade equipment, since the armory couldn't really afford the good stuff. I made a huge profit on the Bladed Shield before, so some of the girls probably wanted this, too. *Time for another auction, I guess.*

Now that we were all the way down to the 16th floor, the spellstones were starting to improve, but there still weren't very many of them. I supposed this dungeon wasn't finished developing. It was still all cramped and crawling with pathetic, crap-tier monsters.

"Oh, so is this, like, the end of the line?"

Miss Armor Rep nodded.

I had no hope of fixing my sex appeal with a dungeon that was a measly seventeen floors. I hadn't even found it in a dungeon with a hundred floors. Did that mean my sex appeal simply didn't exist?

The dungeon king seemed to reside on the 17th floor. As expected, there was a single massive spellstone lying on the ground, beside a spear and some armor. That must've been its equipment.

An armored dungeon king, huh? Could a Living Armor or a skeleton knight really have died by drowning? I wondered what exactly this dungeon king's job was, in any case. I always heard that fantasy worlds were full of mysteries, but with no leads, I had no hope of solving this one. The dungeon king probably didn't know either. It could at least have done the polite thing and left a note before it died! Maybe it couldn't write while it was drowning?

Ah, there seemed to be a passageway here, leading to another hidden room! I wouldn't have been able to spot it without my Area Analyze skill. *Hands down the most useful dungeon ability,* I thought. It did get rolled into the Jupiter Eye skill, so I could still use it even though it wasn't listed in my status. *Miss Area Analyze, you help me so much even though I hardly ever acknowledge you, thank you.*

"This way. It's a hidden passage! Or a hidden room! One of those! You know what I mean, right?"

There was an obvious boulder which revealed a hidden passage when I pushed on it. I was coming to detest mysterious developments like this—every time something here seemed exciting, it inevitably disappointed.

Since there was a treasure chest at the far end of this tunnel, it probably qualified as a secret chamber. This one didn't require a key either, so what was the damn point of that Magic Key I picked up? Was it encouraging me to become a master thief? Well, I was an unemployed sixteen-year-old living in a cave, so it seemed like I had all the qualifications for banditry. *If I can't get a job, I may as well become a thief, right?*

There was a ring inside the treasure chest: "Ring of the Dungeon Master: Dungeon creation, dungeon control."

What?!

"H-hang on a second, Dungeon King! Why didn't you have this equipped?! Why was it hidden?! This is the kind of ring you wear, not forget about! What kind of dungeon king were you?! Did you hate your job or something? Is that why you hid the ring? Did you ditch work to go see the world? I guess the conditions were grim and exploitative, right? I mean, even the head honcho, the dungeon emperor, quit. Folks really hate working in dungeons, don't they?"

Wait, if I put this on, would the dungeon emperor be working for me? Did a new dungeon emperor take over yet? Wearing this ring would probably cause all sorts of upsets in the dungeon hierarchy, so I stashed it away for the time being.

With a dungeon creation skill, I could do more than remodel, I could make my own dungeons! It wouldn't hurt to keep, just in case.

The dungeon king's drop was pretty typical: "Plate Armor: Defense bonus (large). Magic resistance (medium). Autoheal."

It was just basic armor, though it had a pretty elaborate design. Even so, it wasn't as over-the-top as the Spike Armor. Miss Armor Rep didn't want it, but it had good effects, so it was perfect for the auction.

That was enough dungeoneering for the day. There was nothing else here, not even any lotions or massage oils—what a waste of moisture. There was no point resting here. I'd hoped that the final treasure chest was on a rotating platform that I could convert into a bed, but this dungeon was a bust from start to finish.

On the way back, I told the farmer that the dungeon was dead and there were no more monsters, and he was really happy for some reason. He even brought the village elder out to meet me. Ugh, now I had to talk to another ancient geezer, as if I hadn't seen enough of those.

After bowing to me about a hundred times, they gave me tons of vegetables. Why won't they just shut up for once! That's all I ever wanted. According to the elder, a flood destroyed the walls around their town, leaving them defenseless against monsters. That sounded scary, especially since the people of this hamlet weren't equipped with war clubs like the folks from that bloodthirsty town I hailed from.

They gave me a bunch of fruits and veggies. A hamlet this small didn't need a huge wall, and I didn't get to do anything all day—literally just climbing up and down stairs for hours—so my magic power was totally full. I placed my hand on the ground and imbued the earth with all my magical might.

If I settled on the area of effect first, I could just visualize the results and make them happen. With my magical reserves, I could probably go a bit overboard, controlling the depth and height of the wall so that it could withstand any monster attack.

"You just need a wall, right? No moat or anything? Hazards like that are probably a bad idea, not very safe."

The wall I created was ten feet high, and thick enough that a boss goblin probably couldn't smash through it.

Maybe a kobold or wolf could scale it, but if I made it too tall, it might topple over. I carved out a ditch around the wall to make it harder to climb—perfect.

"I felt guilty just taking all these vegetables, so I made you a wall to keep you folks safe, yeah? More or less?"

The villagers were speechless.

When they collected themselves, they decided to give me even *more* vegetables! Considering all the farmland, they probably had a massive surplus. Without my item bag, I never could've carried them all, not even with a horse-drawn cart!

They seem happy, so all's well that ends well, right? The village elder wept with joy. Why was he making such a big deal out of this? Was there no one around who could've channeled Earth magic? I was going to make way more profit off the vegetables I got from making this wall than from raiding that dungeon.

Tourism really had its upsides. I felt like making hot-pot tonight. *Can I make a clay pot with Earth magic?* I wasn't sure.

EVENING

Knead it into shape, let it dry, fire it, fire it again, and I'm done, because I can't glaze it.

INTERLUDE:
THE WHITE
LOSER INN

HARUKA-KUN HAD DECIDED to make hotpot tonight. He looked thrilled.

He spent some time sculpting and firing a clay pot for the purpose. *What is his ultimate goal, anyway?* The hamlet near the dungeon had given him a bunch of vegetables. At first, I assumed it was a reward for slaying the dungeon king, but it was actually because he transformed their humble village into a literal fortress.

To be precise, they did give him vegetables for killing the boss, but then they gave him even more after he built a wall around the town. Of course, the culprit had no common sense at all, so he thought he'd made an ordinary town wall. In reality, it was far more suited to defending a castle.

Even a goblin king wouldn't be able to take down that wall. It was only about ten feet tall, but he added a ditch around it, and the walls were so straight they were nearly impossible to scale. He even installed giant spikes along the top. What in the world was he trying to defend them against?

The farmers, thrilled with their fortified hamlet, gave Haruka-kun even more vegetables. He felt bad for getting so many, so he distributed clubs, too. *Monsters and bandits, please avoid that hamlet at all costs. You'll never get out alive!*

If some hapless monsters attacked that hamlet, they would get obliterated before the town could even send soldiers to help. It couldn't even be called a hamlet anymore!

The person responsible for this was just pleased that he got a huge load of vegetables, and the villagers were happy, too. If everyone was satisfied, then there was no problem, right?

He kept saying the villagers were overreacting, but it was only natural to be happy about their change in circumstances. They lived near the evil forest, and only had a broken-down fence to defend them against the hordes of monsters that emerged from dungeons. They must have spent every night filled with stomach-churning terror; of course they would be ecstatic if their hamlet suddenly became a fortress. Haruka-kun even gave the farmers weapons. There wasn't anything weird about their reactions.

"It's hotpot time!" sang Haruka-kun, "mystery meat, mystery veggies, ludicrous loads of fungus, y'know what I mean, soon we'll eat!"

He seemed like he was in a good mood, but he'd totally forgotten about the dungeon. It was the reason he went there in the first place!

His only nod to the dungeon was in declaring that he killed it, leading to the first wave of vegetable reward. The dungeon was destroyed now. He babbled for so long about hotpot dinner, and could only spare a single fact about the dungeon: it was dead. He also mentioned some sort of inexplicable landscaping tools, but I couldn't handle any more of his prattle, especially not with the smell of hotpot wafting through the room.

What an amazing scent! Some of the mysterious vegetables seemed similar to napa cabbage. Others resembled scallions, but I wouldn't be sure until I tasted them. *Is it ready yet? Can I eat them?* The lord of the hotpot was a dictator of the kitchen!

"Haruka-kun, I'm *so* hungry, I'm wasting away!" I groaned.

"Still thy wagging tongue!" Haruka-kun snapped. "The good lords of broth, chicken and mushroom, must first comingle, then they shall get familiar with the scions of vegetable. Once I have agitated them to a boil, we shall lower tensions until they are barely simmering, and finally the heavenly hotpot shall be ours to consume...y'know?"

Vice Rep A said, "It smells so good."

"I can't wait," said Nudist Girl.

"I want it so bad," said one of the mean girls. "I can't stop thinking about hotpot!"

Despite all our efforts, none of us had the knack for cooking. The melee fighters among us could use blades in a thousand destructive ways, but we were useless when it came to dinner. No one dared to question the whims of the hotpot despot, so we simply sat there and waited, stomachs growling in concert.

"At last, it is completed, cooked, hotpotified! The simmering tensions as ceramic, flame, and ingredients began diplomatic exchanges. Soon, they joined each other with love in their hearts, as well as friendship, bittersweet joy, and an ambivalence raw from the harshness of reality, yet still able to reconcile into harmonious fluttering—"

"Stop ranting! We're starving and you won't shut up!" a mean girl said.

"Let's eat!" we chorused.

"Hot! Yummy!" said Nudist Girl.

"Wow! Incredible!" said Vice Rep B.

"This is great! Seconds, please," Fish Girl demanded.

I was too busy eating to say anything—it was *that* delicious. Indeed, I was so impatient that I burned my mouth on the steaming hot food.

"It's so good, it hurts!" I cried.

"I'm so happy, but my throat is on fire!"

Damn, it was delicious, even if Haruka-kun kept complaining about the lack of kombu. That hotpot might be the best hotpot I'd ever eaten. How could Haruka-kun *still* find something to complain about? He was way too demanding. His constant pursuit of new ingredients had forced the small general store to expand its inventory by a massive amount. At this rate, it'd turn into a department store before long.

After dinner, we took turns reporting on the regional dungeons we investigated, making plans for future raids. Each dungeon needed a different approach, so after some discussion, we formulated battle plans that took advantage of our individual skills, gear, strengths, and weaknesses.

Finally, I asked the absentminded hotpot czar, Haruka-kun, "So what happened to the dungeon? Did you reach the lowest floor?"

I should've known I was only rolling out the red carpet for more of his nonsense. He whined nonstop about the dungeon's lack of climate control, not to mention the inadequate safety measures and poor signage. He went on to claim that its deplorable condition ruined property values and made the place dangerous for adventurers.

Could a dungeon with proper climate control and compliance with local safety ordinances still be considered a dungeon? I couldn't tell if he went on a dungeon raid or a house hunt. I could easily imagine Haruka-kun breaking into the homes of strangers and menacing them. Although, he did say that he faced some monsters, so maybe he was talking about a dungeon after all. The culprit's report couldn't be trusted, but it was at least clear that he wasn't talking about a condo—I hoped.

At one point, he said, "The humidity was just so awful; I was so hyped to do some dungeon crawling, but I ended up wading through wet muck. A terrifying, awful experience, right?"

"You're the one who flooded it! It's your fault!" we shouted.

It was a recently formed dungeon with only seventeen floors. Angelica cut a swath of destruction through the dungeon, slaying the few weak monsters that remained.

"We got a real workout from climbing up and down stairs, even if it was in that mold trap. I mean, the dungeon king was already dead before we got there, clearly weakened by the toxic environment!"

"Even a dungeon king in a healthy environment would die from drowning!"

"Ohhh, I get it. So the real perpetrator was a lack of healthy exercise habits. That's why it died so quickly underwater, right?"

"The dungeon king would've died no matter how much exercise it got! An exercise routine doesn't prevent drowning!"

He complained that the dungeon was boring, but he did bring along the former emperor of the Ultimate Dungeon to a wimpy seventeen-floor dungeon. She was total overkill!

Nonetheless, I was relieved that Haruka-kun was safe.

It was so easy to forget that he was still under level 20. Even level 20 adventurers couldn't form their own dungeon raid parties, they needed to tag along with senior groups as apprentices.

I couldn't decide what was in greater danger, Haruka-kun or the dungeons. In either case, what they did would've been deadly dangerous for any other pair of adventurers under level 20.

That's why I was still relieved when he came back safe.

Then he started mumbling about how the dungeon king's armor was just lying unused on the lowest floor. That obviously meant that the dungeon king died without ever facing its foes. It drowned as an innocent, possibly without ever even seeing a human.

Haruka-kun didn't know what kind of monster it was—he didn't even fight it! The life of the dungeon king, along with its dungeon, was cut short.

I got the feeling that I should be more worried about the dungeons than about Haruka-kun. Typically, defeating the dungeon king would be a feat worthy of praise, but after hearing what happened, I actually thought the dungeon king sounded a little...pitiful.

Haruka-kun said that he was going to take his automatic landscaping tools to make a garden around his cave tomorrow. His cave was going to become even more luxurious. What was so great about dungeons and caves?

Then, he began another auction. There was a sword, a spear, a shield, and the dungeon king's armor. The participants flooded in, shouting in their bids...but everyone fell silent when it came to the deluxe item: the Spike Armor.

We couldn't get items with abilities attached or high-grade armor in town, and it was difficult to equip thirty people in the best-case scenario. Furthermore, because we all swapped between different weapon sets, every one of us needed their own swords, shields, spears, and armor. Considering our lack of good equipment, the auction was fierce for all except the Spike Armor.

He even started lowering the price after getting no bids. Eventually, he begged us to just take it off his hands and tried to force us to accept the armor, but we all ran away. No one wanted it.

No girl would ever wear such sinister, spike-covered armor! Even the boys recoiled from it. Only a true villain would ever wear that stuff—the kind of gear that suited a post-apocalyptic warlord.

Only Haruka-kun would consider wearing something so obviously evil. It was only suited for someone more wicked than a demon lord, and he was the only person I could imagine qualifying for that title. Even the former dungeon emperor shook her head with tears in her eyes.

How dare you suggest a girl put on something so vile!

LONER LIFE
◆IN ANOTHER WORLD◆

I didn't do anything wrong, so why doesn't anyone believe me?

TIME FOR A GIRLS' MEETING in the baths. As we undressed and washed each other's backs, we asked Angelica about her day. Her speech was still halting, but she was somehow easier to understand than Haruka-kun, who could only vomit a stream of inexplicable untruths.

"A small hamlet," she said, "so poor. But the people were kind, gentle."

So close to the evil forest, yet their only fortification was a busted-up, unmaintained fence.

Of course, Haruka-kun failed to mention that he received so many vegetables because he also distributed food and potions to the farmers on top of everything else.

The villagers wept tears of gratitude.

Angelica beamed with pride as she spoke of Haruka-kun, as if he were a shining hero.

The villagers were overjoyed when he built a wall to barricade the hamlet. He bought all the potatoes they couldn't sell, and even taught them how to cook with them. Then, he scythed down the evil forest surrounding the village, so the villagers continued to express their gratitude with even more vegetables.

Angelica filled us in on the many things Haruka-kun left out. Our eyes turned red from crying so much.

Now we understood: Haruka-kun always presented his actions in the worst possible light.

We all knew hypocrites that painted themselves in a positive light—I could think of plenty of adults like that. They flattered themselves, pretending their meaningless acts were great deeds, profiting off their own bullshit. There were a lot of people like that in the world we came from.

Haruka-kun, on the other hand, was the exact opposite. He never said anything good—about himself or anyone else. Every word that came out of his mouth dripped with venom, so even when he did incredible things, we could only see the problems he caused.

I had never heard him say he did something right.

Even though he was always helping everyone, he acted like it was all a coincidence—an accident, nothing to do with him, he didn't know, he didn't do anything, he was surprised. He was innocent but wore the mask of a criminal.

He was an anti-hypocrite. Looking and acting like the bad guy, he ended up helping everyone he came across and refusing to take credit.

Today was another day like that. When all the villagers wept their thanks, he retreated as if this was his ultimate weakness.

When he was totally alone in this world, he faced a horde of monsters, and later escaped from the Ultimate Dungeon all by himself. Yet, when anyone tried to thank him, he lost his cool and fled the scene.

He only knew how to play the part of the villain.

That's why all our eyes were red.

We moved the girls' meeting from the bath to our rooms. Angelica cheerfully showed off the dresses and lingerie Haruka-kun bought her.

No one could deny that this world had fabulous clothes. She had beautiful dresses and lingerie, and countless elaborate accessories. We looked on with envy and passed them around...but the more we looked, the more we realized how revealing the clothing was. We suddenly understood exactly what Haruka-kun was doing. *I mean, this dress—*

"What is this?! The slit on this dress goes all the way to the hip, like a qipao?!" I said.

"This one is so cute... Hang on, the neckline is down to your navel," Vice Rep B said.

"This black one is gorgeous, with its open back," one of the athletic girls said. "Wait, everyone could see my ass if I wore this! That's so indecent!"

"This one is all lace with no lining! Can you even call it a dress?!" Vice Rep A shouted. "It doesn't cover anything! It's more holes than fabric!"

"Not to mention this one," Fish Girl said. "It's literally mesh netting!"

The dresses were brightly colored and made from high-quality fabric, but when I took a closer look, they all revealed way too much!

"They even have lingerie in this world," said the Queen Bee.

"This one's cute, but it's so skimpy, it only covers half your butt!"

"Oh, look at this one! The sides are just string, but it's kind of cute in a sexy way? Actually no, it's all sexy, no cute."

"This covers less than a handkerchief! It's just saying, 'look at all the exposed bits!'"

"Oh my god, look at that one! It's mesh underwear! Mesh!"

"If these were a little more normal, I'd want them, but they're way too revealing!"

At first, we were excited that there was cute underwear in this world, but the more we looked, the more we realized that none of it covered anything at all. Most of it was tiny or see-through!

"You—you wouldn't even need to take this off to be naked," Nudist Girl said.

"Don't tell me you wore this—you did?!" I said.

"All this...where did Haruka-kun buy it?"

"The *general store?!* I've got to see that!"

"I don't think this underwear would survive combat—it would disintegrate in the middle of a battle!"

"Yeah, it's for sexy purposes only."

"I mean it's cute, but why would I ever wear it? Even if you think of it like lucky underwear, I don't want the kind of luck these would bring."

The dresses and lingerie were completely impractical, but they were apparently getting daily—or should I say nightly—use! *That* was the only kind of combat they were for!

Angelica, with an innocent smile on her face, explained in *way too much detail* exactly where his hands went, why there were holes in this or that garment, and so on. It was way too explicit for our impressionable young minds!

The girls couldn't take it and literally started to faint from the descriptions! Her expression was so erotic, too.

I mean, I understand getting caught up in your feelings, but this was TMI! Her eyes and face melted with the heat of remembered pleasures!

For example: She told us she got blue stone earrings today. We all told her that sounded great, until she showed us the blue dress with the extreme side-slit they were meant to accessorize.

We realized immediately that the earrings were just an afterthought for the dress!

She kept going, pointing to where he licked and bit her, the things he did with his tongue, hands, and fingers—*this is totally out of bounds!*

Such vivid descriptions made even the girls with the stoutest hearts recoil! Our eyes rolled back, we practically blacked out from her recollections.

Everyone's eyes were red. Mine were bloodshot from all the excitement, too.

I'm getting the sense that this is about revenge, so why does it feel so good?

BEFORE WE LEFT for the Adventurers' Guild in the morning, I just needed to do one little thing. I needed to get my morning glares. Getting bombarded by cutting glances and piercing stares was a balanced, wholesome part of any teen boy's morning.

"Okay, I've had enough. The job board still hasn't updated?! Does this guild even try? Whoever's in charge of this bulletin board clearly doesn't work at all, right? I'm a NEET and I've worked harder than this! I come every single day and for what? There hasn't been a single update! How long will it take before you post a get-rich-quick scheme for me?! Where's my cash cow?!"

The head receptionist said sharply, "Can you knock before slithering in here? Why do you come here every single day? Do you think you get a prize for perfect attendance?!

I tell you every day that these job requests are for adventurers *only*, and last time I checked, you're still not registered, right? Yet you come every day. I'm starting to suspect that you only come to whine about the bulletin board!"

Another round of glares from the morning receptionist. Between the glares from the girls at the inn, the death stares from Miss Armor Rep, and the spicy narrowed eyes at night, I could honestly call this world a paradise of glares! *All right, I got my glares in, time to go.*

I took my considerable load of spellstones to the trade-in counter and tried to explain as simply as I could that I got them from the dungeon by the hamlet downriver. That old guild master showed up, so I explained as quickly as I could before sprinting away.

Why couldn't they understand that the dungeon drowned and died? I explained it three whole times. That should've been more than enough.

Ah, the forest—home sweet home! I'd decide whether to stay the night after taking a look around. It wasn't going to be easy for a teen boy to throw away the chance for some romantic hot tub fun, but if we did that, I didn't think I'd get anything else done.

Anyway, time to mow the lawn! My objective was simple: a detached cave home with a garden!

I'd already tested out the demon scythes on the forest by the hamlet, where they easily felled massive trees. *This is going to be a piece of cake!*

"The trees are imbued with magic, so they're tough... but when I use some magic myself, it's no problem."

First, I wanted to take care of the trees surrounding the cave. They'd been bothering me for a while, but it'd seemed like even more of a pain to fix it than to leave it, so I'd put this essential chore off. My nearest neighbor was so far away it didn't seem like a priority. I didn't even have any neighbors *in* the forest.

The demon scythes had remote control autopilot and autonomous slicing capabilities, not to mention how huge they were. With a single command, I could fell the entire forest, decapitating any goblins that stood in my way. This was a huge win for me! I could have a garden! Should I start cultivating the land next? For the time being, I would just cut down the forest around my cave.

The scythes glittered in the sunlight as they spun and swept away the stubborn undergrowth, felled the gargantuan trees, and massacred any passing goblins. *These are awesome.*

With my scythes before me, we advanced through the forest at a brisk pace, but Miss Armor Rep was starting to get bored since the scythes were doing all the work.

"Uh, you do realize that that's what you do to me all the time?" I said. "You always leave me out of the fun. You did it all day yesterday, remember? I couldn't do a single thing in the dungeon besides climb stairs!"

She looked away from me. But seriously, right when I was ready to kick some monster ass, they'd already been annihilated! It was a tragedy. After all that effort I put into extending my staff, the fight was over. It's pretty depressing to not have anything to do as soon as I entered a battle stance. Such was my life.

There were few monsters left in the forest now. I heard that soldiers and adventurers even started to enter the forest to thin out the population, rendering this area fairly unprofitable. Not like there was much hope for profit anyway; the goblins had worthless loot, and mushrooms were, for once, scarce. I wanted to go back to the cave.

Occasionally the demon scythes brought back spell-stones—how?! Did they have secret hands?!

After much slashing and felling, we arrived home, but it was too soon to relax. Leaving the demon scythes to finish their landscaping job, Miss Armor Rep and I headed for the center of the forest.

I wanted to gather more mushrooms and hunt goblins and kobolds. I finally had a chance to practice my skills.

Not that getting beat up by Miss Class Rep wasn't worthwhile, but it couldn't be considered practice. Not combat practice, anyway. It just prepared me for surviving death!

Lately, Miss Armor Rep had been practicing beating the hell out of the Class Rep and the others by the bathhouse. I snuck into the back garden to take a look, and I witnessed with my very own eyes the surreal sight of twenty-nine half-dead bodies heaped high under the glittering starlight, with the Poster Girl performing some sort of mysterious dance in a panic. It was wild.

Now it was time to practice Magic Entanglement. It allowed me to power myself up by imbuing my body with skills and magic. But if I made the wrong move, my body almost tore itself apart as my HP plummeted. This skill was a double-edged sword.

Taking a breath, I aligned my magic power with my skills. I tried to synchronize my movements with my skill use so that they worked seamlessly together, as if by instinct.

I would only feel like I succeeded if I could do all of that as effortlessly as taking a breath. If I didn't have perfect control, my own skills would tear my flesh apart and break my bones. I healed with Regeneration whenever that happened, but I couldn't sustain an endless cycle of breaking myself, only to regenerate. That's why I'd decided to practice until I literally couldn't move anymore. *Actually, this is starting to sound like a terrible idea!*

"I don't think I'll be able to use Magic Entanglement until I can use it by instinct, y'know? It just works too fast…and I'm too weak."

Miss Armor Rep nodded.

This skill allowed me to overcome my low stats by forcing my body beyond its limits. It was an extremely reckless technique because I had to manipulate my body from the outside with Holding magic.

I took damage whenever I used the skill, but if I didn't try it, monsters would easily kill me. That's why I pushed myself to improvise new techniques, taking all the shortcuts I could and cheating when I couldn't, hacking together the best parts of my skill list—all to survive. The pain would be worth it when I mastered Magic Entanglement. If I didn't, I'd still get beaten up in the name of so-called sparring. It was going to hurt either way.

I readied my mind and let my emotions blaze.

I let out a battle-cry as I smashed a goblin: "Hiyaaaaaah! …Oh, you died already?"

Magic Entanglement took out level 15+ goblins in one hit. Well, I always killed them in one hit, but now I could do it without relying on sneak attacks, so that was amazing progress.

I could finally defeat them without erasing my presence and ambushing them one at a time. Even so, I was burning through my HP at an alarming rate. It hurt like hell!

Somehow, I was using Magic Entanglement, even though I hadn't mastered it. Next up was the real challenge—*Teleport*. Magic Entanglement was a combat skill, but Teleport was pure magic.

Magic Entanglement not only allowed me to "entangle" my body with magic power, but with my skills and magical talents as well—in other words, I could even imbue my body with Teleport.

Now kobolds were attacking me, so I smashed those hideous, dog-headed monsters. I was certainly fast, but I could barely control the instantaneous movement.

The world seemed to vanish for a moment when I moved. If I could master this style of movement perfectly, I would be able to vanish a moment before attacking, a technique that couldn't be blocked. When I got the hang of it, I would have an undefeatable one-hit-KO move.

"This isn't easy to control. Every time I slay a monster, I take some damage myself. If I push myself too far, I'll tear myself apart!"

Miss Armor Rep gave a sharp nod.

Forcing my blurry limbs into alignment with the rest of my frame, I pumped magic power into my body to speed up after Miss Armor Rep. Teleporting would be easier if I was focused on a static target, but I couldn't calculate precise spatial coordinates by instinct.

Consciously choosing where I would teleport in the middle of battle had to be impossible—everything was in constant flux!

"Maybe if I used Teleport while my target couldn't move," I ruminated as I dodged a kobold's slavering jaws. "God—don't bite me! I'm thinking about something really complicated! My brain's a no-chomp zone!"

Though my movements were clumsy, my body blurred and vanished for a half step as I felled the bitey kobold. I moved faster than my speed stat should've allowed. If I could master instantaneous movement and make it work with Life or Death, I'd be able to keep up with Miss Armor Rep when we sparred. I might even avoid some painful beatings! Although somehow I still had the distinct impression that it wouldn't be enough to win a match with her.

Honestly, despite my lack of control, I had started using Teleport when we sparred and Miss Armor Rep *still* beat the crap out of me. I got wrecked even though I could literally vanish with a thought!

She was on a whole other level. When she was consumed by darkness in the very depths of the Ultimate

Dungeon, she transformed not into a mere dungeon king, but a dungeon *emperor*, something that could have easily destroyed the world.

She'd leveled up since, but even when Servitude had reduced her to level 1, she was unbelievably powerful. If she ever fully recovered her strength, I wouldn't be able to defeat her. No one could!

"Er, if you kill them all, my turn, my chance to practice, uh, my very reason to continue this miserable existence, will go out like a candle in the wind! You know, where I'm the candle and you're some sort of high-powered LED light, right?!"

Miss Armor Rep shook her head no.

Well, at least she seemed to have fun prancing around the forest. She was probably smiling beneath her helmet as she trampled the corpses of goblins and kobolds. At least she got to enjoy herself...

The moment I took my eyes off her, she annihilated another horde of goblins and kobolds. Her merry massacres felled the forest around the cave, turning it into a vacant lot. *I guess that's fine,* I thought to myself, gritting my teeth. Now I had a longer commute if I wanted to gather mushrooms.

We carried on slaying hordes of monsters for a while. I kept trying to entangle my best skills into my body and manipulate them into a single, flawless strike, but all my practice partners had died, and I still wasn't confident.

I decided to head upstream. This area had no king-class monsters, so there was no point in lingering here anyway. At least the monsters upstream were plentiful. Maybe Miss Armor Rep would do me the favor of holding back and leaving me some to fight?

Spoiler: she did not. I heard the blood-curdling cry of another fallen kobold.

"At least put up a fight, you monsters! Why do you all die as soon as we counterattack? You're not stupid, worthless goblins. You're kobolds, damn it! Work together, kobolds! How could you allow Miss Armor Rep to break your formation so effortlessly? Don't you have anything to live for? Is it not easy being kobold or something?"

There was no other explanation. They must've had a death wish. From the moment Miss Armor Rep attacked, they were finished. Couldn't they buy me some time? *Useless dog-headed jerks!*

Losing sight of Miss Armor Rep's ongoing assault, I approached a pack of surviving kobolds. I dodged and attacked with the same movement, over and over. I let each move flow into the next, cheating my way into a combination I still couldn't control.

"Whoa! I think I did it that time. I definitely didn't not do it!"

Next, we headed toward the orcs' hidey-holes. I felt like I spent a lot more time collecting mushrooms than fighting! If I kept this up, I'd get the Mushroom Hunter job added to my status, though that was probably more respectable than being unemployed. On the other hand, being a NEET was way less suspect than a weirdo who hunted mushrooms for a living, wore all black, and wielded a stick.

With a cracked, rasping roar, another orc fell before Miss Armor Rep's blade.

I was aghast. While I was over here working hard to master Teleport, careening through the air and crashing into trees, Miss Armor Rep had already finished obliterating the orcs!

I did explode a few by mistake when I crashed through them, but I didn't properly fight any of them. This was total orc annihilation. No doubt, the one-woman war on the orcs of the forest ended while I rolled around by some trees.

Despite my intentions to practice combat, I only got to practice tumbling. To be fair, I wasn't practicing how to fall on purpose. Worst of all, I only got to fight one lousy orc king, despite all my begging!

The platinum-clad culprit had killed the rest. She looked on as I fought the orc king, nodding occasionally. She often sighed and shook her head as I entangled myself, marionetted, and went flying uncontrollably. She didn't need to make her disappointment so obvious!

Combine my magic power with my skills, entangle them, and let them flow as one—create a single stroke and cut with it, I told myself.

On my seventh attempt to hit the orc, I managed to pull off something like an upgraded Life or Death. I was pretty sure it worked, since I managed to kill the orc king in one hit. As soon as I felt the impulse to move, in the space of a single breath, the orc had died. *That's it?* I felt like I still needed to work on it. Unfortunately, there were no more orcs to use for practice.

Out of options, I spent the rest of the afternoon getting my ass kicked. Miss Armor Rep wrecked me within the very garden that my demon scythes created!

Before I could even take a breath, she beat me up. When I finally did attack, she avoided the strike and still beat me up. Even with my constant teleporting and instant movement, I still managed to telegraph all my attacks. She predicted my every move and played me like a fiddle. By which I mean, she beat me up, and she kept doing it until dusk.

But I had my revenge, and what a sweet vengeance it was, for the hours of night were the time to live out my fantasies! We thoroughly enjoyed my vengeance, though she would probably get her own re-revenge tomorrow.

Still, I had no regrets. My revenge was absolutely worth every moment, even though it couldn't technically be called revenge. Another amazing night!

DAY 43
MORNING

How could you take away the timber I worked so hard to procure?

OMUI
ADVENTURERS'
GUILD

I F YOU FOLLOW THE RIVER out from Omui, you reach a sleepy hamlet called Shimomui. This miniscule hamlet formed in the name of mutual defense in the closest agricultural region to Omui.

Whenever Shimomui grew too large, monsters raided, and the farms were ruined because they couldn't defend themselves. So the town shrank, and in time, began to grow and develop again, only to get attacked by monsters again. And so on and so on. We would send patrols to the area to cull the monster population as best they could, but it was never enough.

The hamlet didn't even have a proper fence, let alone something truly defensible, like a wall. They didn't have the labor, resources, or capital to maintain what they had. It was a poor hamlct, with hardly anything of worth.

But the cycle broke. Because of the regional influx of spellstones, the farmers of that hamlet enjoyed an unprecedented economic boom and now had a civic budget. Still, they lacked the labor and resources necessary to protect themselves. They may have bordered a forest, but they couldn't get much lumber from those woods because of the monsters.

Today, that all changed. We received a large shipment of timber from that boy who showed up at the guild every day.

He said, "Wait, you want timber? This town is literally in a forest. Are you serious? I'll deliver it soon. Be sure to pay me then."

With those words, he left. Difficult as it is to believe, he delivered on his promise. Soon after, stacks of dried, prepared lumber arrived en masse.

We sent a missive to the duke, and he purchased all our recently acquired lumber and gathered adventurers to begin immediate construction of perimeter fences for the towns of his duchy, beginning with nearby Shimomui.

But the Shimomui I'd described no longer existed. It had vanished.

In its place, we found a castle town, surrounded by massive walls. The village elder appeared at the gate and told us of recent events. It was an absurd, incoherent story, like a fairy tale. He told us a child put his hand on the earth, commanded a wall to rise, and transformed their hamlet into the fortress before us.

Our most recent report from Shimomui simply stated that a dungeon entrance had emerged by the river. We had planned to raid the dungeon and end the threat, but we didn't have enough adventurers available, leading to delays.

The day before yesterday, a knight in shining silver armor and a boy in a black hood appeared. He bought up all the surplus produce in the village, and gave them grains and valuable medicine in exchange. Then, the two left for the dungeon.

They acted as if it was all a game.

On the following day, they went back to the dungeon, and, upon their return, they proclaimed that the dungeon was defeated.

The people of the hamlet were in shock. There was no doubt, for the boy held the legendary ring of the dungeon king in his hand. The villagers showered him with praise, glory, and vegetables for his acts of generosity: buying their worthless produce, and destroying the dungeon.

The boy accepted the vegetables with an open heart. Then, he placed his hand on the earth and beckoned a wall into being with the phrase, "Uh, come on, wall." The fortress emerged from the ground just like that.

The villagers didn't know how to thank a sorcerer of such immeasurable power, so they gathered their most valuable vegetables and gave them to him. As if his generosity knew no bounds, he gifted them rare weapons, expensive medicines, and even money in return.

The poor village tried to tell the boy that they could never repay his generosity, but the boy smiled and told them that he only wanted the vegetables. The villagers tried to pool together the few precious metals they had, but the boy looked troubled and instead thanked them for the vegetables. For some reason, he thanked *them*.

When they thought he was going to leave, he ran off into the woods and felled the trees in his path, slaying any monsters he encountered. Then he vanished into the distance without a single glance over his shoulder.

The boy left behind a magnificent wall. He cleared the forest and defeated the dungeon. He supplied them with money and grain. He even taught them how to preserve and prepare the potatoes they couldn't sell. Just like that, Shimomui became a prosperous village, stocked with medicine and even weapons. It was now a place where anyone could find happiness.

The village elder and his neighbors wept as they told us they couldn't believe their own fortune—they now felt like they lived in a dream. They even forgot to ask the boy his name.

It was the stuff of legend.

In this cruel, uncaring world, their tale could only be a legend or a fairy tale. That sort of story was the stuff of gossip that only happened to a farmer's cousin's uncle.

But we could not deny the evidence before our eyes. The magnificent wall stood there. The villagers knew that better than anyone. They couldn't bring themselves to laugh at the absurdity.

I had an inkling of the identity of that black-hooded boy. More than an inkling, because I spoke with him only this morning.

That black-hooded boy stammered something about a dungeon dying. I had no idea what he was on about, but he did say that. I came here, in part, to confirm his testimony.

That black-hooded boy had also shipped in the timber. He cleared the forest of trees and monsters—perhaps I should've expected this of him.

But he left without reporting anything about Shimomui, so no one was prepared for this fairy tale.

In time, it really would become a tall tale passed down through generations in Shimomui.

He brought such joy, won such gratitude and praise, and left without anyone knowing his name. Their gratitude could only become the first small stirrings of legend.

I knew the boy wouldn't say anything. This story could very well have slipped into obscurity. Instead, it became a new local legend for the people of Shimomui.

They would've been surprised to see the boy from their legend walking around Omui, but it was but a cheerful fairy tale until then.

I decided not to tell them that the great sorcerer with the sylvan staff was little more than a boy who ran around beating monsters with a literal stick.

The boy could only blame himself for his obscurity. He never explained himself and didn't even remember to give his name. He would just have to put up with the stories they're spreading about him: the legend of the Black-Cloaked Sorcerer and the Platinum Knight.

From an outside perspective she looks like a weirdo, but at least she's having fun.

THE CAVE

I T RAINED FOR THE FIRST TIME in a while. Was this the start of the rainy season? The rain veiled the outside world in gloom.

It'd rarely rained before today, and even that rain was only drizzle at night. The rain looked like it would stop before too long, so we decided to wait it out in the cave.

Still, I didn't think that continuing our nighttime activities into the morning was a particularly good idea. The idea certainly had its appeal—its delicious, delicious appeal—but it was definitely a bad idea. She glared at me as soon as I imagined it.

I decided to pass the time doing some general remodeling of the cave and building new furniture. I got into a groove, and even tried to make a hammock. Afterward, we decided to test the hammock out. *Don't ask for any details about our testing procedures, they're strictly confidential.*

Having done enough, ahem, testing, I used magic to prepare my garden from the comfort of my cave. I planted fruits, built a terrace, diverted the river to make a small pond, and arranged tables and benches around it.

My magic definitely got weaker with distance. Even using the ground as a medium was easier at close range, so I thought of this as practice! *That's definitely why. It's not that I wanted to stay dry in the comfort of my home!*

Just for kicks, I made a paving stone walkway along the riverbank, an arched stone bridge across the river, and some benches along the opposite bank until the downpour finally turned to drizzle.

"Looks like the rain's gonna stop soon, y'know? It's light enough now that we could go back to town if you want. Or we could just stay here…"

Miss Armor Rep looked hesitant, but it seemed like she was leaning toward going back to town.

She was the one who wanted more alone time with just the two of us, so why did she glare at me so often? Was I trying too hard? *I'm just a teenage boy!* Worthless during the day, but night was a whole other story—know what I mean? *Since I wasn't the hero of the story and I wouldn't get any cool action scenes, at least let me have these love scenes!*

Miss Armor Rep looked like she wanted to go back and see the other girls again. I enjoyed spending time alone with her, but she seemed to enjoy having female friends to chat with. I was happy for her, but I couldn't help but wonder what they talked about together. Every time I asked her, she said it was a secret between girls. In any case, we could always come back later. We set off toward town.

The forest was behind us already, that's how fast we moved. Having killed all the monsters and picked all the mushrooms, there was no point loitering in the forest. Because of my Walking Mastery skill, I got out of the forest in no time. Teleport and my other movement skills certainly helped, too. Miss Armor Rep followed me without a problem. If we didn't stop, the trip would take less than an hour at this rate.

Soon enough, I saw that town, whatever it was called.

I shoved open the front door to the general store and said, "Get any good merch? I'll buy 'em, I'll buy 'em all! Rich man walking, over here! Where's the general of the general store, y'know?"

I was rich from the mushroom hunt! Miss Armor Rep's eyes sparkled as she looked at all the latest foreign fashions. She was exuding some kind of a terrifying bloodlust by looking at the racks. *I'll just slowly back away?*

Despite expanding, the shop was still small and cramped from all the new inventory. I felt like I was at a flea market; they clearly didn't expand the premises enough.

"Are you not making enough profit? With all these mushrooms, you should have plenty of capital, so why haven't you expanded your store yet?"

"Sales are going great, but we have a lot of supply chain issues. Everything's a bit chaotic, right now. We only just expanded but a certain someone keeps flooding us with more inventory, so there's never enough room!"

She had bought the adjoining building and claimed the extra floor space by knocking down the wall between them. The floors of the two buildings didn't match each other, and the whole store looked like a jumble with products scattered all around the store.

"Didn't you buy the lot behind your building? If you need more money, I'll lend you some. You can pay me back with sexy lingerie if you want. I'll take revealing dresses, too! You have such an amazing stock! Please! I'm not kidding! Thank you! Please?!"

"H-h-hang on," the woman stuttered, "We have new arrivals, so please calm down! I did buy that lot, but we couldn't find a carpenter that was free! Also, I couldn't decide between building a warehouse or another shop, not to mention the lack of architectural plans. This place is busy all the time now because of a certain someone. To be clear, this used to be such a quiet town until that certain someone—you—came along."

Expanding into the neighboring shop wasn't enough, so she bought the plot behind the store, too. But she still hadn't started construction.

I provided loads of capital, mushrooms, and spellstones to this store in exchange for two of the three basic necessities of life: rice and skimpy dresses. Sleep was a necessary sacrifice to satisfy the other two needs!

"Since you already own the land, I can just build it for you. With stone construction, you're limited to four or five stories, so it would just take a sec. I can even put in a basement! Would you like me to throw in a dungeon feature?"

"How could you build it so quickly? Why would a general store need a dungeon?! What do you think this place is? What do you want from this store...besides lingerie? Although a basement would be useful, so long as it's not a dungeon!"

Did that mean she didn't need a dungeon? Dungeon kings had rings and stuff she could sell, or maybe you could turn the dungeon king into dungeon chef for some fresh dungeon-to-table ingredients.

"We'll deal with the interior after I connect the two buildings. Can you move the inventory away from the back wall?" I said. "Miss Armor Rep, can you help, too? I'll buy all the clothes you want after, okay?"

A square building made most sense considering the plot I had to work with. Nothing special: the first two floors would be retail space, with the third in reserve if there still wasn't enough room. The fourth and fifth floors would contain the warehouse, office, and private residence of the general store lady. The basement would also function as additional storage.

I could add more floors or expand the basement later if need be. I began the real work.

I used Jupiter Eye to make accurate measurements of the current store, wrote them down, and laid a foundation based on those calculations. Next, I poured my magical power into the ground to carve out a basement. With the soil and stones I gathered from that, I erected walls that surrounded the old building and created support beams and pillars to keep the structure stable.

Hmm, I doubted that I could do more than five floors with my magical reserves. Slowly working magic in, I compressed the earthen walls with Holding magic until they were solid. The buildings were now inseparable, as I created reinforced pillars in the four corners and the center of the structure, with sturdy buttresses to support the upper floors.

If the architecture is fun, it will make the shopping experience more fun, right? I summoned a staircase that spiraled around the central pillar. Once I was satisfied with those stairs, I decided the walls needed a bit more ornamentation, so I added that and strengthened them a little more. Finally, I added a delivery entrance with direct basement access!

Damn, I spent most of my magic power on that. I was cutting it pretty close. The sexy outfits had better be worth all this effort! *Nothing motivates teen boys better than horniness,* I thought. *All this for the sake of infinite romance!*

One could never have enough clothes, after all. Miss Armor Rep looked amazing no matter what she was wearing, so it shouldn't have mattered, but it would've been a total shame if she couldn't wear clothes that matched her looks.

Besides, half the fun of trying on new outfits was when she took them off...though there wasn't much mystery, since I only bought revealing outfits for her. *I can't help myself. I'm a teenager.*

Regaining my train of thought, I returned to the old general store interior to find that the lady was taking her sweet time to move her products out of the way. I put in so much work, and she was only halfway finished!

"It's built," I said, "so what's taking so long? I just want to connect the interiors before calling it a day, y'know? Going to take an Out-of-MP break for the day."

I reinforced the load-bearing walls and merged them with those of the new building, integrating them and opening up the space! *Damn, I'm spent. Just a little more...a little more... Yes!* Wow, that was close! I would have to finish decorating and renovating tomorrow; I had no magic left.

"The rest of what? How much did you do today? You... you... Ahhh! What is this?! Where am I?! What have you built?!"

The general store lady lost her mind and sprinted out of the store to gaze up at the new building, mouth agape. For some reason, a crowd had gathered around the building. Was there something weird about it? It was just a stone building.

"You can stare all you like, but it's just a rectangle right now. I don't even have the energy to paint or decorate it yet. Well, I'm famished, so I'm going to go, okay?"

The general story lady didn't respond, she just continued

to stare with her mouth open. Her reboot cycle was taking a while.

I felt like I was going to faint from hunger. Why wouldn't she respond? Can't she hear my stomach growling?! Am I that despised?!

If she didn't snap out of it and go back into her store, Miss Armor Rep was going to shoplift all the outfits we were promised. *I'm not kidding, she's holding armfuls of clothes—is it okay to just take them?*

Miss Armor Rep couldn't stop smiling from all the cute new clothes she got. I wore a matching wolfish grin, thinking about all the titillating outfits.

She absolutely had to try them all on, though I suspected that we wouldn't get past the part where she took her clothes off...but I could think about that when it happened.

Not that I could even begin to think in that situation, so this plan was foolproof. I doubted that she would have any interest in trying clothes on at that point...though if she didn't put anything on, how could she get me excited by taking it off? Oh well, at least the result was inevitable.

I returned to the inn.

"We're back!" I shouted, pushing open the door to the

common room. "Can I have, like, an extra huge serving? As soon as possible, okay? I'm ravenous, I could eat a whale. I feel a vast emptiness inside me, you know what I mean?"

"Welcome back," said the Class Rep. "How was your garde—what's with all the clothes?! Where'd you get them?!"

As soon as the girls heard about the new arrivals at the store, they ran out immediately. Some of them even resorted to using Blinding Step and Ground Shrink to get there faster. Unfortunately, I had just bought up all the best outfits to keep this shopaholic next to me sated!

I slurped up serving after serving until I was stuffed.

The Poster Girl sprinted pell-mell around the place, doing chores, so I decided to thank her by giving her one of the outfits we bought. She responded with one of her inexplicable dances of joy. She looked out of her mind when she danced like that, but at least she was having fun, right?

I took a bath and prepared for bed. *We're going to sleep the hell out of each other. So much relentless sleeping, I might even forget to sleep.*

We slept all night long, if you know what I mean.

But you always tell me to stop spending so much money?!

THE WHITE
LOSER INN
INTERLUDE:
GIRLS'
MEETING

WE SCRAMBLED TO BATHE as fast as possible.

It wasn't the best display of manners, but we couldn't help ourselves. We finally got cute, new clothes and we couldn't wait to try them on!

Most of the clothes in this world were either undyed or dyed a dark green, with an occasional and very expensive gray or dark blue. Until now, I hadn't seen any clothes in vibrant shades of red, blue, teal, or pink—not even white!

But the new clothes we bought came in a variety of pale colors, not quite pastel. They had new colors and patterns, and even came with ribbons and frills. They were *adorable*. At last, a boutique!

"Oh my god, I totally love our new clothes," said Vice Rep B. "But what happened to that store?"

"Yeah, their selection is incredible now! But the building seemed weirdly modern."

"This is so much cooler than what they had before! I don't remember the store being five stories."

"These fabrics are great, not scratchy or stiff like you'd think. Did you see they had stairs going down into a basement?"

"They're going to, like, get more new arrivals soon. We *have* to go back," the Queen Bee said. "The hicks in this town couldn't stop staring. Ew, I meant at the building!"

"They even have lace! It's super expensive, so I'm gonna start saving up. This is the first time we've seen a building that big in this world, right?"

Sighing, we all said, "The usual suspect..."

We knew who the culprit was from the start; we just ignored it. Clothes mattered more.

You could tell even at a distance that it was a building bigger than any of the others in this world. We had burst through the crowd without even stopping to look, but a close look really wasn't necessary.

We crowded into the store, tried everything on, hotly debated our selections, and rushed to buy whatever we could afford... Somehow, none of us gave the new building any thought until after we left.

"They even had hair clips! They were wooden, but even so, *accessories*! The kind that aren't a type of equipment!"

"I've seen equipment with gemstones before, but it's too fancy. It's hard to pull off flashy jewelry like that when you're sixteen!"

"OMG, this ring is super cute, right? It's also carved out of wood!" one of the mean girls squealed.

At last, the store carried a real selection of cute clothes and fashion accessories. It even had a few cosmetics!

The proprietress looked like she'd been crying as she restocked. Restocking so often in a store this size had to have been exhausting. She needed to hire some help before she keeled over.

One person could never run a shop the size of a department store by themselves! To be fair, the store's transformation was sudden.

There was no need to ask who was responsible for all this, we all knew. There was always only one truth! Angelica-san had quite a bundle of evidence in her arms.

"I heard they ordered the latest fashions from the capital, though it'll take a while to get here. They're supposed to be the best clothes in the country!"

"Yay! I need it!" several girls shouted.

We held an impromptu fashion show to show off our clothes, giggling the whole time.

We wore armor most of the time, though there were some decent robes and cloaks. Leather, chainmail, and plate armor didn't have an ounce of charm, so we couldn't contain our excitement at the thought of wearing some nice clothes for once. Everyone was dying to dress up.

Sure, we couldn't wear these clothes often. This was a dangerous fantasy world, so we had to wear armor most of the time, and our clothes had to be practical, rugged, and easy to move around in.

After all, there was no point wearing a cute outfit under my armor; the clothes would eventually get ruined.

Despite that, we just wanted to have something nice for ourselves. Even if we lived as adventurers, we were still girls. That's why we had a fashion show that lasted all night. We could finally be ourselves.

"Here, these would look so hot together," said Shimazaki-san, passing over some items.

"Wow! You look like a model!"

"The pattern on that skirt makes your legs look *super* long with those shoes."

"You're so right, thank you!"

"Your legs look so long now!"

"I want to try it on next!" Vice Rep C declared.

"Only if you let me borrow those shoes!"

"Deal!"

These clothes wouldn't have warranted a second glance back in Japan, but in this realm, we treasured them.

Haruka-kun made all of this happen. He invested in the store, made the new building, and ordered lots of adorable women's clothes. He even ordered different sizes, so no one had trouble finding clothes that fit. But I couldn't ignore that he happened to order a lot of revealing clothing.

Nonetheless, we were all close friends now. Naturally, we had a blast relaxing, swapping clothes, and putting on a fashion show.

This was the first time any of us could say we had made true friends, and now we had so many of them.

"Hey, not fair, you got two shirts!"

"Well, I couldn't choose a color, so—wait, you bought two pairs of shoes!"

"Let's swap, then!"

"This is great! I missed shopping!"

The general store lady even gave us a special "black-hair, black-eyes" discount. Even the girls who didn't have enough cash could buy what they wanted on credit. That was probably another directive from the store's not-so-silent silent partner.

He knew...he probably knew we were all holding back tears. He wanted to make us happy again, able to laugh.

That was why he spent all the money I couldn't confiscate—he spent it on clothes and building materials...all for our sake.

Of course, he could've used some of that money to pay off his mounting debts at the inn. He even tried to hide his bills from us until he risked getting evicted. We owed an unbelievable amount!

Angelica wanted to show off her new outfits, too.

The dresses she tried on seemed normal at first, but we soon noticed how provocative they all were!

He got her more of those, I thought. *Is she going to wear that tonight?* It was a strapless dress with a low neckline, cut so short that we could see her upper thighs. It left almost nothing to the imagination. She looked so happy with her clothes—an amazing, beautiful model. Her confident attitude made her look even sexier!

Our Presence Detection was probably going to level up again tonight. I felt like mine was going to hit max level. We had enough trouble sleeping as it was without hearing Haruka-kun trying too hard through the walls! At least Angelica seemed happy.

Then she started telling us about what they did in the cave last night. We all got knocked out in the first round. The explicit story mowed us down, knocking us out left and right! *I mean, they did it in a hammock?! It's too much!*

Angelica, satisfied with her story, headed over to Haruka-kun's room with an entrancing smile and a dress that left nothing to the imagination.

Even her footsteps sounded perversely delighted. When she finished her story, she said, "I w-want, with e-everyone." *Is she inviting us to join?!*

She said those words as her eyes sparkled with anticipation, a beatific, dreamy smile on her lips. *She wants to do* that *with all of us?*

Do *what?* What exactly was she imagining? All of us in a hammock?! Well, there's nothing weird about the hammock itself. Left to our own imaginings, we were in a hammock harem panic.

We couldn't bring ourselves to respond, as usual. *Everyone?!* Was she trying to become the dungeon emperor of harems or something?

I knew better. If we all showed up at Haruka-kun's door wearing sexy dresses, he would definitely escape at maximum speed. He'd run straight through a wall, leaving a Haruka-shaped hole behind.

Even though he was a pervert, he never could survive

a harem. The boy was hopeless around girls. He even ran out of his own home and lived in a tent by the cave entrance rather than stay with us. Seriously.

No matter how dirty his mind was, he was too timid. He would definitely run away from his own harem.

**DAY 45
MORNING**

With limited space, the display counter and sales floor
end up competing with one another.

**OMUI
GENERAL
STORE**

FIRST THING IN THE MORNING, I went to the store to finish working on the exterior and reinforcing the structure.

Upon entering the store, I said, "Good morning or whatever? It's morning, right? I'm here in the morning. Hey, you look tired."

I was about to get started on arranging the interior and setting up displays when I saw the general store lady wavering on her feet, dark circles under her eyes. I almost mistook her for a ghost—a raccoon ghost?

"Why are you so rude?" she growled. "Yes, fine, good morning. A certain someone forced me to work through the night! I'm *still* not done arranging the merchandise. I feel like I'm rolling a boulder uphill! As soon as I open, all my work will be undone!"

151

LONER LIFE IN ANOTHER WORLD

"No duh. How do you expect to display merch without shelves or tables? You were wasting your time. Anyway, I guess I'll make some shelves and tables for you now, okay? All that merch is in the way—do you think you can move it?"

She was crestfallen. I'd never seen a crest so fallen. She looked so low, I wonder if she remembered I only created one basement level? If she went too far down, another dungeon emperor might pop up. *Trust me, I've seen first-hand, the proof is standing right next to me!*

Since I felt sorry for the shopkeeper, I left her to her own devices. Turning my attention to the wall, I created wall-mounted racks while Miss Armor Rep activated Super-Speed and started shelving the merchandise.

She never failed to impress—she was still a genuine dungeon emperor even after quitting her job. She stocked the shelves so swiftly that her hands appeared to be in ten places at once. *So, this is the true power of the Emperor of the Dungeon?! Atatatatatata! You are already shelved.* The store owner finally came back to her senses while we were messing around.

We cleaned up most of the area. I figured I should consult with the store manager about the final store layout.

"What do you think? I don't think it should look too fancy, since it's supposed to be a general store, and we don't want to intimidate anyone. This place could use a bit more light, so I was thinking about making the windows bigger, although all that sunlight could damage some of the merch—you know how exposure to sunlight causes colors to fade—so the safest option is to paint the interior white, to make this place a little less dark. Also, regarding the shelves, installing a lot of them would let you display more products, but there's something really chic about that minimalist unused-space look, y'know? We want to inspire the customers to spend their money, right? That means we need to cultivate the right atmosphere. Make them feel like their next purchase will finally give them the happiness they desire. Oh, speaking of which, cheaper items should be placed near the counter instead of scattered throughout the store as they make for perfect impulse purchases. Let's use that wall over there for clothes and accessories, with a lot of shelves and displays to show an abundance of merchandise. And, for the sake of appearances, you should stock up on cookware and cutlery—your main business is in providing necessities and people will always need to replace them when they break, after all. Oh, some high-end glassware would be nice, too. Even if it's expensive, people might treat themselves sometimes, and it'll make people think your other products are reasonably priced. Which reminds me, we also need price tags, but those..."

"SHUT UP!" the general store lady roared. "Enough! No more of this! I stayed up all night, I'm exhausted, and I still have so much work to do! The store is too big, there are too many products! Why did it have to get this insane? What did you turn this store into? Even the capital doesn't have any stores this massive! What sort of nightmare is this building?! Because of you, all the townsfolk keep walking by and gawking at my store! Do you have any idea what a general store is supposed to be? Why are you doing all this? I don't know what you're trying to pull! Why do tables and shelves keep appearing? Why does everything look like it was measured to perfectly fit together? This is supposed to be my store but you're arranging it however you please! What, you're going to overhaul the second floor, too? Seriously?! You're putting larger items there? Who buys beds and sofas from a general store? Where did these come from, anyway? I've never seen tables or chairs that looked like those! How could you sell them for so cheap? Wait, you made all of these, and they cost you basically nothing to make? I didn't know you made furniture! You also designed and built this whole building, too. And you go dungeoneering, don't you? Why are you unemployed? You can clearly do every job on earth! You also cook and make your own medicine! This is what you did just to get by? This is not normal 'getting by'! It's too much!"

Ugh, you've gotta learn to chill out a bit, I thought. The definitely-not-old store owner should avoid staying up all night and getting so angry—it made her crow's feet way more visible. It made her look like a middle-aged—*uh, never mind, I should get back to work.*

Despite more incidents like that, I continued to work on the interior, arranging and shelving products, until it was time to open.

To cover up all the empty space, I put my own home-made furniture, medicine, cookware, and mid-century-modern style curios. Of course, of course, I couldn't deny that I redesigned the store to suit my preferences, but the results were pretty stylish. I did all I could, so... time to bounce.

"Okay then, good work? Have a good day running the store, there's a huge crowd outside. Wow, I've never seen people line up for a general store! That's awesome!"

The general store lady waved her hand, staring into the middle distance. She looked completely resigned when she saw how long the line was.

I decided to go to hit up one of the dungeons my classmates were in charge of exploring next. Though my precious assistant, my ally, my savior—Miss Armor Rep— seemed to have mixed feelings about it?

"This is the only dungeon where you guys haven't made any progress yet," I said. "It's only been one day, but y'know, I want to try taking on the dungeon more seriously. I've only gone into two dungeons and they both died on my first day there! Why haven't I been able to fight them normally?"

I shouldn't have expected the dungeon emperor to be able to provide me with an answer. Maybe taking out the dungeon king ahead of time was the trick?

"Anyway, that's why I'm here. Y'know, I just want to give you all a hand, okay? Besides, why are you taking so long to kill the dungeon, anyway?"

"We can't just take on a dungeon without preparation!" Vice Rep B shouted at me.

"We normally spend the first day on reconnaissance!" Vice Rep A added.

"We're not slow compared to a sane standard!" said the Class Rep.

The Class Rep and her Vice Reps were a united front, but their last party member didn't chime in. It took me a moment to recognize her—she was the girl with the big shield who kept getting thrown around in battle.

"What's with this, are the Class Reps excluding Shield Girl? Is it because she's not on the student council?" I turned to Shield Girl. "Why don't you try running as Shield Treasurer or something?"

"We're not bullying her," the Class Rep insisted, "and her name is Miwa-chan, not Shield Girl! Stop calling us the Class Reps!"

So her name was Miwa-chan. I thought they were imitating cats meowing or donkeys braying whenever she got knocked into the air, all of them shouting "Meeewaa! Meeewaa!" but apparently that was her human name.

"Why am I Shield Girl?" she cried. "Why do I have to run for Shield Treasurer?!"

Unclear if she was related to cats, donkeys, or humans, but it sounded like she wanted to be shield treasurer.

With a title like that, I was sure she would get along with Miss Armor Rep. Speaking of, her platinum armor was totally unnecessary, since she was untouchable in battle, obliterating all who stood in her way before they could even attack. At this rate, she was bound to lose the next election for Armor Representative. Maybe they actually wouldn't get along? To be honest, I had no clue.

"You should never listen to anything Haruka-kun says!" the Class Rep told Miwa-chan.

"His words are the honeyed venom of a devil!" Vice Rep A said, giving me an icy look.

"Yeah, he's so evil that he even butchers other demons!"

"Hey, aren't you being a bit too cruel?" I cried. "This is bullying! Harassment! Slaying demons is to be praised, isn't it? Saying a demon slayer is worse than a devil is defamatory! I might cry! I'm going to do it, y'know! Seriously! Maybe?"

Gossip was a real problem in the fantasy world, and rumors like these decimated my sex appeal so thoroughly I was almost knocked out of the running!

"The demons are the only ones who deserve to cry!"

"Yeah, we can all see from the way you fight—you're more vicious than the worst demon!"

"We can't help but feel bad for them!"

A noble and just high school boy defended himself against demons—what was so wrong with that?!

"I didn't hear any of you complaining when I sold you all of those demon blades," I said. "You're holding one now, Vice Rep A! I had to trap them under a net and skewer them to death! You were so desperate to buy them that you're guilty by association! I deny all accusations!"

They shook their heads in disappointment. I definitely joined the wrong group.

"Anyway, how come you only reached the ninth floor after three days?" I asked, trying to move on. "You're all at least level 90! What were you doing all that time? Slacking off? Having a dance party? A dungeon dance party—a dance with death—don't you know how dangerous that is?!"

Why am I thinking about dancing? I'm definitely not fantasizing about Miss Armor Rep dancing in a bodycon dress so tight and short that it's practically a holy artifact...sweet lord!

"We weren't dancing or slacking off!"

"I have never been more annoyed in a dungeon," Vice Rep A said under her breath.

"Why would we go to a dungeon to dance?!" said Vice Rep B.

"Besides, you're the real danger in this dungeon!" added the Class Rep.

"This dungeon is full of nothing but golems and they send me flying in one hit!" Shield Girl pantomimed, "Flying!"

I remembered that back in the forest, the orcs launched Shield Girl through the air with some regularity. For a Shield Girl, she seemed pretty delicate. She was tall, but not exactly a powerhouse.

How did she end up as the tank of the group? She was an excellent customer, though, having bought the Counter Shield and Plate Armor from me. Without a doubt, she was one of my most frequent customers—sometimes I even gave her a loyalty discount!

"So? Golems break up into bits if you drop them down a pit," I said. "At least, that's what always happened in my experience."

"You're the only person adding more pits to dungeons! Most people can't do that, and even if they could, they won't! Also, you can't punch holes through the floor in a dungeon that's still alive!"

Huh, that was news to me. No wonder it was so easy before. Apparently, we couldn't damage the dungeon itself until the dungeon king died.

I was able to renovate the first floor of the Ultimate Dungeon, but if I tried to punch holes into the floor while the dungeon was still alive, it wouldn't have worked. Would that have made the dungeon emperor mad at me? She always gave me an angry look first thing in the morning, anyway.

At last, we went down to the tenth floor and found it teeming with level 10 Stone Golems. I tried to whack them, but they weren't breaking up.

Whoa, Vice Rep B the Archsage entered the fray! She hits and she hits again! What a brutal beating! Not very sagely of her, though. What happened to her magic?

With every strike, her whole body swayed! That swing! That bounce! And bounce! Left and right, up and down, bouncing, bouncing, bouncing! Maybe they were so round because she was an Archsage... Uh, I wasn't looking at anything. *The golems are your enemies! I'm on your side!*

Was this some sort of "the friend of your friend is an enemy" situation? That didn't sound right. The girls gave me such disappointed looks even though I was just trying to help!

Vice Rep B wielded a long staff with a heavy lump of metal on the end. It was such a weird design. I'd seen war hammers and maces that looked kind of like that, but never a staff. Ah, but her shirt strained at the seams to contain her true fighting spirit, and she had so much spirit to contain. *Forget the golems, this is the real struggle—my god they're huge...not that I'm looking!*

Afterward, she insisted that it was a staff. She smashed golems into rubble with it, but it was still a staff. Well, I could kill them with my staff, too, so I suppose it made sense.

Anyway, I decided to scout ahead because the atmosphere here was too terrifying. Not because of the golems, but because of the girls. An oppressive aura of bloodlust practically radiated off of them. *Gotta go.*

It's the best. It can clean, wash, even polish, even get out stains, and even relieve stiff shoulders!

STONE GOLEMS: giant living statues covered in tough stone armor. They were the only monster type in this dungeon. These gargantuan monsters were unfeeling engines of destruction who pressed their attack without fear or caution. They would attack relentlessly unless we shattered their cores. They were so *slow*, though.

One of them raised its massive rock arms, leaving me with just enough time to use Magic Entanglement to Teleport out of the way as the arms came crashing down. Before it could do anything else, I stabbed it with my staff, and in a moment, it shattered into bits.

"Whoa, how'd you do that with one hit?" asked Vice Rep B

Vice Rep A asked, "What kind of sorccry was that?"

As durable as stone was, it only took a second to destroy it, thanks to Vibration magic. This was a technique I'd developed—a new application of Holding magic. I used Holding magic on my staff to vibrate it at ultra-high speeds.

For mere level 10 golems, all I had to do was stab them with my staff, letting the vibrations break them apart. It broke apart their core in seconds, like using a jackhammer.

"That's amazing!" the girls shouted.

The student council struggled against the golems, so they were very excited about the technique. I realized that golems had to have been really annoying enemies for sword fighters.

I wasn't sure if they could handle Vibration magic, but maybe if they had something like a vibrating sword, that could work. I wasn't sure swords could handle the stress involved, but they could hypothetically chainsaw their way through tough enemies. It should work if they didn't have a way of dealing blunt damage. You could come up with all sorts of techniques.

"I developed Vibration magic from sparring with Miss Armor Rep every day," I said. "It even proved itself effective against her...when I used it at night. Every night. Why are you all glaring at me?"

It was true, I honed my Vibration magic every night with Miss Armor Rep. I diligently did my best to hone my craft.

I had to be careful not to overdo it, because Miss Armor Rep was really peeved the next morning when I did. The weapon I developed and used at night dealt no physical damage, but maybe it caused psychic damage?

"It's only Vibration magic," I continued. "It's just a simple matter of magically moving an object so that it oscillates at extremely high speeds, producing vibration."

"You invented a vibration function for magic?!"

"And you developed it for use with Angelica?"

"Did you just say that vibration was super effective on Angelica? On a dungeon emperor?!"

"Pervert!" they chorused.

"Hey, it's a legitimate technique! Did you see what I did to that Stone Golem? I destroyed it in one hit. Besides, it has many other uses!"

"Ugh, just stop talking!" they screamed.

The oscillating, elliptical vibration was actually just a result of the excess energies leaking out from my magic, but it proved so useful in itself.

I was trying to have a serious discussion, but my classmates just stared at the ground, their faces scarlet.

I mean, it was handy! You could use it for stain removal, cleaning, laundry, polishing the floor, even for relaxing body parts...even big ones.

"Why don't any of you want to learn it? I'm willing to teach you all my secret technique, the ace up my sleeve! Why are you all blushing so much? With vibration you can make things so relaxed and soft and oozy, it's amazing. You just witnessed its power!"

After Miss Armor Rep beat me senseless, we continued to the next floor.

Apparently she did it because she was embarrassed. What's embarrassing about being able to make mayonnaise anytime I wanted? Is mayo awkward for people in the fantasy world?

"Should I be more discreet about my vibration magic? I just love whipping stuff into shape, stirring up all the wet stuff so easily—Ahh!"

"Shut! Up!"

Homemade mayonnaise was so much better than the store-bought stuff. They would know if they agreed to learn vibration magic! With a steady supply of eggs, they could have mayonnaise whenever they wanted! But for some reason, it was embarrassing. Was being a mayo stan shameful here? Their faces were bright red!

We headed from the 11th to the 12th floor. Miss Armor Rep easily dispatched the golems without the aid of vibration magic. She didn't even need to aim her strikes—even a grazing hit sliced right through them.

To be honest, the Class Rep and Miss Armor Rep had similar figures. Both had amazing bodies, ample chests, slim waists, curvy hips—ahem, I meant their fighting styles! Their forms and stances! *I'm honestly only thinking about combat!*

An errant slash would've cut me in two if I didn't Teleport out of the way.

But it was true—they cut very similar figures in battle. They were both melee generalists who were just as comfortable dual-wielding swords as they were with wielding a sword and shield for a more defensive fighting style, and used a little bit of magic.

Both also focused on speed over power, and evasion over trading blows. They both had such lovely forms. *In battle of course, I'm talking about battle!*

The Class Rep's stats were way higher. She was over level 90 and she had nearly 1,000 speed and 700 vitality, so she could tank a few hits if need be.

On the other hand, Miss Armor Rep was only a smidge past level 20, which meant that her stats were a third or a fourth of the Class Rep's. Her stats were high for her level, but she still couldn't take a hit, which was why she relied so much on evasion.

Maybe because her race had changed due to Servitude, but she sure did level up slowly. Even so, she already out-leveled me. My stats seriously needed to pick up the slack.

Anyway, that's why I studied Miss Armor Rep's form with such diligence—the ex-dungeon emperor's sword-play. I had to study her technique, steal it, and master it. First, I had to learn what she did differently from me, then I had to take some fraction of her strength and make it my own.

She had the strength to protect her friends, to defy death. She never lost that power despite all she'd gone through. No one cared about my struggles and my experience—no one even wanted to learn my secret techniques! I couldn't blame them. Miss Armor Rep's were way better.

Reflecting on my fighting style, no matter how many different things I tried, I always did the same basic thing: charged straight at an enemy and beat them up. My only technique was a surprise attack. Barely a technique! Whether I was ambushing a goblin from hiding or lung-ing straight at a golem, it all boiled down to the same principle of jumping in and swinging my stick. Honestly, what else could I do?

Kill first, that's all I know, I thought. *Kill them before they can react, kill them before they swing their weapon, kill them before they kill me.* I'd get killed instantly if I tried to tank. With my stats, I'd die before I could even get knocked into the air.

It was no wonder that the others didn't care about my techniques. Miss Armor Rep showed off technique after technique, each more amazing than the last. But we shared the same flaw: we couldn't get hit. She would die instantly, just like me.

It was fine to learn her techniques, but no one should learn to become like her. The swordplay of the dungeon emperor was much the same as her: delicate, ephemeral, and beautiful. *Hey, I'm just as delicate, but for some reason everyone thinks my techniques are hideous! Let's not follow this train of thought...*

"I'll help!" said Shield Girl.

"Thanks!" Vice Rep C chimed in.

"We need support here!" said Vice Rep A.

Shield Girl leapt to her side and said, "I'm on it!"

Legendary heroes should learn from Shield Girl instead. She got launched into the air, time and time again, but only because she worked so hard to protect her friends.

She had plenty of HP and vitality, and enough speed and dexterity to reach her allies in time. She had the skills to endure the enemy's blows and deflect their attacks. That was the kind of strength needed to stand toe to toe with an enemy, even if she ended up flying through the air practically every time.

"Waah!" she yelled as she hurtled past.

"Miwa-chan!!" the girls cried.

Then the Platinum Knight appeared at the front. With a silver-white flash, she reduced the golem to rubble. That's how powerful, brilliant, and unbeatable she was—Miss Armor Rep, who had been held captive by the darkness and made a dungeon emperor.

And I couldn't let her become like me. Since coming to this world, I have done nothing but kill—I even murdered a classmate. I couldn't protect friends—I only knew how to destroy. All my techniques existed only so that we could kill faster.

I didn't have what it took to be a hero...but I couldn't let Miss Armor Rep end up the same. So why wouldn't they at least learn vibration magic? *It's seriously useful!*

"Wow, she's incredible! Such jaw-dropping power!"

"There's no way I can learn how to do that!"

"Her sword moves with such speed and precision! I can't even follow it!"

"Haruka-kun, how did you survive your fight with her?!"

I was getting the feeling that each floor would end with a display of Miss Armor Rep's peerless strength. I was very familiar with that turn of events.

"When I fought her, she was still controlled by the darkness," I said. "I felt like I fought that darkness more than I fought her. If I tried to seriously fight her now, she'd probably kill me instantly."

She was holding back on purpose, trying to fight in a way that could help the girls learn. She purposefully let some attacks land, letting her armor absorb the shock. If they watched and imitated her, they might be able to narrowly dodge attacks, too.

"Are you telling me that I can cut through stone if I slash with enough speed and hit the right angle?"

Miss Armor Rep nodded.

I *had* to teach the girls Vibration magic tonight: it would be way more disastrous if they learned how to slice through any material like Miss Armor Rep!

The ability to trade blows was of utmost importance in this world. Weapon techniques were all seemingly designed around the users exchanging blows and crushing each other until there was but one survivor. The way Miss Armor Rep and I fought didn't belong in this world.

The Class Rep shouted, "Aim for the knees!"

"Too hard!" said Vice Rep C, diving out of the way.

"I can't do it!" Vice Rep A admitted.

"I'm having so much fun!" Vice Rep B shouted, as the end of her staff smashed into the golem's side.

Swordfighters had a tough time fighting golems, but there seemed to be one person who had the time of her life pulverizing golems with a hammer. Maybe it was my imagination.

After all, that wasn't how an Archsage was supposed to fight, especially not with a staff. It could still be my imagination, but I got the distinct impression that something was bouncing. The only thing I knew wasn't my imagination was that I'd get killed if I tried to look. *It's a trap!*

At the rate we were going, we wouldn't reach the 20th floor, and Class Rep and the Vice Reps wouldn't get much practice, either.

Shield Girl was working hard, though. She learned as much as she could from Miss Armor Rep about how to improve her parrying and how to close the distance. Before the golem could finish swinging its heavy stone arm, she stepped in, broke its stance, and shattered the monster. Shield Girl was improving so much, I could hardly recognize her. I needed to learn how to fight that way myself—after all, they had the benefit of cheat skills!

Despite their protestations, I decided that I would teach the girls all about Vibration magic when we got back to the inn. Tonight, I would practice my own Vibration magic technique. I would shake things up until dawn!

No, you need to really strongly vibrate it, just below the collarbone. Huh? Why are you mad at me?

THE WHITE LOSER INN

INTERLUDE: GIRLS' MEETING

WE TOOK A CRASH COURSE in the forbidden art of Vibration magic.

I had assumed that this class was just a prelude to sexual harassment, but it turned out to mostly focus on whipping mayonnaise. Only the girls who succeeded would be allowed to eat dinner, so we all vibrated our hearts out.

"Huh?" Miwa-chan said. "What do you mean, make it more elliptical?!"

"You know, let the vibrations spread through, get it emulsified. You know you're doing it right if you feel it buzz and twist." Haruka-kun said. "Got it?"

"No, I don't get it!"

Piping hot croquettes and mushroom salad lay before our eyes, just begging for some mayonnaise to complete the dish!

We tried our hardest to make these wooden spatulas magically vibrate. If anyone tried to whip mayonnaise by hand, he would confiscate that person's croquettes, motivating us even more to master the art of vibration.

"To put things simply, just visualize vibration, and channel your magic while focused on that image. It's like, if you believe in your heart that it's vibrating, then it does, y'know?"

"That doesn't help at all!" I shouted.

Haruka-kun demonstrated Vibration magic for each of us individually. We held the spatulas in our hands, and he made them magically vibrate. *Yep, I've heard about this from Angelica-san.*

She told us in excruciating, lurid detail all about the power and danger of Vibration magic and its potent effect on pure-hearted maidens.

"Mayonnaise would be such a hassle without this technique, and making large batches would be out of the question," Haruka-kun said. "Not that we can make too much mayonnaise, since we don't have that many eggs. Still, this is good practice for tonight's dinner. You'd end up whipping them all night long before it came together, otherwise."

Somehow, his explanations only made us think of Angelica's extremely vivid descriptions. She'd gone on and on about the incredible power of Vibration magic, tears in her eyes, shivering and shuddering as she attempted to capture the sensation in words.

None of us could stop blushing after that, including myself. Haruka-kun was likely the only person who could make a class in mayonnaise-making sound like sexual harassment.

"Whoa, I can feel it vibrating! I can totally feel it vibrating in my hand!"

"Oh yeah, sometimes the vibration is unexpectedly strong. This might even hit the Richter scale. I mean, look at how much bouncing it caused!"

"Eyes up here, creep!" Vice Rep B said.

As Haruka-kun went from girl to blushing girl and made their spatulas vibrate, I couldn't shake the feeling that this scene would need heavy censorship—why was everyone breathing so hard?

"And with a vibrating sword, this kind of vibration makes it easier to penetrate enemies?" another girl asked.

"P-penetrated with vibrations?" the Queen Bee gasped.

"Hey, it's just cooking! What's with those faces?" Haruka-kun exclaimed.

With a bit of practice, most of us got the hang of Vibration magic. We stared, blushing, at our vibrating wooden utensils, and, after a moment, started to whip together our own mayonnaise. For something so inno-cent, this whole scene sounded way too explicit.

"Oh yeah...it's getting really thick!"

"Y-you're talking about mayo, right?"

I focused with all my might on not crossing my legs. *Just stand normal...*

"It's so creamy now, look how it drips..."

"We're talking about mayonnaise here!" Haruka-kun shouted.

It should have been an innocent scene of mixing eggs and vinegar, but instead it desperately needed pixelation. The eggs weren't getting mixed—Angelica-san's spicy story was getting mixed up in our heads instead!

"Look," Haruka-kun said, "It's mayonnaise. It's going to be wet and sloppy at first, but when you get in the groove, things will stay moist, but they'll thicken up before long—be sure to use enough oil, especially if you want a creamy result."

"Stop joking around. Everything you say is gross!" Vice Rep A yelled.

I needed to banish Angelica's gossip from my mind. If I didn't focus on the croquette in front of me, I'd start thinking about vibration instead!

This whole situation was way too risky!

This must be what Angelica felt, vibrations this strong,

*and the things they did with them...it would be enough to
knock you out...I can't keep thinking about this!*

After the awkward struggle, we finished making our
mayonnaise. It was finally time to eat! Haruka-kun re-
heated our croquettes, and we all feasted on piping-hot
croquettes topped with mayonnaise and mushroom salad.

"Let's eat!" everyone shouted. "Oh my god, this is
amazing!"

"Since when was mayo this good?!"

"It tastes better because it was hard to make."

"The ingredients were all-natural, too."

"It's so rich, but somehow light?"

"So good!"

Since we made too much, we gave some to the Poster
Girl, who loved it so much she broke into her mysterious
dance. *Is she tap-dancing?*

We all lost our minds when Haruka-kun brought out
the okonomiyaki. Maybe we were tapdancing ourselves.
I wept when I tasted it. It tasted like home.

Apparently, he spent a lot of time researching how to
make it. He couldn't make the sweet soy sauce no matter
how many times he tried, but the general store lady came
through with a replacement: a salty sauce derived from
pickled vegetables.

"This is amazing! I want more!"

"Yeah, me too!"

"You only have cabbage and pork? Where's the seafood?"

"I want mine with soba noodles and eggs!"

Even the guys, who kept quiet until now, couldn't stop raving. Tears streamed down their faces from the nostalgic taste. Haruka-kun complained that it wasn't perfect without dried bonito flakes or seaweed, but it was still delicious. I couldn't help but cry.

"Thank you for the meal!"

"That was amazing. Painful, but amazing!"

It tasted like our memories of going home from school. It probably didn't compare to the okonomiyaki we would get back in Japan, but it was still delicious. Even more delicious.

Eggs and sauce weren't easy to come by, but Haruka-kun searched high and low to make this happen, all for our sake. Something with that level of care put into it couldn't not be delicious! That's why we couldn't stop crying.

The girls' faces were puffy from the tears, and the guys continued to stuff their maws with okonomiyaki even as they wept. We thought we would never experience that taste again. The memories, the taste, the joy—altogether, they were too much, and nobody could stop themselves from crying.

While everyone else gave up on these flavors from home, Haruka-kun kept searching, kept researching, and served it to us like it was an average day in Japan. That's why it tasted especially good. *Thank you, Haruka-kun.*

With stomachs full of happiness and okonomiyaki, the girls all went out to the back garden to practice the Vibration Sword technique before bed.

Apparently, the guys weren't having much trouble fighting golems, but still wanted to learn Vibration magic to make mayonnaise.

"Oh my god, this vibration is incredible...I think I might get addicted to this!"

"My whole body is shaking. This might be a wild night!"

"It feels like an electric shock traveling through my entire body, I can feel it coming—another wave!"

"What's coming? A wave? What?!"

Class Rep B moaned, "Ah, mmm, yes... It's too much, it feels too good!"

We were being trained in the Vibration Sword technique, right? Everyone had swords in their hands, but that's not what it sounded like at all. And one unnamed individual wasn't holding a sword at all!

"Ahhh! My whole body is shaking!"

"This, this feels illegal! It's too much, it's too strong!"

"I'm literally going to die!"

"If I keep it up, I just might..."

She meant she was going to die fighting golems, right? Why are the swordfighters making clubs vibrate instead? *You just might what?*

Clubs should definitely be banned! We need to censor all the vibrating clubs! It was too inappropriate, no one could stop staring! This was so wrong.

"I couldn't call this a Vibration Sword, right? It's too gentle, more like a Massage Sword?"

"What would that do, help the golems relax?"

"Are they easier to kill if they feel relaxed?"

"I don't know, I don't think so."

"We won't be able to kill them in one hit, but maybe we could break them, bit by bit."

"That's horrifying! Disintegrating slowly is something straight out of a horror movie!"

Even trying my hardest, it wasn't easy. I got a sense for it, but the vibrating wasn't nearly strong enough. I didn't know if it was because I didn't have enough magic power or couldn't properly control my magic, but it was nowhere close to the destructive power Haruka-kun demonstrated. *Oh, I think I did it right!*

This was good practice for my Magic Manipulation skill. Normally, my cheat skills functioned automatically, so this was good practice for manual control. I'd have to use it in battle tomorrow, so I wanted to get as much practice in as possible tonight. I doubted that I could destroy a golem with one hit, but I felt like I was improving.

"Oh, there you are," Vice Rep B said. "What are you up to? Still practicing Vibration magic? It feels *so* good. Haruka-kun is so good at it. I felt like I was going to literally melt away..."

Vice Rep B had left for a little while, and when she got back, she drifted listlessly around, a dreamy expression on her face. What did she mean by "really good?" What were they up to, together? Did she do *that?*

"What the hell did you do with Vibration magic?" I said, "What felt so good?!"

I figured that she didn't need to practice making a Vibration Sword since she just smashed monsters with her staff that happened to look like a hammer. What kind of Vibration magic practice did she get herself involved in?

I didn't know she was that kind of girl! I could hardly believe what I was hearing.

She let out a deep sigh and said, "Well, Haruka-kun went over my whole body with Vibration magic. I feel like I'm about to melt—he turned me into putty. It was so amazing, everyone should try it. He's so good at it, and he looked so cute, blushing as much as he did."

We hunted down and interrogated the perpetrator. He was in the dining hall, hanging out with the guys, bullying Oda-kun and the nerds, calling Kakizaki-kun's group the kings of idiocy. *What is wrong with him?!* Regardless, we surrounded the criminal, captured him, and interrogated him until he confessed his crimes! The jig was up!

"Huh?" he said, "You want to know what I did to Miss B? She said something like, 'I wish I was more like Miss A. Then my shoulders wouldn't get so stiff every day.' So, I taught her how to use Vibration magic for massages, but she told me that it was too hard to massage herself so I…got to vibrating… I shook things up, you know what I mean? I made things shake!"

So, he claimed it was a simple massage—a simple, full body massage. He made every part of her shake and bounce. *Guilty! The criminal confesses! She said she felt like she was melting, that's a criminal offense!*

Even if the rest of us didn't mind, Shimazaki-san was incensed. She knew exactly what was meant by "I wish I was more like Miss A" …As in, not so heavy in the bust area. That wasn't exactly Haruka-kun's fault, but he couldn't avoid the scolding.

"H-hang on, when I said, 'full body,' I just meant that I vibrated the parts she told me to! She said stuff like 'right here' and 'a little lower' and 'stronger, harder' and 'aah, don't stop, yes, right there!' so I deny all accusations! Only the meatheads made a fuss about how she sounded! The nerds, too! They're slipping out of the room now, but they clearly got nosebleeds from her moaning and facial expressions! It wasn't my fault that certain assets started bouncing as well! I didn't do that on purpose!"

They were all guilty, every last one of the guys! Their guiltiness was as guaranteed as a murder on the Orient Express! A serious lecture was in order! Exactly one person seemed not to realize he'd committed a crime, as usual! No matter how I looked at it, making a girl moan like that in public was an obvious sign of guilt! Seriously, where did she mean when she said, "Yes, right there?" Right *where*?

Oh, apparently Vice Rep B meant between her shoulder blades. Still! By his own admission, he leered at her 'assets' bouncing! A lecture was inevitable! He literally confessed!

LONER LIFE
◆IN ANOTHER WORLD◆

No one bothered to tell me the name of this place, so of course I don't know it! Not that I was listening.

MY MEETING with the emissary from the capital was over. I hurried back to my manor to issue instructions to my subordinates. The kingdom knew of the dilemma, and it was far too late to take any meaningful measures in response, but that's why I took this matter so seriously.

"So they already know?" I sighed. "In that case, I can only ask for your brief attention."

I had sent a report telling the capital that we were investigating the death of the Ultimate Dungeon, but I kept the precise details secret. But now the death of that dungeon was public knowledge. Somehow, the nobles caught word of it and spread it like gossip. If the royal family couldn't keep a secret, their days were numbered.

The emissary didn't *officially* tell us they wanted us to relinquish the equipment of the dungeon king to the kingdom, that the spellstone of the dungeon king belonged to the royal family, or that we should send those who slayed the dungeon to the capital, but they did *imply* many demands of that sort.

"Enough is enough! You shouldn't even have to look at requests like these!"

My attention had flagged throughout the meeting, as it was nothing but a procession of absurd, insulting demands. I couldn't stop myself from thinking, *If you wanted the dungeon's treasure, then you should've destroyed it yourself! Where were you?* but I kept such thoughts to myself.

To be sure, we were indebted to the kingdom and the royal family. But I could not be so ungracious to our true benefactor. I could not throw him to the jackals at court.

Protecting him was a point of pride!

"We will not tolerate any traitors in this territory!" the emissary declared, "It will not benefit the kingdom, either."

Yes, that was all obvious. Yesterday, I received the guild master's report on the Miracle of Shimomui Village. The hamlet was saved—the villagers wept with joy, and professed their gratitude unceasingly.

Then, there was the matter of a small general store in

our town. The proprietor was a former adventurer who went out to fight dangerous monsters to procure rare ingredients, and even sold her products at a loss to the poor folk of our town. That humble shop supported our town with all the necessities that peddlers and traveling merchants couldn't provide.

That general store had helped our town more than I could even conceive. It aided the townsfolk without asking for anything in return, obtaining anything the people needed without any regard for the dangers involved. Unacknowledged, that store made life in our town possible. Now, the general store had transformed into a massive edifice, as if it was a symbol of the prosperity of Omui, a symbol of a brighter, happier future.

That mountain of merchandise, the dazzling decorations, the cornucopia of food and spices—they all symbolized an end to the lean times, and a beginning of a new, prosperous age.

The building itself became a point of civic pride, bringing out admiring crowds of people. The people of my duchy could finally dream of a bright future.

Even now, the proprietor sold food and medicine at cost to those in need—it's not like the store was excessively profitable. That new building announced the rebirth of our town.

And I knew who to credit, without even having to launch an inquiry. A single boy created that symbol of our rebirth.

As usual, he didn't tell a single soul; he refused to take any credit for his deeds. That boy was the very portrait of humility as he brought such merriment to our town.

We owed more to that boy than to any of the nobles of the kingdom. What did the nobility even do for this town?

They provided us with a minuscule aid fund, sending less every year.

Those parsimonious nobles sent no soldiers or adventurers to deal with the threats we faced. They never even entered the Ultimate Dungeon, yet they deigned to make demands of me and my town!

To begin with, the treasures of that dungeon were not mine to give. Those belonged only to the boy who conquered the dungeon! No one else had the right to lay claim to his spoils.

He wasn't even a subject of our kingdom. They had no authority over him. He had received nothing from the kingdom, no aid or succor.

On the contrary, he aided the whole kingdom—nay, the world! Indeed, all the people of this world owed him a debt unpaid!

This much was self-evident. No one could even reach the halfway point of that great labyrinth until he defeated it single-handedly. If he wasn't our savior, then the word held no meaning.

Were the monsters of the Ultimate Dungeon to spill out into the surrounding land, it could have spelled the end of not only the kingdom but the entire continent. Could they not see that they were saved from catastrophe?

Instead of expressing the least bit of gratitude, those greedy nobles wanted to steal his rightful earnings!

How could they even think of demanding treasure from our savior? They ought to bow down before him! These demands are unthinkable!

"It is essential," I instructed, "that they do not discover the boy or his companions. Nothing else matters before that. I will not permit any disturbances to our benefactor!"

"Y-yes, My Lord!"

Those greedy aristocrats, those nobles rotten to the core, they only thought of plunder and profit! The incompetent royal family only had the authority of their crown.

Those noble families were all gutless cowards. They did nothing to aid the people of the kingdom!

"Begin preparations at once," I commanded. "Protect the borders of our domain to the bitter end, be it from monsters or from fools blinded by their own greed! Our benefactor must remain untroubled!"

"I shall make the necessary arrangements without delay!"

If they threaten us with force—we shall not waver! The frontier was not so weak that obsequious nobles, too timorous to fight monsters themselves, could frighten us. They let the kingdom become weak while they wallowed in their decadence.

Even though our soldiers were always under-equipped, without even sufficient medical supplies, they were an elite vanguard who cut their teeth fighting the monsters of the forest and dueling the devils that emerged from that dreaded Ultimate Dungeon.

Now, however, we had ample weaponry. Our fortifications were in good repair, and we had plenty of medicine. Should we be outnumbered ten to one, it mattered not—one hundred to one, it mattered not! We would not falter!

We could only credit all of this to a solitary lad. If we did not take a stand, why did we arm ourselves with this equipment? What purpose did these swords serve? What good was a duke who did not protect the people of his domain?

I could not claim to have guaranteed the security of my subjects, nor to have lifted them out of poverty. It would have been fair to call me as incompetent as the nobles I criticized. But none could call me a coward. None could say that I did not protect the lad who blessed my domain with such prosperity. That alone, I would not permit.

"They may forgo negotiations," I said, "therefore we must increase our patrols. Do not allow any agents of the nobles to approach the boy and his companions!"

"Yes, My Lord. I shall assign our most experienced soldiers to guard our domain."

I would stand resolute against their authority. If they attacked in force, I would accept their challenge. The true danger was espionage.

No, I did not need to worry overmuch. I would have liked to see a spy attempt to visit harm upon that boy or his friends. If there were agents so mighty, why did they not busy themselves destroying the dungeons that plagued our lands? It was simple: they did not exist.

Indeed, those pampered snakes in the royal courts would need protection if they tried to harm the boy. He could easily bring ruin to the entire kingdom.

The royal army paled in comparison to the horde of rampaging monsters led by an orc king. How could they not comprehend the terrifying might of a boy capable of destroying the Ultimate Dungeon on his own?

If they believed that they could defeat him, then they ought to have dealt with the labyrinth long ago. If they could not defeat a dungeon king, how could they believe they stood a chance against a boy who did so with ease?

Were there no limits to their folly? I felt only pity for their idiocy.

What sort of fools thought it wise to provoke a boy who possessed more might than the entire kingdom?

Did they not realize that they would be the ones destroyed?

That they sought to control a power greater than their own only spoke to their hubris.

Perhaps they sought to destroy themselves. If so, it all made sense. He could grant them oblivion with ease.

They would be destroyed in an instant. All would be gone in the blink of an eye.

As he did to the great forest, as he did to the Ultimate Dungeon, he could destroy the entire kingdom before anyone noticed what was happening.

After all, he didn't even bother to remember the name of the kingdom, never mind the king. Just like that, a nameless kingdom would perish, its name never to be spoken again.

Apparently, it turned into an adult animal, but what's the
difference between an animal and a monster?

FOCUSED ALL MY strength, speed, magic, and skills
on the tip of my staff and thrust.

I aimed in a straight line, putting all my sped-up force
behind it.

"How did you shatter it in one hit?!"

"You didn't even use Vibration magic!"

"Is your tip special?"

The golem splintered into jagged chunks of rubble. As
I thought, brute force attacks worked without a problem,
so I didn't need to focus on slashing so much.

"Okay, no matter how much you glare at me, I just
wanted to demonstrate that you could defeat golems
without Vibration Sword, okay? My employment status
is a bigger challenge than these golems! I'm just trying
to show you that your weapons are more versatile than

you think, y'know? I mean I'm literally using a stick to fight!"

"Yeah, and that stick went through the golem like a knife through butter!" the Class Rep shouted at me.

Well, I did fuse a divine sword into my Wooden Staff, so I didn't actually need to use Vibration magic to cut through my foes. It could cut just fine.

Besides, I got plenty of Vibration magic practice last night. I didn't even need any more practical experience. I already tried it out in *real* battles, you know? I got scolded all over again this morning!

"Look, it's easy as can be. If you swing it, it's a baseball bat, if you make it vibrate, it becomes a jackhammer, and if you drop it…it falls. So long as I can whale on stuff with my stick, I'll find a way to make it work. It's part of my Vibration Shinto-Muso Cane Style, y'know?"

"That doesn't exist!" said the Class Rep. "Your Shinto-Muso whatever makes no sense! You keep saying, 'stab like a spear, swing like a halberd, slash like a sword,' like that explains why your stick can do everything sticks can't!"

Hey! I have yet to receive any complaints from practitioners of Shinto-Muso in this fantasy world. I relied on smacking and stabbing. Sticks are made for poking things, after all. Besides, I imbued the stick with Weight magic to max out its destructive potential. According to my vast experience, most of my problems could be dealt with by beating the crap out of them.

"There's no point in even trying to keep up with what Angelica's doing." said the Class Rep.

"She's literally disintegrating the golems into clouds of dust!" said Vice Rep A.

The Class Rep's group kept glaring at me as they struggled to fight golems with the Vibration Sword technique. *Business as usual.* It was pretty dangerous to glare at me in the middle of a fight, but it's still to be expected.

The student council surrounded the golem and attacked. They cooperated splendidly, flanking the golem from every angle before cutting it down. Their swords vibrated enough to eat into the stone, without making a clean slice. That actually made their attacks far more damaging.

I dodged a clump of rock the size of my fist. By evading the way I did, I closed the gap with my enemy and used my momentum to strike. Whacking and stabbing broke the golems apart, thanks to my mighty Wooden Staff! Indeed, with my fantasy Shinto-Muso Cane Style, I didn't have a single care in the world, everything was just fine! *Probably. Hopefully.*

"Thanks for the help yesterday, but what we did in the back garden last night is none of your business!"

"We're trying so hard, and you destroy them in one hit—it's just not fair!"

"I can tell, especially the Archsage! She's going all out smashing the golems."

I got a guilty verdict because of that Archsage last night. *I'll maintain my innocence till the day I die!* It wasn't like I went out of my way to make them shake! It happened on its own!

"Miss B is just swinging her hamme—staff with all her might. Her swings have such wild, destructive momentum. Just look at them go! Bouncing and swinging all over the place," I said.

"*Stop being a creep!*" the girls screamed.

I couldn't help it—Jupiter Eye made me see everything, even when I looked in the opposite direction. I literally couldn't not look! She really was swinging them!

Now everyone was glaring at me, so I fled through an opening between the ranks of golems. With a stab, I intercepted the huge, stone fist of a golem to my right, fracturing it to the elbow. It looked like it had stiff shoulders, so I decided to give it a gentle stick massage, shattering the golem into debris. From there, I continued toward the center of the golem crowd.

Able to see in every direction and predict all of their attacks, I evaded their blows and pulverized them as I walked. Whenever they tried to hinder me with their attacks, I parried with the gauntlet on my right hand.

I finally did it! I got to use a Spearshield Gauntlet to nullify a physical attack. At last, it had a chance to shine, but I forgot to do that cool sound effect!

I reached the center of the golem horde. As their massive fists hurtled toward me, I put my hand on the ground and channeled waves of magic power—ripples of devastation tore through the golems in every direction, the vibrations pulling them apart stone by stone. *Vibration magic rules.*

I dodged through the avalanche of collapsing, dead golems. Stones heaped high behind me.

So, this was the 19th level. *I have to say, it feels no different from working with normal stone.* All I had to do was smash, drill, pulverize, and move on. I did that so often in the cave that it was no wonder I was a natural.

We reached the 20th floor.

"Hey Haruka-kun, what's the rush?"

"Yeah, you're really flying ahead, is something wrong?"

I supposed that killing all the golems at once while my group fought them one by one made it seem like I was in a rush.

"You should be asking Miss Armor Rep, she's on a real rampage right now! Not that she's listening at the moment, but she gets sloppy when she's rushing like that. It's much better when she takes it slow and gentle. Y'know, when her every thought, her every feeling can be sensed from the way she moves, and how she...uh, never mind! I am not speaking a single word or remembering anything at all!"

Miss Armor Rep said nothing, but I felt her blood-thirsty aura from here. *So she is listening!*

Yeah, this wasn't normal. She had joyfully massacred those golems, without a care in the world for what I or the others were saying.

"It's not that I'm in a hurry or anything," I said. "It's more that if I don't kill them, they'll get annihilated before I get the chance. They'll all go extinct before I even get to fight one! In the last dungeon I went to, I didn't get to do anything besides climb stairs, and it sucked. Miss Armor Rep stole all the kills on her one-woman extermination mission. Seriously!"

Miss Armor Rep didn't need to coach anyone today, so she went buck-wild, slaughtering all who stood in her way.

Dungeons were a real rat-race: first slay, first loot. If I didn't give it my all, I'd become an even more irrelevant background NPC. Recently, I only got a chance to do my best late at night. *I'm giving 110% at night, but that's the only time!*

The monsters on this floor were level 20 Iron Golems. They must've evolved from stone to iron.

Speaking of monsters evolving, the Queen Bee still hadn't evolved into a Girlboss. For some inexplicable reason, she was furious with me when I asked her about it.

"Spread out!" Class Rep commanded.

"What?" I asked. "We're underground, there's nowhere to spread."

"We know," the girls shouted. "Shut up!"

They were having real difficulties fighting the Iron Golems. Even with Vibration magic, iron was much harder to cut than stone.

"They're so hard, I'm only scratching the surface!"

"Target the joints!" said the Class Rep.

"Got it!"

I sped myself up with Magic Entanglement and approached the Iron Golems. When facing huge enemies, staying close was the safest position. I identified the core with Jupiter Eye and pierced it without any wasted movement—with my stick, of course.

"I can't believe I'm still using a stick in a fantasy world," I complained. "Even though I fused a divine sword into it, it still looks like an old branch. I look like such an NPC!"

Pulling my stick out, I turned and stabbed the core of the Iron Golem that was trying to flank me from behind, shattering it. I was doing so well but no one paid any attention to me. They were too busy for little ol' me. *Well, fine then!*

Having destroyed the Iron Golems that surrounded me, I checked in on the student council. It seemed like the tiny Vice Rep C was having the toughest time. She moved with such speed and cleverness, striking non-stop as she dodged golem fists, but she wasn't doing any damage. She must've been too small to have any effect.

Compared to a golem, she was like a tiny animal. Vice Rep B was way bigger and she didn't have any problem bouncing from golem to golem smashing them to bits. Hell, they were so big that she could've used them to smash the golems directly, right?

Oh shit, Miss Armor Rep had returned without my noticing. She glared at me as she raised her sword overhead. *Teleport!*

It didn't work. I tripped and fell. Miss Armor Rep scolded me.

Anyway, the tiny animal targeted vital areas with sneak attacks while her enemies were distracted. She had a tough time fighting the golems one on one. Being an assassin or ninja-type, she wasn't well suited to direct combat in the first place.

Her weapons weren't useful against these enemies,

either. Her twin daggers lacked in reach and damage potential. With her high speed and dexterity, she could probably use plenty of different weapons skillfully.

"Hey Small Fry, can you come over here? Try using these. With their size, even a tiny animal could use them. Besides, it's a throwing weapon, so you can attack from whatever range you want. I picked them up off of some minuscule war puppets I fought, so they should be just right for you."

I fetched two francisca throwing axes from my item bag—I kept them around thinking I'd find a use for them eventually. Those war puppets formed a phalanx to attack me, but in addition to the expected shields and spears, they also dropped swords and axes.

"I'm not small, I'm petite!" Vice Rep C roared. "Besides, I'm still growing! I'm going to grow really fast, you hear! Just you wait, I'll be a big animal soon, got it? Ooh, you're giving these to me? I'll take them!"

Despite her complaints, she snatched the axes out of my hands and sprinted away. I had to be careful. This tiny animal was turning feral! *She should return to the wilderness. She can take the mean girls with her!*

If the axes didn't work out for her, I could give her a falchion. I didn't want to let her choose between them, since she would've just grabbed them all before running away.

For now, the francisca axes were enough. As a throwing weapon, they didn't have much reach, but they hit much harder in close range. They were also made of wood, so they were perfect for a tiny little animal!

Without delay, she held an axe in each hand, waved them through the air, and started spinning on her feet and charging into golems. She looked just like a spinning top! She was the right size, too!

She was so small that maybe she still *played* with tops. With her speed and all that centrifugal force, she smashed the Iron Golems into scrap metal. *Looks like it's working*, I thought. Even her movements seemed practiced and confident. She probably had a spinning attack named Whirling Squirrel Strike or something.

"Yay, yay, I got new weapons! Throwing axes! Axes! Like a real grown-up! I feel so mature!"

She happily showed her new axes off to everyone. She obviously had no intention of paying for them! She kept claiming she got them for free, but I only asked her if she wanted to try them! She had no intention of returning them. I should have expected nothing less from a wild little animal.

But why would wielding axes make her an adult? Tiny animals were truly mysterious.

LONER LIFE
◆IN ANOTHER WORLD◆

Swords are awesome, but you'll never be celebrated
for wielding a bunch with your mouth.

THIS DUNGEON had literally nothing but golems.
I was starting to get bored.

Waiting for the student council to finish their meetings—I mean, catch up—meant we barely made any progress. Checking in, I found that they developed a terrifying level of control and potency with their Vibration magic, but for some reason this didn't improve their Vibration Sword technique.

Why in the world had they been practicing focusing all the vibration energy on one point? Finally, they finished off the last of the golems right before lunchtime.

I found the hidden room on the 20th floor, and I decided to check it out alone. How did groups normally split the stuff they found in treasure chests?

It seemed like a real pain in the ass. When it was just Miss Armor Rep and me, we used a simple method: Miss Armor Rep decided which items I was permitted to keep. *Wait, why is the servant giving permission to the master?*

It should go without saying, but we obliterated the golem lurking behind the secret door. I didn't even get to see what kind of golem it was before it vanished in a flash of silver-white light.

"Okay, I'm opening the chest. What a bunch of slackers. They didn't even lock it. The least they could've done was install a trap."

The chest's lid clanged open and I Appraised the sword inside: "Remnant Blade: Invisibility (medium). POW, SPE, DEX +10%."

Kind of a weird item, and the stat boost wasn't impressive. I didn't want it.

An invisible blade that you could only see remnants of sounded badass, but if I slotted it in my wooden stick, then I'd just be swinging around an invisible stick looking totally nuts. That'd send me straight back to kiddie games on the playground.

People would think I'd lost it, right? Killing monsters with an invisible stick, it just wouldn't look or feel right. Totally cringey. I returned to the girls.

"I found a Remnant Blade. What does medium invisibility mean? It has visible afterimages, was that it? Or it's like a translucent sword, I guess? I wish it was translucent clothes instead!"

Besides Shield Girl, who used a short spear, and the Bludgeoning Archsage, everyone used swords or daggers, with most of them dual wielding.

"Whoa, that's awesome—you said it was in a hidden room?"

"A sword! Remnant Blade sounds powerful, and it's invisible!"

"If you could only see the afterimages of the blade, wouldn't that be overpowered? Nothing could beat it!"

This was going to be a bloodbath, a war of Valkyries, a battle without honor or humanity, a fantasy world catfight, a total melee. *What if there's a wardrobe malfunction?* Where was the best place to spectate? Hmm, they didn't start anything, even though I made a big show of taking the sword out of my bag.

"It's yours to keep," said the Class Rep. "If we find something together, we share it, but if one of us finds something on their own, they get dibs."

Miss B said, "Yeah, Haruka-kun, it's all yours."

"If you decide to auction it, you keep half the proceeds, and we split the rest. Haruka-kun, what's wrong?"

Well, this sucks.

"We weren't exactly a party—it's just me and Miss Armor Rep—so it was a simple system. Any items she didn't confiscate, I got to keep. Basically, I took everything aside from all the valuable weapons, and most beautiful outfits and accessories. Makes sense, right?"

Everyone turned to Miss Armor Rep, who frantically shook her head no for some reason. Did I explain it wrong? That's how I remembered it working, anyway.

"You got dibs—just choose what you want to do with it," Vice Rep C said.

Miss Armor Rep didn't need it, so I could just give it to the student council group. I still had plenty of left-over weapons I got from the minotaurs of the Ultimate Dungeon, and those were better anyway.

That reminded me, I had been waiting for a chance to try my Sword Rain attack, but there were never enough monsters to make that attack worth the effort. Combining Sword Rain with my three demon Scythes would be devastating. I had been practicing controlling them and throwing them with Holding magic, but I still hadn't gotten to show them off even once.

"Here, you can have it," I said. "Miss Armor Rep doesn't want it, and I want to avoid looking like a lame teenage dork swinging an imaginary weapon, so it's all yours, okay?"

Vice Rep A exclaimed, "I want it! Do I need to pay for it? You're sure you don't want it? I'm a bit short on money right now, but I can pay in installments!"

She seemed to really want the Remnant Blade. Vice Rep A bought a ton of swords at my bargain sale, too. How many swords did she want? Was she going to wield a sword in her mouth, too? Triple wielding? Somehow, I didn't think that fighting style was going to catch on. Everyone would just think she was a freak.

The student council group had a rule that they gave each other the equipment they needed free of charge. Since I didn't want it in the first place, I let it go for free. A tiny animal already stole two of my throwing axes, so I might as well give Miss A something too.

Since she dual wielded swords, the Remnant Blade seemed especially appropriate for her. She now had more than five different swords, though. *Maybe she really does intend to wield one with her mouth?* But that would mean a sword in each hand, and *three* in the mouth. *Terrifying!* Enough to terrify goblins and kobolds alike. If I faced her, I would want to run in fear myself. Maybe this fighting style had its merits!

Some time later, we engaged Iron Golems on the 25th floor. Miss Armor Rep and I exterminated our share, so we studied the girls. Not that they had many monsters left to practice on, obviously. My precious monsters.

"Left flank, your turn!" the Class Rep commanded.

"Okay!" Vice Rep C squeaked.

"Right flank, push them back!"

"Target the kneecap!"

"Aahh!"

Vice Rep A held one sword in each hand, but she didn't hold any in her mouth. Why not? At least the Remnant Blade fit her fighting style perfectly. *Holy shit, it's awesome!*

"H-hang on, I want to use it like that..." I sighed. "Now it seems so cool! She doesn't need that many swords. Maybe I'll swipe it from her later."

Then Vice Rep A activated a skill that let her wield two more swords with spectral hands, so she was quadruple-wielding. Two more and she'd look like the six-armed demigod, Asura.

Any junior high school edgelord would die to have a skill like that! Then, if she held even more swords with her mouth...no, somehow that immediately seemed less epic. Not that there was any indication that she would start doing so.

Miss Armor Rep drew her swords and started coaching Miss A.

"Y-your sword, part of body. Wh-when slash, sword extend from b-body in straight line."

"This is harder than it looks!"

They both had beautiful, long legs. Even in armor, they looked amazing. It was a shame that the armor prevented anything from bouncing or jiggling, though Miss A didn't have anything that could bounce, anyway. *I wasn't saying anything! I was just observing!*

"Charge!"

"Surround the golems!"

"On it!"

Unfortunately, Miss Armor Rep seemed to have the only form-fitting armor in this world. The rest of the armor was totally unsexy. In a sense, I was relieved that I didn't actually have an armor kink. It was the pure sexiness of Miss Armor Rep radiating through the outer shell all along. *Beneath* her armor lay the problem.

The Class Rep fought alongside Vice Rep A, learning from Miss Armor Rep. Meanwhile, the itty-bitty animal spun wildly from enemy to enemy, and Shield Girl was getting blown around left and right. The Archsage fought in her usual style, without casting any spells. Did Miss Archsage not know that was her job?

I found another secret chamber on the 28th floor with a level 28 Metal Golem waiting inside. What kind of metal? Was it an alloy? Regardless, Mr. Metal wasn't very friendly, so I decided to turn him into scrap. I hadn't used Inferno in a while. I stressed the metal body with high-speed Vibration magic and scorched it with Heat, then crumpled it with Holding magic and Weight. The monster stopped moving.

"Mission accomplished, I guess?"

"It's hot in here!"

"Now it's cold! Couldn't you have killed it normally?"

No matter what I did, I got no respect. None of my companions could act even a little impressed? Whatever. I approached the treasure chest.

It contained: "Fairy Ring: Illusion effect (medium), Evasion (medium). Speed +20%." This was a pretty good item.

"Anyone want this? If not, I'll buy it off you. It's pretty useful no matter who gets it. I'd especially recommend it to Miss A or Miss C."

"Hmmmm. It does look nice."

If Vice Rep A got it, the illusion bonus would totally synergize with Remnant Blade. Meanwhile, Vice Rep C darted around so much, so the evasion bonus would make her even safer.

The evasion and speed boosts made it a good choice for anyone. It was even slightly better than my Evasion Cloak. What a good find.

"If you want it, Haruka-kun, feel free to keep it," said the Class Rep. "You just gave away your last find, and you gave away those axes, too."

"No objections!" the other girls chorused. "You gave us delicious okonomiyaki!"

Looked like it was mine. I gave them the Evasion Cloak in exchange, and after some discussion, they gave it to the Class Rep.

I wondered if fusing my Fairy Ring and Demon Ring together was a bad idea. Would they start fighting? I had to warn the demon scythes that there would be no bullying allowed. Could a Fairy Ring get bullied?

I decided to show my gratitude by giving them some sweets as we stopped for a break. I kept them a secret because I didn't have a lot to share. They were limited edition snacks.

"These are my latest creation: steamed buns filled with jam," I said. "They're limited edition, okay? I can't mass-produce them yet. The mystery fruit jam is so sweet and delicious, it's mostly sugar. Actually, it's more sugar than mystery fruit."

"Oooh, steamed buns with jam!"

"Look at that powdered sugar! So fancy! Yum!"

"They're so sweet! The mystery fruit is so sweet!"

I only got one variety of mystery fruit in that hamlet.

It tasted great, but it wasn't very sweet and not too juicy either—very weird, for a fruit. Perfect for jam; they kind of reminded me of strawberries.

My creation got rave reviews. Next time I stopped by that hamlet, I'd teach them how to make jam. They've got to cultivate more of this fruit.

We were approaching the 30th floor, but at this rate, getting to the 40th might be out of the question. How many floors did this dungeon have, anyway? I wanted to go back to town and sell some clubs. There was no point in trying too hard here. And anyway, the only enemies were golems.

I had no hope for encounters with monster girls. Stone Golem monster girls would be unacceptable! *Absolutely forbidden!*

Inorganic monsters were a definite turn-off. They were way too rigid—no softness at all. Although, I did find myself attracted to Miss Armor Rep's sexy armor. *Does that mean golems could be sexy, too?!*

Impossible! As intriguing as the idea was, I couldn't get over the rock-solid skin.

Revival turned me into a perpetual teenage-boy machine.

AFTER DINNER AT THE INN, Miss Armor Rep went to the bath with all the other girls. They sure seemed close.

"So how far did you guys get?" I asked the guys.

A meathead said, "Bro, our crew almost ran out of HP on the 28th floor! Those bastards were nasty, man. Mega-nasty!"

"We ran out of MP on the 30th floor," a nerd said.

"It's tough to conserve our MP when we're the only party in our dungeon."

"Dude, there were so many monsters in our dungeon, too!"

"Bro, Haruka-kun, spill. How far did you get?"

"36th floor," I said. "But by that point, the student council was having a tough time with the golems, y'know?"

"Sounds tough!"

We turned around at the 36th floor. If the student council couldn't handle the monsters anymore, there was no point pushing forward, since they wouldn't level up by standing on the sidelines. If I let Miss Platinum Armor do everything, we'd all get demoted to background character status. *She's stolen my limelight plenty of times already!*

I guess they were having another girls-only meeting today. It looked fun, as usual. Whenever I saw them, they were all smiling. They went out for dinner and shopping, and now they were headed for their girls' meeting with conspiratorial grins. If they were going to let Miss Armor Rep be a part of their group...well, it should have been my role as the master to keep my servant happy, but her rapacious appetite for luxury goods did seem like a serious issue?

We discussed our dungeon raids over dinner. The student council didn't merely catch up to the other groups, they were now the furthest ahead.

"Let's get some training in before the bath, bro," said one of the meatheads.

"We'll join, too!" said Nerd A.

"For real? You guys are down for sparring and shit?"

"Sounds painful. No thanks," Nerd B said.

"Okay, uh, can I join?" I asked.

"Are you kidding me?!" another meathead shouted. "For real?!"

"Like...'Are you kidding me, of course you can'?"

"Nah, bro! Like, hell no! You stay away!"

I was being excluded for some reason. Were they bullying me? I had planned on scorching some nerd's head, so that was off the table.

None of the parties had defeated their dungeon yet. I suppose everyone needed to get stronger to continue now that we reached the middle levels.

The dungeon Miss Armor Rep and I had destroyed was the only small one. Every other group faced dungeons with at least thirty floors. Their pace cratered around the same point, too. The meatheads were the furthest behind now, but it was surely for some idiotic reason. They couldn't possibly have any problems in combat, so I assumed they were just getting lost. Obviously. Because they were idiots.

Tomorrow was a rest day. The girls needed a break, too. They looked especially exhausted lately.

Wait, what if they're so broke that they started a secret side gig? I was also broke. Well, that's why I planned to sell some goblin clubs, so a day off was just what I needed. I should check on the general store lady, too, but I could only assume she was still in tears. Seriously, hire more workers!

"I guess I'll get a side gig by myself," I grumbled. "But if the store is doing so well, why does the general store lady never have any money? And with so much profit, why am I still stuck getting such a small allowance? Life sucks, man."

It was tough living on a fifty thousand ele—about one thousand dollar—budget. Technically Miss Armor Rep received her own stipend, so we had a hundred thousand ele between us, but still.

I had a handy arrangement with the general store lady where I traded her mushrooms under the table, but I wanted to check out other stores. When would that shady trader come back to town? There were new stores popping up all over, too. Where was the hot nightlife scene, hm?

I was a bit worried about my cave, but the goblins or mushrooms weren't likely to be a problem at the moment, and if we went back, I'd want to spend the night, so I nixed that idea. *My jacuzzi is too awesome,* I thought, *those slender legs and gorgeous curves enveloped in bubbles, they make me want to...* [CONTENT CENSORED]

Still, I couldn't spend the entire day wandering around a town this small. It actually wasn't that small, but it didn't have many stores, so it *felt* small. It was too hard to kill time here. If there were a bookstore, I could spend hours and hours...but there wasn't. There were barely any books in this world in the first place.

Miss Armor Rep loved shopping, and she could spend hours trying on different outfits and accessories, so that might be a good way to pass the time.

Miss Armor Rep came to town ten days ago. Before then, she was utterly alone. Even now, we've kept ourselves so busy that she hasn't yet had a chance to relax. Tomorrow would be the perfect day to let loose and have some fun.

She had a lifetime of catching up to do, after all. I couldn't be the only one having fun, so I wanted to help her enjoy her time as much as possible! *Teen boys are experts at having a good time!*

I whiled away my time doing nothing in particular. I'd been avoiding something. I really didn't want to look, but I had to check...my stats. Everyone else checked theirs every single day. *Yeah, because they didn't get depressed every time they looked!*

Checking my stats wouldn't have been a problem if they didn't call me a Loner, a NEET, a Shut-in, Master of None, and a Blockhead! If they didn't insult me so much, I would look!

They genuinely made me upset. I kept worrying that I'd see something new and horrible whenever I looked at them—something like a Servant occupation, or even worse, Sugar Baby!

Look, at least Alpha Male and Super Horny had a good reason for being there. I was fairly content with those skills at this point. *Bring 'em on, I say.*

"Status—without the insults, please."

NAME: Haruka   RACE: Human

LV: 19   JOB: —

HP: 340   MP: 369

VIT: 315   POW: 313   SPE: 372

DEX: 360   MIN: 374   INT: 397

LUK: Max (Above Limit)

SP: 3747

COMBAT SKILLS: Peerless Cane Mastery Lv7,
Avoid Lv5, Magic Entanglement Lv4,
Life or Death Lv9, Rapid Movement Lv9,
Bubble Lv5, Eye Mastery Lv1,
Diamond Fist Lv2

MAGIC: Heat Lv9, Teleport Lv6, Gravity Lv5,
Holding Lv5, Four Elements Sorcery Lv5,
Wood Lv8, Lightning Lv8, Ice Lv9, Vibration Lv5,
Alchemy Lv1

SKILLS: General Health Lv9, Sensitivity Lv8, Body
Manipulation Lv7, Walking Mastery Lv6,
Servitude Lv9, Uncover Lv4, Magic Control Lv4,
Presence Concealment Lv8, Stealth Lv9,
Hiding LvMax, Insentience Lv5, Physical-Proof Lv2,
MP Absorption Lv4, Revival Lv3,
Supreme Thinking Lv4, Dash Lv8, Airwalk Lv7,
Overclock Lv9, Jupiter Eye Lv3, Super Horny Lv5,
Alpha Male Lv5

TITLES: Shut-In Lv8, NEET Lv8, Loner Lv8,
Bane Sorcerer Lv3, Sword Master Lv2,
Alchemist Lv1

ABILITIES: Corporate Proactiveness Lv7,
Master of None Lv9, Blockhead Lv9

EQUIPMENT: Wooden Staff?, Clothes Set?,
Leather Glove?, Leather Boots?, Cloak?,
Jupiter Eye, Ring of the Destitute, Item Bag,
Monster Bracelet Power+44% Speed+33%,
Vitality+24%, Black Hat

Somewhere along the way, I grew a level, although I didn't feel any different.

"So close," I said to myself. "A little bit more and I would've hit 400 intelligence. It still insulted me, but at least it didn't call me a sugar baby."

My power and vitality weren't growing as fast anymore, Neither was my HP. My stats trended toward a glass cannon build. Getting to level 20 was probably going to take a while. Level 10 also took an extra-long time to reach.

"How did I become a Sword Master when I can't even equip swords? All I need to do to become a Sword Master is swing a stick around? Everyone would think I was a lame fraud if they knew my titles!"

I got Alchemy and Alchemist, too. That must have been from my cooking and science experiments. Without any kitchen appliances, I had to use magic to make my life easier. Without real medicine, I needed to become my own pharmacy, too. *Not to mention the wood stains and varnishes I developed for the furniture I made.* Varnish gave a modern look, but having monochrome detailing wasn't aesthetically exciting. Thinking about this made me want to shut myself up in my cave and do nothing but research. Even though I was a shut-in, I couldn't go back to my cave. She would inevitably distract me from my research.

In total, several skills leveled up and I gained four new skills. I had no comment regarding how many levels I gained in a couple of those skills. *Let's just say I practice them more than any other skill—all night, every night.*

But why did my Revival level up if I hadn't taken any injuries? What was regenerating? I was wondering where I got Super Horny and Alpha Male from. *Could it be? Is Revival healing my stamina in that way, too? Of course!* Revival was to blame! This wasn't good—Miss Armor Rep would be super exasperated if I tried any harder.

Then there was my SP, which seemed to increase and decrease for no reason at all. What was I even using my SP on, anyway?

If that number only went up, that would make sense, but sometimes my SP decreased for unknown reasons. If it didn't have a use, then I didn't really need to care, but even so.

Fretting about it wasn't going to help. Tomorrow was a day off, so I decided to take Miss Armor Rep shopping again, her favorite. She was really starting to fit in. I had gotten used to having her around, like she had always been part of my life, even though only ten days had passed.

She looked like she was on cloud nine every single day. I wanted to give her the perfect day tomorrow. This was her first day off, and we had to make up for lost time. *Dungeon emperors are terribly overworked.*

After all, if we just spent all our time doing what teenage boys wanted to do, we wouldn't ever go outside. *I have to show restraint! Yeah, I have to be patient.*

Still, tomorrow was a day off, so it wouldn't hurt to do a little extra tonight, right? If Revival really did what I suspected, then I could possibly go forever. That was a good thing, right?

Was this the true purpose of Revival? *Is it really meant for sex? Really?*

**DAY 46
NIGHT**

There's no problem as long as you follow the rules, right?

**THE WHITE
LOSER INN
INTERLUDE:
GIRLS'
MEETING**

W<small>E DECIDED</small> to take the day off. We had no choice—we were all terribly sleep deprived. One problem was our Presence Detection, which leveled up every night. The higher the level, the more precise and graphic details we could sense, making it far harder to focus on other things such as sleep.

As if the timing could get any worse, he decided to teach us Vibration magic, too! The girls were in a state. Everyone's Vibration magic leveled up several times in a single night. It was too much. We needed sleep. Mornings had become unbearable.

After getting our beauty rest, we planned to go to the general store. We also invited Angelica, but despite seeming pleased with the idea, she couldn't decide what to do.

She had to choose between hanging out with friends or going on a date, and she wanted to do both. But apparently, she was going to the general store either way, so I really didn't see what there was to think so hard about.

"Sooooo sleepy," murmured Vice Rep C. "Nighty night."

"This inn is more exhausting than the dungeon," Vice Rep A said.

"Vibration magic is *banned* tonight!" I said.

"Awww," groaned the girls.

We made good progress over the last couple days. Although Haruka-kun and Angelica killed most of the monsters, they split the spellstones with us evenly. Thanks to that, we had plenty of money to spend on shopping.

Of course, pushing ourselves to catch up only made us even more exhausted. The more I saw of Haruka-kun in action, the less sense it made. *How can he be so powerful?*

"Do you think they have new clothes in stock?"

"Didn't the owner say so?"

"Yeah, but that was a couple days ago."

"Still, we'll be able to do lots of shopping tomorrow!"

"I want new clothes, new gear, and delicious food. Somehow, my money never lasts."

"Yeah, I'm going to go bankrupt if I keep spending like this!"

"At least we won't have to worry about any surprise auctions since Haruka-kun hasn't been going off on his own lately."

"And if he did, it would be because he wanted to buy more clothes, obviously."

"Yeah, he can supply his own snacks, so he's definitely after outfits and accessories."

"Hang on, isn't Haruka-kun in cahoots with the general store owner? What if he sets up his own snack stall?"

There was no way that building could've been built without Haruka-kun's meddling, after all. No matter how I looked at it, it was obviously modern architecture.

"Good point," the girls said, "R.I.P. my wallet!"

"I think Haruka-kun is going to make bentos tomorrow," I said. "Angelica said she saw him preparing something."

"So cute! Will it be sweet? Delicious? I don't mind getting fat!"

"Haruka-kun seems so irresponsible, but he's actually quite diligent, isn't he? Even when he looks like he's just having fun, he's doing something for all of us."

"At school, he just looked scary, right?"

"I don't think Haruka-kun has changed, just the way we see him," I said.

"True. He pretends not to notice, but he does have his own kind of charm. He just does things his own way."

At school, he always sat by himself reading books. He came across like he didn't care about anything or anyone. No one knew how to approach him. Oda-kun and his friends tried, but that was only because they were too clueless to take a hint. Haruka-kun brushed them off the same as anyone else. He was still rude and dismissive, but his secret was out—he was a loner with a heart of gold.

I said, "You know why the nerds always tried to be his friend? Oda-kun told me that whenever it seemed like some delinquents were going to bully them, Haruka-kun would get in their way and he would go off like, 'Lame. What kind of dumb crap is this? Are you idiots? Has the lameness completely infiltrated your brains?' and stared them down until they ran off, tails between their legs. Then, he went off like nothing happened."

Everyone nodded. "Oh. Those encounters always looked like coincidences, but they happened a lot, didn't they?"

Yeah, Haruka-kun was certainly good at putting up a scary front. It was easy to misinterpret his actions because he hardly ever spoke, and he never tried to clear up any misunderstandings.

"Have you ever noticed that, even though he didn't stand out in particular, he always had kind of a *presence*?"

"He was only ever average in gym class, so I figured he was just bad at sports."

"Kakizaki-kun and the jocks said something like that, too. He had this terrible presence that made them feel like winning was impossible, so they steered clear of him whenever they could. Whether soccer or basketball, they didn't invite Haruka-kun."

"So that's how he flew under the radar for so long!"

"I don't remember ever seeing him participate!"

Our class instinctively kept our distance from him. Ever since Haruka-kun was a kid, he did whatever he wanted so long as it didn't break any rules. He was the only kid who wore a disguise during a game of hide-and-seek. He was the only kid who ever set traps when playing tag. Because he had no common sense, he made a habit of bending the rules as far as they would go without breaking. He was unstoppable at those games.

"In the real world, in a world full of natural laws and common sense, Haruka-kun couldn't help but stand out. He always went against the grain. He's not any more sensible in this world either, right?"

Angelica nodded aggressively. She was probably remembering all the crazy things he did in the Ultimate Dungeon, like saving the life of a dungeon emperor.

"They always said to stay away from him," the girls exclaimed, "but it wasn't because he was dangerous. It was because he was nonsensical!"

I couldn't imagine the sort of bizarro world where Haruka-kun's actions made sense. A world of people like Haruka-kun would be so tranquil. In a world where the average person was as intimidating and powerful as Haruka-kun, villains couldn't survive.

"The delinquent squad sure was dangerous, too."

"Didn't they have, like, black belts and boxers in their group?"

"It's true, though. Even Kakizaki-kun's group steered clear of Haruka-kun..."

Being dangerous themselves, the delinquents instinctively recognized how dangerous Haruka-kun was. They knew that they shouldn't mess with him. That was wise of them. Bullies, whether student or teacher, simply made themselves scarce when Haruka-kun was around. He was untouchable.

Even in this world, if people knew that he had a dungeon emperor literally serving him, it would be a huge scandal—an unmitigated disaster. But here, in this town, everyone was used to seeing a girl in gleaming plate armor follow Haruka-kun around, so even if they learned her true identity, they would just take it in stride.

He caused far greater outrage and bafflement on a daily basis, after all. Compared to Haruka-kun, that armored girl seemed decent, level-headed, and reasonable.

Haruka-kun's complete lack of common sense seemed to spread to the townsfolk, so they accepted all sorts of questionable things. All the problems he caused had to have been for Angelica's sake. Though he was probably unaware of how they were viewed. *Absolutely clueless.*

"I want a new bag, but cute shoes or boots would be so nice!"

"Yeah, my feet have been killing me. I should ask the owner what she recommends!"

"I'd love to find a pair of mules! Maybe in yellow?"

"Sounds super-cute!"

"Right?"

"I'm so excited to buy new underwear!" said Vice Rep B.

"No lace!" we yelled in unison.

Angelica, with many rapid hand gestures, told us that she wanted to buy a new hat. Her gestures were getting easier to understand than her speech. Although she had no trouble talking about explicit topics. Probably because that's all anyone asked her to talk about. We learned way too much.

"I can't wait to buy a new bag!"

"Yeah, a stylish bag is an essential accessory. All our bags are beige!"

"You're right!"

"Lately, I've only considered the durability and storage capacity of my bag! What happened to us being girls?!"

"I need a purse ASAP!"

"I actually got used to this ugly sack. What sort of monster have I become?!"

I hoped that the general store had a lot of new items. Everyone was so excited for tomorrow. *It's been such a long time; we're going to have a blast shopping for stylish clothes!* No wonder Haruka-kun spent so much of his free time there.

He traded a lot, and when he still wasn't satisfied, invested in the store itself and constructed a new building for them. Already, the general store owner talked about inventory, turnover rates, discounts, expanding the customer base, and so on. Haruka-kun had to have given her a crash course on modern business principles.

The general store was already like a large-scale mall, certainly the first department store in this world. He even made a stand-out building just because he felt like it, and I knew he was thinking about expansion...without the owner's knowledge, of course.

"The only makeup they have is lipstick, right?"

"Yeah, and it's a little too red for me."

"I want a warm nude color!" Vice Rep C chirped.

"We can't expect anything besides the basics just yet. Maybe before we turn twenty..."

"Forget makeup," said Vice Rep B. "What I really want is Regeneration like Haruka-kun. It even regenerates your skin!"

"Is that why his skin's so smooth?!" we yelled.

"I was wondering why his skin looked so clear and shiny every morning! So it was Regeneration all along!"

I also had Regeneration, but I wasn't about to tell them that. I valued my life too much. We were only sixteen. There was no way that Regeneration helped him that much. It definitely had more to do with how he spent his nights.

Our laughter echoed through the inn. Since coming to this world, everyone had given up so much. We thought that we'd never get to see so many things again, so we tried to forget them. Haruka-kun didn't. Instead, he was bringing it all back, and it made everyone happy. We were having real fun.

I knew that he'd continue to do whatever it took to make everyone happy. According to Angelica, he spent his spare time gathering materials and finding different uses for his magic. I couldn't wait for tomorrow.

All the things that made us happy were sure to be in abundance tomorrow. I was even starting to dream again.

237

"Good night! See you tomorrow!"

Every day was like a dream—an indulgent, sweet dream. Our days of struggling in an uncaring world had turned into days where I could sincerely laugh from the bottom of my heart.

We lived happily now. He delivered on his promise—a life where we could smile. *Thank you.*

AN ELEGANT MOMENT in the morning of a nobleman: For one of true refinement, completing one's toilet before a magnificent mirror was an essential duty. Only the most tactless fool would dare interrupt a gentleman at such a time!

"I am clearly occupied. What irksome boor dares interrupt me?"

"Milord, it is a royal envoy."

I dealt with an endless procession of envoys and messengers—a parade of meaningless courtesies. I sipped tea of the finest quality, assigned my attendants and civil servants to deal with trifling matters, and listened without concern to the rest. There was nothing remotely charming about their low-class behavior.

Unable to bear any more, I dismissed the messengers with excruciating politeness and threw myself down upon a plush divan.

"Did they speak truth? Their reports seemed so unbelievable."

"Both the royal family and the noble houses reported the same, milord. There is no mistake."

This city was the lynchpin of the kingdom. We used deadly force to control the frontier lands, and to gather spellstones from those lands in order to maintain the royal monopoly.

"Knights from across the land have gathered in secret. Each noble house has sent a few capable men as well, milord."

If our city fell, the price of spellstones would soar. Here, we collected spellstones through tariffs, bypassing the royal family and the market to guarantee the wealth and prosperity of the noble houses. This was key, not only to prevent the king from becoming a despot, but as the basis for our alliances with foreign kingdoms.

"The lords under the sway of the noble houses dislike these orders. They disregard all convention. Even so, it brings me some pleasure to see those hyenas snarl at each other."

"However, the mercantile class is not pleased with the

high tariffs imposed on spellstones. The cost of goods throughout the realm have soared, milord."

Due to the declining rate of spellstone acquisition on our frontiers, our domain has suffered long-term economic losses. Now that there are more spellstones in circulation, we had to raise tariffs to rebuild our wealth.

"Forget them," I declared. "They'll simply learn to live with it. After all, those frontier merchants still reject the slave trade."

The people of the frontiers were crude and barbaric, but they knew how to endure. The men were renowned for their strength and their long lives, while the women had their own rustic charm, drawing many admirers. I was reminded, much to my annoyance, of the many nobles and foreign dignitaries that praised their women.

"We have as yet failed to abduct any members of the House Omui," my retainer whispered. "Is it not dangerous to pursue them further?"

"Danger? If they dare take that path, then all we must do is wait."

If they attacked, we would face them in battle. Blockading the roads, we could simply allow the barbarians to starve, but we knew not how long they would last. I could not disregard the rumors of adventurers, either. I would like to make them mine. The treasures of the

Ultimate Dungeon would have been a fitting prize for our glorious House Nallogi.

Using those adventurers as leverage, I could gain the title of marquis, and put the riffraff in its place.

"Summon Chief Shino to begin an investigation, for first we must confirm the veracity of the rumors. The information from other houses cannot be relied upon, is it not so?"

"They reported some balderdash about the arrival of a mighty hero. Surely, their information is wrong, milord."

Our only intel on the state of the region was a dubious report that a mere child had descended into the dungeon, only to return safely before the town could send a rescue party after him. Though the sources of these rumors claimed, "A boy *felled* the Ultimate Dungeon," they had to have meant, "A boy fell *into* the Ultimate Dungeon." Yet, according to our reports, the frontier garrisons had new weapons, and the frontier economy was thriving.

"Even if the dungeon has fallen, we must assess the worth of its treasures. Begin an investigation at once!"

The Shino clan were lowborn scum, but they were useful scum. It would've been far easier to dispose of them, so that they would never have a chance to betray House Nallogi, but I chose to retain their services. They were perfect tools for espionage, well-suited to dangerous tasks in place of more valuable lives.

The people of the frontier, though brutish, were canny and suspicious, so it would be a waste to send soldiers or adventurers to do a spy's job. It was simpler to use the clan, as they had a skill that guaranteed their success— Complete Invisibility. Our victory was assured.

**DAY 47
MORNING**

The general store lady sells for cheap, but was still exhibiting
mushroom-addiction withdrawal symptoms.

**THE WHITE
LOSER INN**

WOKE UP FEELING totally refreshed. This was an absolutely wonderful, exhilarating morning. Indeed, last night was full of wild, thrilling, mind-blowing experiences!

Turning over in bed, I was met with Miss Armor Rep's scowling face. I was safe for now—she didn't have the strength to move, so I had no need to rush. That was fine, right?

She was going to scold me later, as usual, but everything was fine in this moment. As soon as she could get up, it would be a different story, but for now, I could simply look back on those vivid memories. The start of a new day and the perpetual exhaustion of the rest of her life was coming soon, as soon as tonight!

After thorough investigation, I confirmed that Regeneration indeed granted me limitless stamina. I could keep it going forever, like a perpetual teenage motion machine.

We diligently investigated for quite some time. I had to know if this seemingly limitless ability had any limits. As expected, she glowered through tear-filled eyes.

She was going to spend the day shopping with the girls. She looked a bit conflicted, so I told her I'd meet her at the general store later. She nodded excitedly.

She had to have been so excited that she couldn't fall asleep. The dark circles under her exhausted eyes made her glare even more intense!

I dashed out of the inn by myself and went to the armory run by that old guy. I desperately needed more money. That Goddess of Greed, Miss Glare, was going to bleed me dry at the general store later!

"What's up, old man? Doing anything interesting today? Want to buy some weapons? I've got some nice clubs for you, if you want. If you can't afford it, I'll offer them on consignment. Sheesh, this place is cramped! Maybe you need a loan from yours truly? Let's talk terms: if you don't pay me back, I'll tear out your beard, okay? You're bald anyway, so it isn't a major loss. Agreed?"

"Don't you dare touch my beard! Besides, you know I'm good for it," he hollered. "Also, stop calling me old! Anyways, I'll buy your weapons on consignment. I don't have nearly enough stock, especially since I expanded the store!"

Since he was bald, I couldn't very well threaten his scalp, so of course I had to settle for his beard.

Anyway, his store didn't have nearly enough space for his weapons and other merchandise, and he was already wasting a lot of space exhibiting items. The store was a mess. Apparently, he bought the building behind the armory and connected the two buildings with no thought given to the layout—there was a lot of empty space. If I built a second floor and a basement, that would clear things up.

"All right, I'll expand it," I said. "You don't need to go as big as the general store, but adding another floor and a basement couldn't hurt. The basement would be perfect for storage, and you could even move your forge down there. It'd really open up the space, right? I'm going to do it anyway, no matter what you say, so sit tight, okay?"

"Now wait a minute, you're going to do it no matter what? I'm the owner here, and I'm telling you not to! Sure, some more space would be nice, but you can't just architect-majigger my store like that! I'm already paying a mortgage as it is!"

This geezer always tried to sell people on the best equipment they could afford, and he didn't charge too much above cost.

And he wasn't wrong to do that. Dead adventurers weren't repeat customers, after all. If he tried to rip his customers off by selling mediocre gear with extreme markups, those customers would get themselves killed and never come back. I seriously doubted any ghosts of adventurers were clamoring to buy clubs. And, since profit margins were so tight, the only way to make money was through volume.

"Listen, your gear sells, and you've got stock. You're letting the store go to waste by not trying to sell weapons as fast as you can. Here's the game plan: make loads of money, pay off your debts, and buy more weapons with what's left. That's how you get rich. I make money by spending money, so I know what I'm talking about. Besides, I've already decided to renovate your shop. In fact, I've already started."

I got the knack for renovations when I worked on the general store, so the second time around didn't require much effort. Since I knew the steps I needed to take, I didn't waste my magical power this time around. The basement and exterior were finished, so now I only had to do the second floor. Since it was an armory, wall space was essential—it was ideal for displaying weapons. *No need to overthink the interior design. Let's just do it.*

"Can I put the staircase here, or should it go further back? A spiral staircase right in the middle would look so cool? Well, where should I put it? Make a decision, I'm getting bored. I made that second floor and basement, but they might as well not be there if you don't add stairs. You don't want to climb the wall outside to get to the second floor, after all. That'd be ridiculous. Is that what you want? You want to climb walls? Is that your hobby? Do you like climbing walls?"

It was no good. The old guy was speechless. He just stood there, slack-jawed. *C'mon, seriously, give me an answer.*

"Hello, if you don't tell me soon, I'll walk out of here without making the stairs. You'll actually need to climb up from outside. You there, old man?"

He's broken. No response. Maybe he really was into climbing. As an experiment, I pulled out the club of a goblin king. That seemed to have rebooted him. He snatched the goblin club, his hands shaking. Even after rebooting, he still seemed a little broken.

"P-please sell it to me! It'll become an heirloom, I'll polish it every single day, just sell it to me! I'll pay anything. Do you do installment plans? How much for the down payment?"

Uh, it's merchandise, don't keep it. Sell it. I had tons more where that came from, but when I started pulling them out, his brain seemed to crash again. I figured it'd be best to just make the staircase and get on with the interior design.

I did all of this in front of him, but he couldn't take his eyes off the clubs. Why was a blacksmith so obsessed with wooden clubs, anyway? I decided to not show him the goblin emperor's club. He'd go completely catatonic.

Since I was pretty much finished with the remodel, I confiscated some money for the clubs. *Yeah, I'm done here.* The old dude looked like he couldn't decide which club to keep as an heirloom. Would his descendants really appreciate a club in the first place? Would anyone be happy about inheriting that thing?

Since this was an armory, a rustic vibe was better than something too slick. There was something inherently wrong about a stylish armory.

I widened the basement for a new forge downstairs and equipped it with some lamps, but the old dude didn't even go check it out. If he didn't look, I couldn't ask him how he wanted it arranged. Well, I was sure that he would offer me some opinions after he used it for a while. I'd adjust things then. I needed to nab some more cash from him and bounce; the Goddess of Greed was waiting for me and my over-stressed wallet!

The general store was bustling. It felt like the whole town had crowded into the store. Apparently, the proprietor had hired two new shopgirls.

When I asked one of them about it, she told me that the owner had been selling medicine and food at steep discounts to her family, even keeping a tab open. So, when she heard the owner was having trouble with her store, she rushed over to help, and got hired soon after.

Well, first, she told me while wiping away tears that she was grateful for all the mushrooms the general store lady shared with her. Was she another mushroom addict? In any case, it was impossible to run a store this big with only three employees. The store was in a state of chaos.

"You guys better work faster or the Class Rep's group will never reach the front of the line," I said. "And I'm telling you, they're big spenders. This won't do at all."

Goods flew off the shelves faster than they could stock them. I figured that, since I installed all of the shelves, built the storage basement, and organized the inventory, I knew better than anyone else where everything was supposed to go.

They looked so stressed that I decided to lend them a hand.

"Pour forth, ye objects of fantasy, an eternal torrent of merchandise to fill all shelves—I summon thee, Merch Rain!"

A ceaseless storm of goods swept through the store, refilling all the shelves in a thunderous deluge.

This is nuts, I thought. *Who could've imagined that the Sword Rain I practiced so many times could be so useful in a general store!*

Until now, I practiced Holding magic with swords and spears, but it was dead simple to do the same with the store's merchandise. I even surprised myself with the flood of products emerging from the basement. Holding magic itself must have been pretty surprised that it finally got its time to shine. I mean, I was surprised too!

The customers gaped at all the products dancing through the air to their proper places on the shelves. So, even in this fantasy world, an Inventory Rain skill must have been unusual. Well, what's the problem with a little rain?

"Thank you so much. You're a lifesaver," the shopgirl said. "We've been so busy that I can't keep track of what's what. I didn't have the time to restock at all. Come to think of it, isn't all this chaos your fault anyway? I suppose I should thank you anyway. Ah, I'm so tired and hungry! Do you have any mushrooms?"

The volume of customers dwindled a bit and the store finally settled down. The general store lady and her employees were so busy today that they hadn't had time to eat. I made too many bentos, so I gave them my extras: grilled mushroom onigiri, fried chicken, french fries, and sweet potato desserts. Thrilled, they devoured their lunches.

For some reason, they became dewy-eyed as they ate. They really were mushroom addicts, weren't they? Were these side effects of withdrawal? The shopgirls said they got their medicine from here. Was that a codeword?! Was mushroom addiction on the rise?!

Finally, I sold my goods to the shopkeeper and went for a stroll around town. The store was so full that the girls never even got through the doors, so they probably went elsewhere to kill some time. I wanted to deliver their bentos to them.

That general store really was packed. This town was becoming more peaceful and prosperous, but there still wasn't anything to spend all that money on. Since money wasn't changing hands, that meant new wares wouldn't come into town. Without money circulating, artisans and manufacturers couldn't even get started. This city needed peace and prosperity, which was why I focused on expanding the armory and the general store.

In terms of net worth, I should've been a millionaire by now. I invested my own money in the general store and the armory, and pretty much took control of the management in one fell swoop. That ought to have made me a successful entrepreneur.

Yet, I somehow never had any cash on hand. I faced a real liquidity crisis over here. *I never heard of a magnate living on a pittance. I've become the first impoverished angel investor.*

If I could just figure out what they want, their preferred colors and sizes, I was guaranteed a profit!

WE WANDERED through the city, window-shopping and strolling the avenues.

A procession of young girls in the full bloom of their youth: that's what we were.

There were a lot of food stalls now—I even spotted a croquette stand. It was called The Black-Hooded Croquette. They were delicious, and so popular people were lining up down the street.

We enjoyed some croquettes while chattering about this and that. The general store was packed, so we ended up killing time walking around.

It really was jam-packed, though! Oh well, I had no complaints so long as there were still clothes left to buy. It seemed like no one was buying the high-fashion modern clothes; they probably cost too much for most townsfolk.

"Have you noticed how many new shops opened in the last couple days?" Vice Rep B said.

"The old stores have tons of new merch, too!"

"The streets are full of people!"

It wasn't just the general store—all the stores had new goods on sale—greater volume and variety. This town was booming, no doubt about it—everywhere we went, people wore radiant smiles.

Of course, none of the other shops could compare to the general store, but we had a blast shopping, bargain-hunting, and admiring the latest imports.

We were such a raucous group, but I was sure no one minded. How could twenty-one teenage girls manage to go shopping without making a lot of noise?!

We ran into Haruka-kun, who said, "It's just about time for lunch. You know I made these bentos, right? I made french fries and everything! Also, the general store isn't as busy now. Oh, speaking of...do you have enough money, Miss Armor Rep? Here, take this, okay?"

He finished rambling and distributed his bentos. They contained grilled mushroom onigiri, french fries, and sweet potato desserts. It smelled divine.

When Haruka-kun gave Angelica her bento, he literally got on his knees, bowed, and extended his hands like he was making an offering... The coin purse he gave her looked especially heavy, too. *Ugh, he should start worrying about earning the title of Simp.* The red flags were there!

"Ugh, it says 'Yamtastic Friends Fries' on the side!" I said.

"Let's beat him up later!" the girls shouted, laughing.

"Maybe we can spare him this once. This is amazing!"

"How is he so skilled?!"

It was our first time having french fries in ages. All the fried food made for a dangerous combination, but we gobbled it all up. I wasn't about to let any of this crispy deliciousness go to waste, no matter how unhealthy it was!

Although, I ate way too many croquettes the other day, too. *Where can I learn calorie-burning magic? I'm asking for a friend.*

Haruka-kun got up and left, telling us he was going to go take a nap. He probably stayed up all night doing his best. *Don't ask me what he was "doing!"* I was getting worried about Angelica.

I'll ask her to tell me everything tonight, I decided. *Everything.*

"Let's go shopping!" the girls shouted.

"Charge!"

Stomachs stuffed, we stampeded toward the general store. A new shipment of clothing had apparently arrived moments before we did. In the blink of an eye, all traces of friendship and camaraderie vanished. The store became a battlefield of fashionable young women who had no use for honor or humanity!

We bee-lined toward some wooden racks filled with chic shoes. They all had an elegant, sort of Italian vibe.

"So cute!"

"I call dibs! I'm buying it!"

"Those're so cute, I love 'em!"

I wanted them all! The white and mahogany-toned ones looked stylish, but the two-tone brown pair emanated elegance, and the black ones were so cool! My eyes darted from shelf to shelf, unable to settle on any one pair. I wanted everything. I adored them all!

"Oh my gosh!" the girls said, "Boots, mules, and sandals!"

"What size are those! I want to try them on! This yellow is *so* me!"

"Black boots!" Vice Rep C said, "I can look like a real adult, so mature and sexy!"

"Look at these mules. They're all so charming! How much? Should I get them all? I wish I had more than two legs!"

"You can't buy them all! Leave some for me! In fact, I call dibs on these! There, I said it, and that's binding! That's the rule, right?"

"Oh my, this shirt is a bit tight in the bust," Vice Rep B said. "Don't they carry anything that fits bigger sizes?"

"Well, how *nice* for you," the other girls muttered under their breath.

"I need this! I'll die without it! But where's my size?"

The boots with leather straps were a classic style, so lovely. These didn't have buckles, so the straps were meant to be tied together, but they were still really cute. The woven leather sandals also looked cool, and the braided mules had a sophisticated feel, like European high fashion.

They even had clogs that looked a lot like the ones from Scandinavia! Totally stylish, the rivet that attached the straps to the clogs were the perfect detail. All the designs looked so contemporary. I had the impression that fantasy world folks just wore leather boots all the time, so where did they come up with all these suspiciously modern designs?

"Wow, look at all these leather outfits!"

"Damn, those look so mature!"

"These skirts are, like, so cute! They must become mine!"

"These long, flared skirts are too nice! Look, it's actually a wrap skirt with a side slit!"

The leather vests and flared skirts looked fashionable enough to be brand-name. Even though these designs weren't hard to make, they still looked modern and cute. I had a pretty good idea who was behind this.

I wasn't born yesterday. All these clothes looked way too cute. There was no way someone from a medieval fantasy world designed these. The designs were blatantly based on fashions from our world. And they all arrived moments before we got here.

"Hey, look at this!" I said. "It looks like it was based on something Angelica wore the other day!"

"Busted!" the girls yelled, some of them pounding their fists into their open palms.

I had heard that a certain someone pulled an all-nighter working on something. When he heard our plans, he clearly worked through the night in preparation.

Haruka-kun knew how much we enjoyed shopping for clothes. He wanted us to enjoy our day off...so he became a one-man fashion label. No wonder he left to take a nap.

"To the fitting rooms!" I commanded.

"Hurry, hurry, let's not waste any time! I'm getting undressed as we speak!" Fukunuki-san yelled.

"No, this one is mine! It was love at first sight! Please let me have it!"

"Oh no, I can't afford both of these, but I want them both!"

"Please swap with me! I wanted the white one, you can have it in blue! Pretty please?"

Everyone had a rollicking good time. *Hell no, I'm not going to give up this find! It's mine,* I thought. I could get through with Ground Shrink! *Let's go!* The ensuing battle of fashion-obsessed young women didn't need to be described.

That was so satisfying. We all wanted to get even more clothes, but we were flat broke. Could any of us afford to pay our bill at the inn?

A lot of the girls even opened a tab to buy more than they could afford. Most of us were in the red. Could we ever escape debt hell at the rate we were going?

"That was the best!" We chorused back at the inn.

"Now we just need to go home and try everything on!"

"That was so sweet of Haruka-kun!"

Still, we couldn't resist buying what we did—they were one-of-a-kind items made especially for our shopping vacation. He worked so hard on it, so of course we bought as much as we could! Any girl who said no to all of that deserved to be punished.

"I want to try on my new clothes right now, okay?"

"Good idea!"

Everyone got changed into their new clothes. Shimazaki-san, the former model, helped coordinate our outfits. Now that I thought about it, I needed a bag, too! *I better go back and buy one! Where were the woven bags?*

Angelica had bought a lot of stuff too, but she apparently couldn't find a hat that she liked. But then Haruka-kun presented her with a hat as soon as she stepped through the doors of the inn. He had to have just finished it. Angelica couldn't quit smiling. *That's adorable,* I thought. Haruka-kun even did custom orders. Her smile was infectious, though I felt a twinge of jealousy as well.

"Like, have you ever wondered how Haruka-kun knows so much about women's fashion?" Shimazaki-san asked.

"Yeah, all the clothes he made were on trend."

"Is he secretly a fashion nerd?!"

"Thank God he is though!"

"Giving her that hat... That was too cute."

"I know, right?!"

Today was almost perfect. I couldn't help but feel a twinge of envy at the end, when I saw Angelica with her new hat. She sure was lucky.

Why are you treating me like a teenage boy that made girls cry by stalking them and giving them candy and bringing them to a hotel?

DISTRIBUTED MY BENTOS to the girls and made my offering to Miss Armor Rep.

I'd make all my money back soon enough. After all, Miss Armor Rep reported all their wants to me. I worked my ass off on this side-gig, but I was desperate for a real payday. My unpaid tab at the inn had been discovered and all my money got confiscated again, with a bonus lecture on the side. All my savings, stolen from under my nose to pay so-called "bills"!

According to the laws of economics, the economy flourished if millionaires spent their wealth, which meant that the best way to make money was to spend it as soon as I got it. Since the richest people in this world were dungeon-delving teen girls, all I had to do was manufacture products specifically targeted toward their interests.

Since I had a monopoly on modern fashion in this world, teen girls with money burning holes in their pockets would naturally choose my clothes. I was confident that the general store suckered them out of every last ele. *Easy pickings.*

Miss Armor Rep had cheerfully joined the other girls, so I could enjoy myself solo today. I doubted that I would have much fun if I tagged along.

But I'm not alone—someone's following me! Were they a burglar tailing me, or were they a stalker? What kind of sicko got their kicks from stalking a teenage boy?

It wasn't like they would catch me in an indecent moment, y'know? If a teen boy exposed themselves in the street, that would be a cause for concern more than anything else.

My stalker didn't seem like the malicious or violent type, so I was probably safe, right? They completely concealed their presence with stealth, silent and invisible to the naked eye, but I could just barely work out their movements with Area Analyze.

Jupiter Eye allowed me to see in all directions around me, too. I didn't get a clear image of them, but according to Area Analyze, they were of slight build, probably a girl. If they were some creepy old geezer, I would've tried to scorch their hair off right away.

If they didn't want to hurt me, why were they following me?

C-could this be l-love? *Is this my fifteen minutes of fame?!* Did she stan me? Did she want an autograph? If so, she was in luck, as I'd spent a lot of time practicing my autograph. I actually had five distinct signatures! She could pick whichever she liked. *Does she have an autograph book? If not, I'd be happy to buy one for her. I'm not kidding.*

She didn't do anything besides follow me wherever I went. Was she just keeping tabs on me, or was she seriously studying my every movement?

Was it even possible that she didn't want an autograph? If she asked, I would even have let her shake my hand as a freebie! I was confident that I was being followed by a petite girl, though she could've been a child, too. It seemed unlikely that a child could erase their presence with Stealth, though. *Which means,* I thought, *this must be a member of my fan club, waiting for the perfect opportunity to ambush me and demand an autograph!* No, that still seemed ridiculous. *Kind of a terrifying thing to do, in any case.*

Seriously, if fangirls used Stealth to stalk their idols, all idols would go insane from stress. I was going to turn neurotic, just like an idol!

LONER LIFE IN ANOTHER WORLD

Which probably meant that I didn't need to buy her an autograph book. *And I worked so hard to develop five unique signatures,* I lamented.

Still, she followed me wherever I went. *This is either stalking or orc...king?*

That was a joke, there was no way an orc king could follow me around town. Besides, if an orc king got past the gates, I'd have to lecture the gatekeepers immediately! *You can't let a damn king of orcs into town! What's the point of gatekeeping if you don't keep the gate, huh?!*

I had no choice but to confront her directly. Slipping into a shadowy back alley, I said, "Pardon me. Do you need something from me? Are you trying to burgle me? I swear to you that my pockets are empty! If you want to mug me, tell them that I need a bigger allowance! The way things are going, I might have to start robbing people myself! I get mugged by my friends before any thieves can even get to me! That's probably why I'm always broke, you know?"

No response. Now I looked like a weirdo talking to thin air.

If I started following my stalker, wouldn't I become a stalker myself?

Oh no, that's definitely a trap! A teen boy that's following a little girl around—that doesn't look good at all! My sex appeal would die and go to heaven. Wait, wouldn't that mean it actually rose? Thinking about it, it would rise until it disappeared from sight, so it still wouldn't help me!

At this rate, my sex appeal was looking like it'd flame out like a shooting star. My affection levels were as fleeting and short-lived as a comet sighting.

Well, I couldn't see any harm if all she did was follow me around, although she'd be in trouble when Miss Armor Rep came back.

She was a tad overprotective, to be honest. After all, when we delved into dungeons, she went on rampages, massacring anything that got near me. Her protectiveness caused her to go on brutal killing streaks… My stalker was dead meat!

"Come on, why won't you tell me what you want? You can tell me if you're a thief. I've already had everything stolen from me. There's nothing left! Lodge your complaints with the Queen of Greed! I might have to resort to stealing, too, y'know? No matter how much I make, it always ends up as tribute for Miss Greed! I'm not joking around, that's why I'm broke!"

Still no response! Now I looked like a confirmed, certifiable lunatic talking to myself.

I felt so embarrassed. Even though I was an innocent victim of stalking, I was probably going to get branded a stalker, harassing a petite girl! My sex appeal was bleeding to death just from considering that possibility. This sucked. How did she flip the script on me and tarnish my reputation like that?! If I had to get turned into a stalker, couldn't my target be someone a bit more, I don't know, voluptuous?

"Why won't you say anything? Miss Sex Appeal can't take much more damage, y'know? Seriously, where the hell is she?!"

I sensed the presence shift. Was she finally going to say something?

"Wait, is that why you're ignoring me? Because I have no sex appeal? If you have no sex appeal, do girls just stop responding to you? I tried to fix things! None of the shops nor the dungeon contained even a hint of my sex appeal! I'm not kidding, y'know!"

I sensed a small movement again. Was she trying to corner me in this alleyway?

Finally, she spoke. "Um, how did you figure out I was here? Also, I understand the words you're saying individually, but they don't add up to anything strung together. You know that, right? I literally don't know how to answer your questions! Oh, I can tell you one thing: I'm not going to lend you any money."

Whoa, Miss Stalker sure knows how to glower! She had to be a grade A, top-class stalker. *I mean, she can glare from hiding!*

There were so many unanswered questions, but if my stalker could give me a flat look that severe, I welcomed her! *How much did her services cost?* Did I need to buy tickets to see that excellent stalker glare again? I was even willing to pay with mushrooms or clubs if need be.

"What don't you understand? *I'm* the one who doesn't understand! Why did I get labeled a stalker just because I tried to follow the girl who was stalking me in the first place? And if my sex appeal escaped the stratosphere, why would it come back down as a shooting star burning to ash? I've done nothing but seriously ask serious questions, and they get brushed off! None of this makes any sense to me! Besides, since you were such a good stalker, can I buy a whole book of tickets for your services? If I can, I will! How much per person?"

As tiny as she was, she seemed like she was no more than a year or two younger than me.

"Ah, just stop talking! I want to go home! I can't investigate someone so deranged! No matter how much I investigate, none of it will ever make sense! Talking to you is even worse! I can't believe you would call me a stalker! I was only tailing you! Also, why are you talking about buying tickets if you have no money? Also, what in the world is that even supposed to mean?! Waahhh!"

Miss Stalker burst into tears. She sounded like she wanted to go home. Why was she stalking me, then? Was she a lost kid or something?

More importantly, it didn't look good for me that I made the girl I was stalking cry. Why was she crying, anyways? She really was lost, wasn't she? Or maybe she was hungry. I took a tentative step toward her, and offered her one of the leftover potato bentos.

She devoured it. "Amazing! Delish! Thank you so much! That was so tasty! I don't think I've ever tasted anything this good before. I'm not lost, by the way, and I didn't start crying because I was hungry. Still, my compliments to the chef!"

Her tears finally stopped pouring when she tasted the sweet potato dessert. I breathed a sigh of relief. But now I looked like a creep who stalked a small girl and plied her with sweets. *That definitely looks worse than making her cry!*

If I tried to help her out by bringing her to the inn, then the story could only be reported as: "Local teen stalks petite girl, brings her to tears, plies her with sweets, and takes her to a hotel!" I had no idea how it could get worse from there.

It seemed like she couldn't understand a word I said,

anyway. *Could we get an interpreter over here? Class Rep, are you back yet? I need your help!*

Later that evening, I explained, "To summarize: The case of the mutual stalkers became too deep to solve, too twisty to navigate, just like a dungeon, but this time the dungeon master wouldn't sell me any tickets even after she partook of the sweet potato dessert. And I didn't even get a chance to ask Miss Dungeon Master about it all. I'm honestly shocked, y'know?"

"Shut up!" the girls snapped.

The Class Rep said, "Nothing you just said made any sense! It's honestly shocking that you consider *that* an explanation!"

What the hell? Now everyone was mad at me. Why did they treat me like I was the sort of pariah that stalked a little girl, made her cry, gave her sweets, and took her to a strange hotel? I left that part out for a reason! There was no way that I would ever tell them the whole truth!

The Class Interpreter began her investigation into the matter. She kneeled down, beamed at the girl, and gently cross-examined her. Why didn't she talk to me like that?

"Okay, so you were hired to investigate the rumors of a very dangerous person in this city," the Class Interpreter said. "You were chosen to investigate someone so dangerous and powerful because you could keep a low profile... but when you got here, nothing made any sense, you were discovered almost immediately, and he made you cry. Do I have that right?"

"Yes," she said.

"Haruka-kun!" the Class Rep yelled.

For some inexplicable reason, a rush of furious glares struck me like a thunderbolt.

"If that's her explanation, why am I still the bad guy, Class Interpreter?" I protested. "I mean, she followed me and spied on me, but I gave her a sweet potato dessert! I assumed she was a lost child when she started crying! I didn't do anything wrong, okay? I deny all accusations! As for my closing statements: I'm innocent, I've already bribed the judges, and I'll take this impeachment trial all the way to the Extreme Court!"

"Objection! An innocent doesn't need to bribe the judges," the Class Rep said. "And you meant to say Supreme Court—but that doesn't matter, because your punishment is going to be extreme if you don't fess up! Besides, *you're* the only one that needs to be interpreted, so don't call me the Class Interpreter!"

It seemed like I'd get a guilty verdict no matter what I said!

"Don't get me wrong! I gave my stalker sweet potatoes! Not french fries, I swear! How could that be a crime? She ate all the sweet potato desserts, right? They're delicious, right?"

"Ugh, forget it!" the girls hissed.

Well, aren't they delicious? See, proof of my innocence!

So he's amazing at cooking and skilled at sewing and furniture-making and he gives you sweets, but he's not a good guy?

INTERLUDE: THE WHITE LOSER INN

SHE CAME TO THIS TOWN knowing only what was reported: One day, a monstrous man appeared on the frontier and killed the dungeon king. He was considered more dangerous than the monsters. And he was fiercer than a monster too, with knowledge of brutal martial skills and a savage heart.

However, seeing him with her own eyes, she only felt confusion. *Could you really call that a monster?*

He simply did as he pleased according to his desires and ambitions.

She repeated the precise orders that her superiors gave her: "A monstrous man has appeared on the frontier. Alone, he massacred the monsters of the forest. Alone, he continued, slaughtering the creatures of the ancient Ultimate Dungeon. Alone, he thwarted an entire horde of stampeding monsters. He monopolized the wealth of an entire town, and treated the town itself as if it all belonged to him. That is the nature of the villain you must seek. Discover where he plans to go, what his next moves will be, and his true objective. Discover what sort of man this monster is. So investigate him...at least, that's what I was told to do."

Hmm. Her dossier on Haruka-kun sounded pretty accurate. She tried to follow him, but instead they ended up meeting.

Miss A said, "He didn't try to do anything to you, right? I mean, like, sex stuff? He's doing it all night long."

"That guy's not going anywhere, either," Miss C added, "If we take our eyes off him, he just holes up in his cave."

"I don't think he even has an objective. He's just living his life...or something?"

Yes, that was right. They were all 100% right.

"Don't lump him together with monsters—that's insulting to the monsters!"

"You want to know what he's like as a person? He's an amazing chef who also knows how to sew. He can even make his own furniture! He's basically a self-sufficient scoundrel."

"Yeah, if you want to know what he's like, he mostly does construction and oversees business enterprises?"

Miss A said. "He likes making money but never has any. He's always flat broke."

"Right, he only cares about two things in this world: food and sex! That's where all his money goes!"

They weren't wrong, but was that information worth reporting? Who would want to know those things?

"You tailed him, right? Did you learn anything?" I asked her.

"Yes, he expanded the armory today, helped out at the general store, delivered bentos, and gave me sweet potato treats."

That intel was just as useless. I considered drafting a report for her, but I had no clue what I would actually put in it.

From what I could tell, the only mistake in her intel was that he didn't defeat a dungeon king but a full-blown dungeon emperor. Also, he didn't exactly defeat her, though she apparently felt like she was about to die every single night.

Other than that, he did exterminate all those monsters, he did frequently control all the wealth in town when he didn't spend it immediately and end up penniless, and he did treat the town like his property, but it would be more fair to say he did whatever he felt like doing.

What would I ever write about him?

"Can you report something like, 'Caution, do not approach, danger'?"

A warning could work.

Miwa-chan suggested, "Don't try to haggle with him, he'll end up fleecing you."

Was she having a flashback to Haruka-kun's last bargain sale?

"You could, like, talk about how good his food is, right?" Shimazaki-san said.

Like a restaurant review?

Vice Rep B said, "Oh, do note that his massages are really good!"

Here we go again with the Vibration magic.

"And he gives sweets to girls!" Vice Rep C shouted.

Without a doubt, that was the most essential detail to report.

Her employers wanted him investigated, so they probably considered him as a threat. They probably wanted to know how dangerous he really was. It's hard to assess the threat of someone who was simultaneously as harmless as a fly, and a walking disaster.

"Are we even sure that he's human?" Vice Rep A asked.

"Good point!" Shimazaki-san said.

And in terms of how dangerous he was...I think the

bigger problem was how dangerously horny he was. Seriously, that was probably the main risk factor.

"Do you need to mention his ambitions? I mean, we'd need to censor practically the entire report!"

"It would be nothing but redacted text. It'd be illegible!"

How would I describe his personality? Half-assed. Flippant. He was fine, but I'm not sure if you could call his personality a *person*-ality because he probably wasn't even a person?

"What do you want to know?" I said.

"You'd be happier not knowing," the girls said in unison.

Though he was an absolute fiend, he devoted most of his physical and magical talent to getting laid. He cooked, but that wasn't his focus in life. His ambitions never grew more significant than increasing his daily allowance, and the only war he was interested in waging was under the sheets in the dead of night.

He complained so much about his allowance, but he had already blown through most of his savings and racked up massive debt at the inn.

What else was there to say? *It's not that you can't understand him even when you're around him, so much as you can't understand why you're around him in the first place!*

Fundamentally, he wasn't a true monster. He just made no sense. The monsters were massacred without understanding how or why. When he saved people, no one could make any sense of how it happened. He slew his foes in absurd ways, and found inexplicable ways to raise people's spirits.

I read over her report:

"This report cannot be completed because the subject is beyond all understanding. Seeing him with my own eyes, I understood less than before. Actually talking to him only made matters worse, as the reasons he didn't make sense stopped making sense! He is beyond all understanding. I have nothing to report because anything I could contribute would make no sense. Do you understand? No? Neither do I. (End of Report)"

Is it really okay to submit this? Would they not draw the wrong conclusions about someone they thought to be so monstrous?

If she returned with this report, she would just get in trouble. We racked our brains, trying to write different reports for her, but seemed to only confuse ourselves more in the process. This meeting was a bust, we all held our heads in our hands, frustrated.

It's impossible to write a sensible report about someone so far beyond common sense.

It's pretty dope that it's a banned book, but I have a serious problem with the title.

THE WHITE
LOSER INN

THEY KICKED ME OUT so they could have an impromptu meeting in the dining hall. For some unknown reason, they rejected my precise and in-depth description of the parties involved.

Apparently, some aristocrat was investigating me. At least that made sense. Folks with black hair and black eyes stood out in this world.

I wasn't the only person around who fit that description. I felt worried that the girls would get caught up in this mess. *The guys can take care of themselves. I don't care what happens to them.*

There was a possibility that the girls would be targeted because people assumed they were my accomplices. Even though I was a loner, the girls treated me like a friend.

It wasn't like I had to stay in this region. *Come to think of it, I don't even know what part of the world this region is in!* Regardless, I could go somewhere far away and live a quiet, inconspicuous life, but the thought of running away pissed me off. In fact, it was firing up an angry fire in my excitable high-school-boy self. You could even call it a new skill—Anger Inferno. *Give me a break, I haven't been very angry lately!*

I didn't need to necessarily leave the region—I could just hide out in my cave. So why did I feel like shutting myself in my cave was the wrong thing to do? *Am I a shut-in or not?* As much as living alone with Miss Armor Rep in that cave sounded like a fantasy, I suspected it would destroy what vestiges of humanity I had left. I was thinking about that jacuzzi, and her body outlined by bubbles. *Incredible!*

The more I thought about it, the more I realized that the cave wouldn't solve my problems.

Dungeon-delving was by far the most efficient way to level up and get better equipment. *Maybe I should go dungeon-delving for a bit.* If I did that, it might make things safer in town for the time being. Plus, aristocrats sounded like a pain in the ass—I doubted that most of them were sweethearts like Meridad.

I wanted to use this city as a base until I finished off all the dungeons in the area, plus it was the closest to home. Ideally, I wanted to stay within a day's journey of the nearest hot tub.

"I looked it up," I'd said before I got booted from the dining hall. "You're talking about the neighboring city, right? It's pretty far away, but we're neighbors right? I mean, there's only one territory nearby...so it's definitely that one."

Then I got kicked out of the girls meeting, so I figured I should have a loner meeting. Party of one.

This region was a monster-infested forest surrounded by craggy mountains. We were situated in a wide, isolated valley.

There was only a single, narrow road through the mountains. If you followed it, you'd eventually reach the neighbor, whatever-its-called, and that was literally it. There was nowhere else to go.

From there, the kingdom expanded, and the royal capital was all the way on the far side of...wherever we were. But here, there was only one road. So there was only one neighbor.

That neighbor levied tariffs and customs duties at the border, which contributed to this region's poverty and lack of resources.

Our nearest neighbor taxed traveling merchants and soaked up all the profits. It was impossible to do business without going through them, so it was an all-you-can-tax buffet. It's what they'd been doing all this time, and there was no reason for them to stop.

Naturally, they sent an investigation as soon as anything happened in this town. After all, everyone else plundered wealth from this frontier domain to line their own pockets. It was the kingdom's lifeline.

I could see how this development could lead to political conflict with the neighboring territory. And while I didn't mind a good fight, politics were a pain. *I'll pass on the conflict and get the hell out of here!*

"There'll be fighting soon, so is it really okay for me to leave?" I wondered aloud. "The neighboring territory? A fight? A possible fight? Hang on..."

I was sure the duke would do something or other, plus the city had its own intel, so I shouldn't intervene. If the other territory made a move, the duke could just counter. But for the time being, I had to make it clear I was moving independently from the girls. *Yeah, I'm in trouble if they attack...*

To be honest, the girls were just fine in combat, and the guys...*honestly, who cares?* But if they had to face more underhanded tactics like backstabbing, poison, mental manipulation, puppetry, traps—*wait, those are all my specialties!*

Well, since those were my specialties, I was sure that I could come up with a few countermeasures. I was also pretty good at sneak attacks and aiming for the legs—oh, and completely obliterating things, that one was my favorite!

"For now, my only option is to focus on commerce, right? We'll need money if anything happens, and business didn't depend on my stats. Did that mean I was going to have pick up another shift tonight? How is it that a NEET never has a day off?!"

If they were going to exploit our exports, we could just stop exporting. Focus on strengthening the local economy. If people wanted something we had, they'd have to come here to get it. *The neighbors will hate us for it, but screw 'em.*

Eventually, other merchants and aristocrats would probably go behind their backs to reach us. Yeah, that would work.

I went to the general store. At last, the owner acquired some books from this world! No novels...but they did have banned books.

This forbidden text was titled *How to Magic Item!* I wanted to incinerate this thing the moment I saw it. Who the hell came up with that title? Well...obviously the author did, but you know what I mean. Between the bad grammar and the offensively cheerful exclamation point, no wonder they banned this book.

I took a look inside. It was a serious treatise on alchemy that explained the workings of black magic, detailing how to make magical equipment and how to infuse equipment with black magic skills.

Indeed, this book would have been a real boon on the frontier, given the low quality of equipment here. It even devoted several sections to monster repellants and combat buffs, not to mention all the items that would be useful in daily life. I really didn't see anything suspicious written there at all. This seemed like a must-read for people who wanted to survive in this world, so why was it banned?

"It isn't even smut! Of all books, why would anyone ban this one?"

Even though the people in this world could technically read, it felt like they were illiterate. There was literacy—most people could read simple sentences and do basic math—but since they had trouble reading anything longer than a few lines, they didn't have much use for books.

How to Magic Item! was particularly unappealing, being an alchemy textbook. Alchemy in this world hadn't yet developed into chemistry, and worse, it was looked at with suspicion. Even if it wasn't banned, it wouldn't have sold well. But the author must have hoped it would be useful to someone or they wouldn't have written it.

With this book, I could make my own magic items, though they would only have basic effects for now. I had already practiced adding effects to all of the clothes the girls bought from the general store.

They didn't even use Appraisal on the clothes they bought? I didn't think the girls had noticed yet, but I had added defense, evasion, and ailment resistance buffs. I did that with every last article of clothing. Even if the effects were weak, at least they stacked.

They didn't compare to the sort of loot we found in dungeons—probably not even 10% as good. However, it was better than nothing when they weren't wearing their armor, and with several pieces on at once, it was likely better than anything local adventurers wore.

"Maybe this is an intro text. It's really easy to understand, but it never goes in-depth on anything...I can't wait for the next volume! If it's not banned, anyway..."

Given our current situation, being able to detect traps and resist status ailments was probably better than straightforward combat buffs. Spellstone rings would be perfect for that. I had too many spellstones anyway, and even if I couldn't produce a powerful effect, I should get some sort of boost from using high quality spellstones. I hadn't attempted rings yet because they were supposed to be difficult. *I have time right now, so I might as well try.*

Accessories seemed pretty profitable, too, so the sooner I made them, the sooner I could cash in. I got my raw materials for no cost, after all, and I had a lot of potential customers with fat purses. *Let's do it!*

Spellstones were imbued with arcane energy. Until now, I only had the vaguest idea of how magic worked, but thanks to this tome of alchemical wisdom, I could avoid blundering about in the dark.

"Wow, the color changed! This could be a bestseller! It'll fly off the shelves! Coming up with a good design was my main problem. I'm limited to using these stones, so maybe a sturdy design that emphasizes practicality?"

Even if I got enough spellstones to sell my own rings, I'd have to stick to the market price. By using my crafting to add value, I could name my own prices. If the spellstone market crashed, I could take my supply off the market, turn them into expensive accessories, and avoid taking a loss.

"Oh, that's probably why they banned this book and burned almost all copies."

Most spellstones in the kingdom came from the frontier. Naturally, neighboring regions wanted to keep prices low. Therefore, there would be trouble if the people of the frontier could process their own spellstones. In all likelihood, one of our neighbors had a monopoly on skilled artisans and craftspeople who could work with spellstones.

That's why the frontier was so poor. Even though most spellstones came from here, they had to deal with razor-thin profit margins, as most of the wealth went to our immediate neighbor.

This caused a vicious spiral, as the ill-equipped frontier folk couldn't easily defeat monsters, limiting their ability to gather spellstones. This caused a shortage, leading to an economic bubble where spellstones were overvalued. That bubble had burst soon after I arrived in this world.

As a result, the frontier military couldn't push back against the encroaching forest, and the population began to shrink from the constant monster attacks, causing even greater economic woe.

The government's policies managed to be both idiotic and inhumane. The kingdom likely profited in the short term, but if things went on like this, it could doom the entire kingdom. There were no checks against the constant growth in monster population.

"A simple jeweled ring would work. Inedible, but so tantalizing. Maybe I need to put in a warning to not eat?"

Unfortunately, I couldn't put the bigger stones on rings. As decorative rings, they worked, but they were too impractical for everyday use.

"Oh, what if I turn the stone *into* a ring? I can shape the ring and all, so it can be kinda like those ancient jade rings? Any kind of stones would work, since I can change the color however I wanted, so those'll definitely sell! Millionaire status, here I come! Probably!"

I had a good feeling about this! Not only did I have a monopoly, but these rings had added benefits and customizable colors! This wasn't just a get-rich-quick scheme. It could work long term! My life of luxury was on the way!

I was starting to get excited—I could even mass produce them myself. Because of Parallel Thinking, I could be a one-man mass-production factory, especially if I was only manufacturing one type of object. Supreme Thinking and Alchemy would allow me to manage an entire assembly-line solo.

I suspected that no one in this world had industrialized to this degree. Spellstones floated into the air, spiraling around me, like they were on invisible conveyor belts. One by one, I reshaped them into rings.

As I got used to the pace, I sped up production. The finished rings piled up around me...I was a one-man factory! *You can even call me a one-man industrial zone!* Except that I had no one to pay me a salary.

I worked my ass off, but it didn't make my life any easier. Wasn't there an old song about this? Something like, "I work and I work, but my life is still hard, and I still get glared at"?

I was like the poor crab from the fable of the Crab and the Monkey, working so hard only to have the fruits of my labor stolen from me! My picture in the yearbooks was going to have "MOST LIKELY TO WORK HIMSELF TO DEATH" written under it, yet I still had no money! Did I get paid in glares instead?

LONER LIFE
◆ IN ANOTHER WORLD ◆

When I overwhelm with my overwhelming acting skills, all I get is abuse?

DAWN BROKE before I had a chance to rest. I ended up working all night! Producing rings was slow at first, but as I got used to it, it became a mindless flowing task of assembly-line production. When I finally took a break, I saw the sun rise!

To be fair, I did take an unofficial break earlier to participate in some private activities with Miss Armor Rep, but otherwise, I was wholly committed to this side gig—the business opportunity of a lifetime.

Though upon further reflection, I realized that I had already wrung every last ele from the girls. If I wanted to make money, I should target the nerds and the meatheads. Would the guys even wear jewelry? I was going to find a way to rip them off regardless.

293

Well, I guess I experienced it, but it's hard to put into words...I-I'll just tell you what happened! I was climbing down the stairs toward the dining room and before I knew it, leotards! I'm sure you don't understand what I'm saying, and I don't really understand it either. I felt like I was going crazy. I felt as if I only got to experience a brief glimpse of leotards.

"Don't stretch out all the way at once—stretch slowly, as far as you can go."

"Got it!"

I didn't think the meat-nerds would have the Presence Sensing to figure out what was going on down here, but then I saw them running away as I neared!

"They're doing morning stretches!" they said. Now this was an otherworldly fantasy!

The girls kept panting and moaning as they went at it.

I wanted to get out of there myself, but Miss Armor Rep came up behind me and pinned my arms. Was she angry?

"Oh, good morning, Haruka-kun!" the girls said.

"So, uh, what's with all the writhing and heavy breathing? I mean, why are you all undulating, twisting, stretching, moaning, and engaging in otherwise depraved acts?"

Pinioning my arms behind me, Miss Armor Rep shoved me into the room, like she intended for me to join in.

"Get your mind out of the gutter! How dare you accuse us of depravity!" Vice Rep A said.

"Yeah, yeah! Don't get weird. We're just doing a morning exercise routine!"

"Ooh, this just feels *so* damn good," Miss B moaned without a hint of shame.

"Okay, she's just depraved!" the girls said.

They were just doing some morning stretches, that was all. Despite the resemblance, this wasn't the kind of exercise that teenage boys were so obsessed with. The girl from the gymnastics club, an all-rounder in combat, taught the class.

"Pay attention to your own muscles and posture," she said. "The cleanest flow is always the most logical one."

Maintaining a balance of offense and defense was essential to martial arts, but with her background in gymnastics, she could flow seamlessly from evasion to attacks or defense. Not only that, but she had remarkable flexibility and core control.

Even in awkward stances, she maintained complete poise. She could easily fool attackers into thinking she was off-balance. This fighting style emphasized technique over strength. That's why she was always the last one standing. *Why did they need to wear leotards, though?*

"If you control your core, your limbs will move naturally. Move from your core."

There was a major flaw with their leotards: there weren't any elastic materials in this world. I'm sure they used a soft fabric, but without any give, it was probably riding up like crazy.

Their completely innocent panting and sweating sounded downright pornographic.

It was going to have a dangerously unhealthy influence on any teenage boy. This was the kind of titillating fantasy that made me lean forward.

Afterward, Miss Armor and I sparred, leaving me beaten and bruised. I swore to exact sweet, blissful revenge later tonight. It was time to sell some rings.

"Cute!" the girls chorused.

"They have built-in skills, too?!"

"They're perfect! Nothing speaks to a young woman quite like a ring!"

"True, female wrestlers are fearless in the ring..." I said. "But no, I can't sell you any wrestling rings. I'm only here to sell jewelry! A wrestling ring won't fit on your finger, anyway!"

"You think I was talking about wrestling?! Huh, do you, punk?!" Miss C chirped. "How dare you call me a wrestler?! I'll see you in the ring!"

I practiced by mass-producing low-quality rings from the more worthless spellstones. I attached Magic Evasion and minor healing effects to them so I could dump them on the general store.

I recommended the "Ailment Resistance (small)" rings and bracelets. Rather than direct buffs, they made the wearer more likely to escape and fight another day. However, it looked like no one paid any attention to the attached effects.

"I like the red one!"

"Yellow for me!"

"I don't think I could pull off a thumb ring."

"You already tried it on?!"

The girls picked out their favorite colors and designs, and before I knew it, I was completely sold out. I made so many, thinking that I could sell the leftovers to the armory, but there was nothing left. Every single girl had to have bought more rings than they had fingers.

I figured that the effects would stack if they wore multiple rings at the same time, and my profits would stack up, too. That suspicious stall would come back one day, and I needed a lot of money for that. Where, oh where, has my sweet Pheromone Ring gone?

I could probably pawn the Shirt of Temptation for a

good price, but I felt I couldn't unleash such an item into the world. It needed to stay sealed away.

"Hand-made rings..."

"They're gorgeous."

"Beautiful..."

"It fits my ring finger perfectly!"

To be fair, I changed the size of every ring sold using a small spark of magic power. I wanted to guarantee that all the girls had Ailment Resistance, so I let the girls trade rings for their shares of any dungeon treasure found. Soon, I was sold out. Two buffs of the same type didn't seem to double the effect, but it did give a roughly 1.7× multiplier. That was more than good enough, but I couldn't believe that these girls ever dared lecture me about not squandering my money.

"It doesn't make any sense," I said. "I've used my whole fortune, but now I've accumulated credit that can't be used to pay down my outstanding bills at the inn!"

"We're not serial debtors like you!" the girls protested.

"You go from riches to rags on a daily basis!"

"And you haven't even tried to get better!"

In the meantime, I gave stalker girl some new clothes so that she could wear something a bit less shady. Weirdly, Stalker Girl and Poster Girl became friends right away, so

I decided to give them matching rings and outfits. As I suspected, they both started performing a strange dance.

We decided to spend the rest of the day dealing with the golem dungeon. The 37th floor was next. The deeper we went, the better the loot, so I had high expectations for the rest of this dungeon. I made a lot of money dungeoneering, but every time I went shopping in town, I'd be broke after ordering a few specialty items. It was to be expected, after all, that some goods had insane mark-ups, but it still felt like whenever I indulged in some modest luxuries, I went broke. This world had some unexpected developments.

We said our goodbyes and left.

Stalker Girl was apparently going to keep tailing me, but I did *not* want her to know about all my business. I'd be in so much trouble if she spread weird rumors about me in her reports.

However, now that I thought about it, if I could control what went into her report...I could control my reputation! All I had to do was act as appealing as possible, leak her report, and watch my popularity—and sex appeal—explode! It was the perfect plan!

Ugh, I couldn't even show off my demon scythes in a dungeon full of golems. At this rate, they were glorified weed whackers. Maybe I should go clearcut the evil forest? Lumber still sold at a decent price—I was honestly tempted.

I muttered, "More golems, no harems. Golems are so boring. Fighting them is as dull as—well—hitting some rocks. Now if I ran into a dungeon harem? Then I'd feel like I was adventuring in a world of fantasy! I say, bring 'em on!"

"Why do you want to get assaulted by a harem?!"

I needed money, I needed equipment, and I was working my damn ass off every day, so why was I still a NEET who always ended up working for free?! No matter how much money I made, it all vanished as soon as I spent it! It didn't make any sense!

"Just ignore him," said the Class Rep. "It's going to get harder from here on out, so stay in formation!"

"Aye aye!"

Right, I was trying to figure out a plan. *How do I improve my sex appeal?* I considered my options while my death scythes parted golem heads from golem shoulders.

If I knew what actions made me more popular, I would have done them long ago. In principle, I understood that doing things that society considered virtuous should naturally make me more popular.

What kind of things were those? Giving sweets to others seemed like a selfless and generous act, but if some loser gave candy to every girl he saw, that would be super creepy, wouldn't it? *Wait, that's me!*

"Are the Iron Golems getting even harder than before?"

"Maybe their toughness increases with level?"

"Yeah, their level probably measures their hardness."

In addition to trying to improve my ratings, I had to make sure Stalker Girl was kept in the dark about Miss Armor Rep's former job, and it was probably best to keep her strength under wraps, too. Apparently, Miss Armor Rep been uncharacteristically cautious as she glared at Stalker Girl all last night. *C-could this be...a fantasy world glare off?! I would've paid to see that!*

"Forget the golems. What the hell is Haruka-kun doing?"

"I think he's trying to improve his sex appeal by striking cool poses in the middle of battle."

"His sex appeal is definitely hitting an all-time low!"

Anyways, that's why Miss Armor Rep and I went our separate ways today. She went over to help out the Art Club because they apparently kept taking injuries.

The Art Club had made a lot of progress in their dungeon, but they were burning through their potions at an alarming rate. They had at least one divine caster who knew the Heal spell, but it would still be bad if they ran out of potions. Sure, they could stop if someone got hurt, but there was always the risk that they'd be too late.

So, I asked Miss Armor Rep to chaperone and coach them. They were sure to improve under her guidance. The Art Club was most effective when they weren't on the front lines of battle. Most of them were skilled at buffing themselves and debuffing their enemies, and were excellent tacticians, but they struggled to fight foes with Magic and Ailment Resistances.

With the Book Club President, I was confident that they'd survive, but just to be safe, they should get better at melee combat.

"Does he really think that pose is cool?" said the Class Rep.

Vice Rep B asked, "Is he trying to look like a dashing young hero?"

"What's so cool about striking poses while his floating scythes decapitate golems?!"

"What is with this ridiculous festival of violence and villainy?!"

If they just needed a tank, I could've asked Shield Girl to help them out, but Miss Armor Rep could both protect and coach them. In addition, it kept her out of sight of Stalker Girl, and it gave her an opportunity to hang out with the other girls. Spending time with her friends was sure to make her happy.

I didn't want Miss Armor Rep to devote herself to me to the point where she'd be willing to sacrifice her own life. I wanted her to forge lifelong friendships with all the girls here, so that if anything happened to me, she wouldn't have to be lonely. Besides, I kind of wanted her freed from Servitude, at least for the sake of appearances. *Seriously! I don't want to be a slaver my whole life!*

"I think he's totally trying to look like a young protagonist struggling to survive!" Were they still talking?

"He should apologize to real heroes everywhere!" cried the girls.

Miss Armor Rep wasn't a fan of the idea at first, but after I bribed her with some sweets and a ring, she agreed to coach the Art Club girls. That was probably a demonstration of the efficacy of Servitude. I even had to promise to make her a new hat before she got back tonight. *Yet another long night.*

I did my best to keep a brave face—I felt sure that, unlike the guys, the girls could keep their cool around Miss Armor Rep.

"And what about that evil-looking hand motion he's doing now?"

"Maybe he's trying to make it look like a real struggle?"

"It's freaking the golems out!"

Okay, I thought, *now I'll play the part of an innocent, harmless, but still dashing young hero!* Yes, I was going to raise my appeal!

"Gee-whiz, that was a close one! Did that sound convincing? How's it going, ladies? Is anyone injured? Anyone hungry? I've got some tasty treats in my sack, my compatriots! Something like that? Did you like that?"

Nothing's more appealing than a brave lad struggling in the depths of an evil dungeon! *I bet I charmed them all!* A glowing report was sure to follow.

The Class Rep took me aside and said, "Haruka-kun, you sound deranged. You kept switching to a creepy monotone after every quip, asking us how we liked it! You've always been odd, but you're at full freak today."

Huh? Did that mean she didn't see me as a dashing young hero?

"How can this be? I fought so valiantly against overwhelming odds, and then I offered you candy! I'm a kind and gentle young hero! I'm a great person! Right?"

Now that they understood how appealing I was, I stuck the landing by striking a dynamic action pose.

"Hmm. I think the main issue is, despite yelling about how tough a battle that was, you weren't in any actual danger." Said Vice Rep B. "Rather than demonstrating a real fight against overwhelming odds, you lopped the golems off at their knees, and while they struggled to stand back up, you lopped off their heads. Massacring a bunch of helpless golems wouldn't convince anyone you had a hard time, would it?"

Huh? I fought that way because I didn't want to inconvenience myself. Besides, they had weak joints, so it seemed like the obvious strategy to me.

"If anything, you made the golems look valiant in comparison; as you monstrously slaughtered all their kind, they struggled to survive."

How could fighting monsters in a dungeon end up *lowering* sex appeal?

"Also, shouting stuff like 'hero appeal up!' and 'sexiness up!' and 'eat shit!' didn't really help. Your entire plan was a disaster."

"Yeah, you're totally miscast for the hero role."

"The only character that fits you is the heel, not the hero."

My plans utterly backfired! Why did they think I was a heel? How could they say such a thing?

I was sure I could still make this plan work!

There was a hidden room on the 40th floor. I gave the performance of a lifetime, pretending to accidentally discover it when I leaned against the wall! *My acting is good enough for the movies!*

"Wow! Yes, indeed! I just found an epic hidden room! What a shock! Would be a real shame if we missed it, eh?" I crowed. "Well, did that sound convincing?"

"You're saying all your thoughts out loud—you know that right? It's not really helping your crappy performance."

"Also, no one was convinced by your so-called accidental discovery. You walked straight toward that wall and dramatically leaned against it, then acted surprised."

"And I think you might have oversold it with 'Yes, indeed!' It sounded like a line from a dumb movie."

My acting coaches were brutal. Now Stalker Girl gave me a flat look. If she was going to simply report what she saw and heard, then my spectacular performance right now surely did the job.

"Great Scott, what's a treasure chest doing in a place like this?!" I shouted. "Boy howdy, what an absolutely astounding discovery! I ask of you in a completely natural way: what should we do?"

"Just stop," begged Vice Rep A. "Stop acting! You sound like an idiot!"

"Why do you think heroes sound like that?"

"No one in the world would think 'hero' when you act like that!"

Even Vice Rep A was dunking on my amazing talents!

I even said those things with a gleaming smile. Where did I go wrong?

"Since when were you under the impression that I'm not a righteous hero?" I said. "Speaking of righteousness, would any of you girls like some sweets from the hands of a trustworthy savior?"

"Haruka-kun, we'd have to be delusional to think you were really a young hero! We'd need to be dreaming—no, we'd need to be in a coma!"

"If I saw a heroic Haruka-kun, I'd know he was a fake! The real Haruka-kun just stands around bribing girls with sweets," said Vice Rep A.

"How shall I say this? You would be much better suited playing the part of a horny teenager. Come to think of it, that's what you're doing presently, is it not?" said Vice Rep B.

"Yay, sweets! Give me sweets!" said Vice Rep C.

All the girls rejoiced when I gave them cookies. Surely, I must have seemed like an upstanding youth now! They happily ate their cookies, didn't they? Their attention was so diverted that they actually forgot about the treasure chest.

I went ahead and opened the poor, abandoned treasure chest. Within, I found a hat.

"Devil's Hat: VIT +10%. Daunt (large)." Damn, this wouldn't help my sex appeal at all.

"Read the damn room!" I yelled at the hat. "Where's the loot meant for a shonen hero?!"

Instead of finding something that would make me popular, I found something that made me more intimidating. *No, thanks.* It looked like a cowboy hat, for some reason. I hadn't seen any gunslingers in this world, so who was this hat for? Come to think of it, did this world not have guns because everyone used magic instead?

Speaking of magic, I did my best not to pay attention to a certain Archsage who hammered her foes with her so-called staff instead of flinging spells—if I paid any heed to her most powerful features, Stalker Girl was sure to put that in her report!

"Can I have it? Can I have it?" Small Fry squeaked, her mouth covered in cookie crumbs. "It's so cute and rugged! With that hat, I reckon I'll be a real grown up, pardner!" *What do cowboy hats have to do with adulthood?*

As a result, wc now had a strange, tiny animal wearing a cowboy hat and leather armor, who spun around with a pair of axes when she fought. There was nothing adult or intimidating about her.

LONER LIFE
◆IN ANOTHER WORLD◆

Sounds like she wrote up a slanderous report to post on some shady website.

A DUNGEON
46ᵀᴴ FLOOR

I WAS TRYING TO AVOID doing all the killing myself, so our progress was pretty slow. I had to be on my best behavior while Stalker Girl kept her eyes on me!

"Ugh, these golems are even harder!"

"I can't one-shot them, even when I aim for the joints!"

"Don't use big, sweeping attacks!"

"Got it!"

Even though the girls could all use Vibration Sword, the Iron Golems got a significant hardness bonus from the 40ᵗʰ floor onward. That's why the girls were taking so long to defeat them. Well, all of them except for a certain Archsage.

"Take that! Teehee!" she said as her staff punched through her foes.

Even without using the Vibration Sword, Miss B made a lot of things shake. It was like an earthquake over there!

"Eyes up here, Haruka-kun!" Miss B shouted as she caved in the head of a golem.

"Er, no, I was just admiring your huge, impressive... magical talents when an earthquake caused a lot of vibrations? My eyes were momentarily drawn away by large, distracting movements...Wait, shouldn't you cast some spells as an Archsage?"

In fact, I couldn't remember a single time that Miss B used magic in battle. Every time I looked at her, she was just swinging and bouncing from enemy to enemy!

"Stay focused, everyone!"

I taught the girls how to use Vibration for destructive purposes, but they still couldn't use it in combat. They leveled Vibration up a lot right away, but something was holding them back from using it in a fight.

Stalker Girl glared at me. I tried to make myself look as weak as I could as I dodged the attacks from the Iron Golems, striking poses of exhaustion and agony and feigning pratfalls where I just so happened to smash in their golem heads.

I was using my Wooden Staff to whack the golems to hide my other skills, but I still had to make sure not to kill them in one hit—especially considering how closely I was being watched! And now she was writing something?

Was she going to report that I was a barbarian who bashed monsters with a stick? *That's unfair. No one can look cool while swinging a branch!*

"Something's off, right?" I said. "I mean, I'm really struggling over here, you know? I don't mind if you glare at me, but I can't focus on fighting when you do. Also, fighting golems is dull, isn't it?"

The Class Rep responded, "That's your main complaint, isn't it? You usually complain that there aren't enough monsters to fight, but when you get as many as you want, you're bored of them! What happened to your hero act, anyway? You're acting like your old self now!"

I'd done nothing but whack metal golems over and over for what felt like forever. With Jupiter Eye, I could always sense the location of their cores, so one-shotting them was effortless. *Of course I'm bored.*

As she scribbled down notes, Stalker Girl muttered, "Report: Easily bored. Whiner. Wields stick. Not dashing!"

She was filling her report with insults. That report was bound to get posted on some shady blog!

I wasn't gonna let her get under my skin! I detected another hidden room, so I continued forward. *Hell yeah, just like that, dashing forth like a dashing young hero.*

"I'm *so* exhausted!" I said, dramatically stretching my arms out and yawning. "I better rest myself against this particular wall—Good heavens, it moved! What in the world?! There was a hidden room here! How could this be?! I'm so shocked that I'm going to drop my stick! Oh my? I dropped it!"

"The only shock here is that you think you can act!"

"I think this is the first time I've ever heard someone flub every single line."

"Ugh, I'm still cringing over you saying that you're going to drop your stick."

Tough crowd, as usual. Anyway, the treasure chest contained: "Impact Pendant: Adds knockback effect to blunt and slashing attacks (large). Attack Bonus." An item like this would definitely impact the market! *Who am I kidding? The only impact I'll feel from this pendant is realizing how little money I could get from it.*

"It's an Impact Pendant, perfect for melee fighters who want their attacks to have knockback," I said. "You could send enemies flying with a slash, and if you get good enough, you could even knock multiple enemies back with a single attack. Who wants it?"

The Class Rep and Tiny Animal were the obvious choices, but even Shield Girl would benefit? Even though the Archsage wasn't supposed to be a melee fighter,

I considered her as well. Miss A whittled her enemies down, so it didn't gel with her fighting style. Meanwhile, I didn't have enough power to send enemies careening.

After much debate, the girls ultimately decided to let Archsage have the pendant. The impact of seeing that pendant nestled in that sweet valley—*Nevermind! I wasn't imagining anything!* I was only admiring the pendant! It was an innocent glance!

They all reprimanded me.

By this point, it was obvious to everyone that the Archsage had no interest in using magic, so they agreed she should have the pendant. She immediately started whacking the golems into the air. Her hammer was called the Staff of Sacred Mysteries and it granted a bonus to divine magic. Why was she using a magical staff to smash things?

The halls of the dungeon rang with each of her swings.

Seriously? It's meant to be a magic staff?

At last, we reached the final floor. There was a hidden room somewhere in there, and I detected no stairs that led further down. I'd know the rest when I got there.

"Finally, the first dungeon king we've faced in such a long time—it's another goddamn golem?"

Tragically, there were no sexy monster-girl golems, just another giant golem, charging straight at us.

"I'll exterminate them from this world...wait, what world is this? Does this world even have a name? Did someone tell me before? Where am I? What in this world is going on?"

"You weren't convincing before, but no one upstanding would ever say a line like that."

The golem was huge, tough, and strong. It glimmered a faint silver. This level 50 Mithril Golem was a gargantuan creature that had Reflect magic and Status Ailment Immunity. Physical attacks were our only option.

"What should we do?"

"This is too strong for one party—I think we need to retreat!"

"Whoa, magic and normal attacks aren't working!"

Its defense was impregnable. *Actual mithril!* This was my first time seeing it. Would it leave mithril behind if I killed it? That seemed like a major event flag to me. I was getting pretty suspicious of anything that resembled an event flag in this world, but mithril was a material recommended by none other than *How to Magic Item!*

The legendary mithril—silvered steel, a sacred metal that could amplify magic energies. Servant of elves, truesilver, the treasure of Moria that glittered brilliant gray. There it was, the fantastical mineral, mithril!

"Uh...Haruka-kun, what in the world are you doing?"

I didn't trust the rules of this world, so I decided to acquire and process the mithril directly while the golem was still alive.

"What? It's mithril! Don't you want it? Don't worry, there's enough to share. I can do bespoke orders if you want. There's plenty to go around, so just let me know, okay?"

I held the mithril steady with Holding magic and shook it free from the golem's core with Vibration. Then, I tempered the metal as I continued to dismantle the golem. *Don't worry, I'll definitely share, okay? As a hero, I have no reason to hog it all for myself!*

The Class Rep said, "You're just ignoring the core? You're just stealing the mithril off its body and forgetting the core?!"

"If I leave the core alive, it obviously won't turn into a spellstone, right? The mithril is way more valuable! Just leave the core over there, okay?"

I could process its spellstone into an item, too. Besides, even if I obliterated every part of a monster, a spellstone still appeared, so there was no need for concern. In fact, my only concern was for the sweet, sweet mithril! *The myth, the thrill, the legend! Mithril!*

"Okay, I'll process the mithril into a long bar so that

we can carry it home. What an amazing discovery! We'll make a killing! Do you think more will spawn if we wait? Please?"

"Please don't forget the spellstone. I'm starting to feel guilty about letting it lie there, neglected!"

Huh? This was the first fantasy material I've seen in this world! All my gear was made of leather, fabric, wood, and other common materials. Everything I owned was 100% natural. Well, natural for a fantasy world, but still, mithril was way better.

For some inexplicable reason, all the girls stared at me with blank expressions. How could their hearts be so small? Even those with busts that looked so b—nope, of course not, it was the mithril! I was looking at the surface of the mithril, not the surfaces of—*no, nevermind, I'm not looking at anything.* I was simply admiring the mithril, nothing else!

I am by no means thinking any dirty thoughts, so please put away your double axes and your quadruple swords! Their glares were only growing in intensity!

"Mithril is amazing, y'know? I can make equipment with it, or improve your current gear. It can boost your magic power, too! It's one of the strongest materials, and might even enhance your skills! This is a real windfall. We hit the jackpot!"

How could they not see the appeal? The girls were probably unfamiliar with fantasy tropes. What was I to do?

Her eyebrow twitching, the Class Rep said, "*We* didn't do anything, Haruka-kun. Sure, it's a windfall, but it didn't exactly fall on its own, now, did it? You tore it from a living monster. That poor core died, stripped of everything, even though it was the king of this dungeon. Such a lonely death. You stripped the mithril off its body so fast that it couldn't even use Regeneration! We all came here to kill monsters, but with you, we end up feeling sorry for them! This was an unprecedented tragedy!"

She's right, this really is a tragedy, I thought. When the king died, the dungeon died with it. I wouldn't be able to farm for more mithril.

If there were only ten or so more of these golems, I would've had mithril left over even if I made equipment for all of us. Why did it have to end like this? *You disappoint me, dungeon.*

DAY 48
NOON

All I did was make a teeny-weeny golem on the way back
and the teeny-weeny tiny animal got all fired up.

A DUNGEON
46TH FLOOR

UNTIL TODAY, I had to bash monsters with a stick in this fantasy world. But now, I acquired a genuine fantasy mineral. Soon, I would have my own mithril stick! I would finally feel like I was a real fantasy adventurer! *I mean, besides the fact that it's still a stick.*

"What a glorious haul—the legendary metal! A fantasy mineral! I can't believe I have to do more work tonight! Though my focus is probably going to be divided, since I have other, more private 'work' to do. Just like every night. I feel like I haven't slept in days, y'know?"

"So, you've lost interest in your legendary mineral so quickly!" one of the mean girls said.

At least I got a good souvenir for Miss Armor Rep. Mithril was a magical ore that could enhance equipment, store magic power, and amplify it.

Since this meant I had to continue working my side job, I really didn't have any time to sleep. Still, this was such a spectacularly profitable fantasy world. I'd be fine. I didn't even know the meaning of "impossible!" If there was no food, I would life off passion! Nah, I was being ridiculous. I would die without food. People needed food to live.

Well, the dungeon was dead, and the sun would soon set. No better time to go back, but before I left, I sensed another hidden room nearby. Which meant a treasure chest, and a treasure chest on the 50th floor was bound to be good. This meant I had to give a flawless performance!

"Oh, how strange, by total coincidence I seem to have stumbled upon—"

"Don't bother!" the Class Rep interrupted.

"—a hidden room."

The girls upbraided me. At this rate, it didn't look like the report was going to help my reputation at all. I would just have to bribe Stalker Girl with some sweets.

She seemed a bit stupid, so I figured that giving her candy would be enough to trick her into calling me an "upstanding young man" in her report. Actually, I should just be direct about my bribery: every time she wrote down "upstanding young man" I'd pay her with a sweet. It was a foolproof sex appeal training plan!

"Um, everyone can hear you," the Class Rep said. "You just said, 'she seemed a bit stupid,' out loud."

They bombarded me with some of the most furious glares I've ever felt. Picking myself up off the ground, I heard the rapid scratching of a pen on paper.

"Not a decent young man! Not a kind young man! Not a gentleman! Not a virtuous young man!"

In the meantime, I sent my death scythes forth to decapitate the annoying golem that lurked in the hidden room. I tried to open the chest, but the lid didn't give. It was locked. *At last, a locked chest!* Oh, Vice Rep B just smashed it open with her hammer before I could unlock it.

I supposed that that worked just as well. *Why does the Magic Key even exist?*

It was supposedly one of the most important items in the world since it was buried so deep in the Ultimate Dungeon. A one-of-a-kind item, so rare that it was useless. Why did I even keep it around? Such a waste!

I identified the ring inside the chest: "Ring of the Golem Crafter: Create, control, and master golems." Oh, I could dig that. In the right terrain, I could totally use it. Probably.

"Okay, could you please let me have this one? Maybe? I'll make you custom mithril gear free of charge! No?

Okay, how about bespoke outfits? I'll even throw in custom rings. After that—ahh!"

"You can have it! Take it! Clothes made to order! Handmade rings, too!"

I felt a shiver down my spine when I looked at their eyes.

"O-oh, thanks, I guess? Are you sure? It can make golems, y'know?"

They weren't listening. They were too busy chatting about fashion, what they wanted to wear, what they liked. As for the rings, they wore intense expressions as they contemplated possible ring styles. What about the poor mithril? Why didn't mithril get any love? It was a legendary ore from fantasy literature!

I could give them major equipment and weapon upgrades with it! Mithril! Precious, rare, legendary— mithril! They were ignoring me. But they got handmade rings just this morning?

I heard an unmistakable scratching. As she wrote, Stalker Girl muttered, "Report: Lures girls with promises of clothing. Ensnares them with hand-crafted rings. A young man without virtue!"

Did she have a grudge against me or something?! Her report sounded like nothing more than a catalog of insults. I would need a mountain of candy if I was going to bamboozle her into writing anything respectable. Looked like tonight's workload had gotten even more onerous. *I'm not a factory worker! I'm unemployed!* From dawn to dusk, I was an unemployed mercenary, and from dusk to dawn, I was an unemployed factory worker! Evil corporations from my world had nothing on the labor rights violations of this world!

Instead of using the dungeon gate, we climbed the stairs to the exit. Compared to the Ultimate Dungeon, it was nothing. Seriously, if only I could've used the gate back then... Using the dungeon gate would've helped me out of so many jams back then.

As we went up, I destroyed any golems that happened to respawn. Apparently, if you took too long to conquer a dungeon, some monsters were bound to spawn again. The girls were so preoccupied with their fashion discussion that they didn't even bother to fight, so I tirelessly smashed golems by my lonesome. I gathered the spellstones by myself. And when I got back to the inn, I would have more work to do!

Yet I still had no money! I understood that it was because there wasn't enough money to go around in town, meaning it never got around to reaching my pockets. I seriously contemplated destroying the neighboring domain.

"If I climbed one of the mountains, made a temporary house there, and enjoyed a weeklong vacation where I flung meteors at them, they would all die, right?"

That domain was the whole reason I was broke! It would be fine if I wiped them off the map, wouldn't it? I was an unemployed NEET who worked 24 hours of unpaid overtime every single day, damn it! I worked so much overtime that I didn't have time to get a paying job!

The Class Rep nudged me with her elbow and said, "Uh, hey, Haruka-kun? Your rambling is causing a scene. Your little stalker is from that neighboring domain, and that rant made her so scared she started crying. If you wipe the neighboring region off the map, your sex appeal will go extinct, got it? Also, since you spent all your money yourself, you can only hold yourself responsible. You'll still be penniless if the neighboring domain disappears, you know? That's a fact."

Huh? Did I say that out loud? *I don't want to my sex appeal to go extinct!*

I responded, "What are you worried about? Another domain should spawn right away. Yeah, if I keep that greedy duke who has all my money half-alive, the people of the domain should keep respawning. That's how it works, right? I mean, I don't know."

"Only dungeon monsters respawn! The neighboring

domain can't respawn! Also, maiming the duke so that he's alive but helpless is far worse than killing him outright! You're making the Stalker Girl cry again!"

Was it a bad idea? Apparently, the neighboring domain wasn't a type of monster.

Between choked sobs, Stalker Girl said, "Report: Will turn our city into a sea of flame if we don't give him money. If we don't bow to his demands, he will treat us the same as monsters. He's no hero!" Tears splashed onto the pages of her notebook.

Why did she want to assassinate my character like that? Turn their city into a sea of flames if they didn't give me money? That made me sound like some sort of evil demon king! *How dare you!*

"Of course you sound like a demon king!" Vice Rep A said. "Raining meteors on an entire region for a week is actually pure evil!"

Vice Rep B said, "You're, like, way worse than an evil demon king; it's a serious insult for a demon king to be compared to you."

"Even a demon king wouldn't keep someone in a permanent state of half-life! They would get it over with! But don't you dare do that either!"

Was my plan really that bad? Even so, I had to defend my character.

"But what about the people?" I asked. "I'm pretty sure Mr. Meridad would fight to protect the people of his domain even if people started calling him a demon lord! And if defense doesn't work, the only option is offense. Unfortunately, there aren't enough people in this domain to even properly defend it, y'know? Just like me, he doesn't have the power to protect his people. People will die, no matter what, so I think we should attack. We need to make the first move, before someone we know dies, or one of the hamlets gets destroyed, right? Just like what happened to the Poster Girl's home village. Her family had to flee the destruction! And they were only able to escape because the legendary White Loser sacrificed his life. They would've died if he didn't do that! Our enemies not being monsters doesn't change a thing. The end result will be no different from an army of monsters invading. I stopped a horde of monsters from attacking the town, but you want me to ignore an equivalent threat? Don't you realize that townspeople will die if I do that? They've already started investigating us, y'know? Gathering intel is a prelude to war! Stalker Girl's report could obviously cause an invasion! Armed soldiers made attempts on the lives of the duke and his family! Twice! The neighboring domain is actively trying to foment a war! Maybe you don't understand what I'm saying, but it wouldn't have been strange if all-out war broke out from the moment they attacked the duke! Clearly, they still haven't had enough. I don't think they'll learn their lesson until their own lives are on the line, y'know? What they're doing is totally insane! Think about it. They heard about the appearance of a dangerous person, and even though the domain where that person appeared has endured abuse after abuse, they send someone to investigate that person's connection to the domain? I mean, after all that, what's wrong with shooting meteors at their damn city?"

Everyone fell silent. *Please, write all of that into your report!* It was my ultimatum. The enemy could decide on their own whether to mend their ways or to invade.

"B-but...the citizens of the neighboring domain haven't done anything wrong," the Class Rep said. "Why do the people have to suffer for the actions of their ruler? They may be good people. You don't know them! So, you can't just attack them like that. You can't!"

"The local townsfolk haven't done anything wrong either!" I responded. "Even the duke hasn't done anything wrong! We know they're good folk! Is it okay for them to pillage our towns, and kill our people? Should we let them keep killing us just because there are good people on their side as well?"

Stalker Girl, unsure of how to respond, bit her lower lip as she wept. Her people had to have known that their domain's actions contributed to the suffering and poverty on the frontier. They were our closest neighbors, after all.

"Even if the nobles are the real problem, that's the consequence of living in that domain. They settled there because they didn't want to tough it out on the frontier. They settled there and paid taxes that funded the armies of the nobles. Their lives of privilege were built on the suffering of our domain, whether they know it or not— that's reason enough for us to attack! They shouldn't feel any surprise if they woke up one day to fireballs raining down upon their city! If they didn't want to die, they shouldn't do things that make them our enemy!"

I didn't know what she would write, but I also didn't care how her incompetent lord would react to that report. Stalker Girl could write whatever she wanted.

But since we met, I wanted her to at least understand some of the reasons for what was going to happen. This wasn't going to just be someone else's problem. *Also, can you please write that I'm a nice boy, just once?*

Everyone climbed the stairs in silence. They finally understood that it wouldn't be unexpected if the war broke out while we were still in the dungeon.

Well, I won't let that happen, I thought. I wouldn't allow anyone to just have their way with the frontier. Sure, I liked to do as I pleased, but I didn't like when *other* people just did as they pleased. When I crossed a line, no shortage of people told me off for it from morning to night. *Therefore, none of you have any right to complain when I get angry at you, got it?*

LONER LIFE
◆ IN ANOTHER WORLD ◆

Stalker Girl delivering an entire monologue? She's barely had any lines until now!

INTERLUDE: OMUI CITY

THE REPORT was complete, but there would be consequences if I submitted it to Lord Nallogi.

Nonetheless, I had to do it. Haruka was so full of rage... Normally, he just mumbled to himself, but today, he was furious.

The Duchy of Omui was so poor that Duke Meropapa couldn't guarantee the safety of his people. Suffering and death were inevitable. Nallogi had exploited the people and rulers of Omui for generations. From what I knew, almost none of their dukes died within the safety of their castle. Their tombs stood empty. They met their fates on the field of battle.

Nallogi, my city, caused so much of the poverty on the frontier. It was founded to supply Omui so its people could hold the frontier against monsters.

The city prospered by embezzling funds meant for the frontier army. It was a city built with the wealth gained from the spellstones of the frontier.

All the people of Nallogi knew this. They all spoke ill of their duke, and they pitied the exploited frontier folk, but they did not act.

Of course, they would be shocked to wake up to fire raining down on the city. They couldn't not be surprised, regardless of how aware they were of their privilege. They couldn't possibly deserve death just for that. I had never even imagined the possibility until Haruka suggested it.

Were it to happen, I would want to save as many of the city folk as I could. Those people had always treated me well. My closest friends and my loved ones all lived in Nallogi. Even if they deserved it, I would still try to protect them.

I wanted to protect those I held dear. The black-haired girls promised me that they would stop Haruka, and I trusted them. When I told the Poster Girl that I was going to leave soon, she gave me so many sweets. She probably got them from Haruka. Imagine—he gave sweets to me, a spy sent from a rival city!

I understood that the situation wasn't resolved yet. Of course it wasn't. Even if the girls could stop Haruka, I couldn't stop the duke.

I had become close friends with the Poster Girl, and she told me her story: how her family lost their home and had to flee, how they eventually reached Omui and built an inn there, and how they made a new life for themselves. She told me how, if no one was willing to fight for them, she would have died.

Lord Nallogi would invade Omui. The Poster Girl would lose her home once again—and this time, she could die. Despite having lived in Nallogi all this time, I had never stopped to think about it before.

Lord Nallogi had ordered attempts on Duke Omui's life several times. There was more than enough cause for the people of the frontier to attack Nallogi, even for someone to raze the city to the ground.

I knew nothing of those matters. I hadn't thought about what it all meant. However, my clan were the ones that spied on Duke Omui all along. I couldn't claim that I wasn't involved. I couldn't claim ignorance.

My clan descended from the scouts that surveyed the frontier—so we should have been working alongside Omui all along!

But, because they weren't strong fighters, my ancestors were part of the rearguard. We were far enough away from the frontier that our clan was incorporated into the territory of Nallogi. Though they wanted to go to Omui, their weakness held them back. We were helpless, forced to help a system that caused our family and friends in Omui to suffer.

When Haruka told us that gathering information was a prelude to war, I understood. Killing me right then and there would have been the obvious thing to do.

Our clan had a similar saying, passed down for generations: "Intelligence is the first step in protecting our allies and destroying our foes." I grew up with those words, yet I failed to think about the meaning behind what I was doing.

My clan taught me to "see with your own eyes, listen with your own ears, and interpret everything with your own mind. Recognize falsehoods, secrets, and lies." Yet for too long, I watched without seeing and heard without listening.

My mind empty, I let the most important truths fall out of reach. I hadn't been thinking for myself. I hadn't understood what I was doing until Haruka told me.

That's why I had to deliver this report, to my clan and to Lord Nallogi.

He would almost certainly have me executed. That would be the obvious thing to do. It was the natural punishment.

As I ran back home, I remembered just how kind the people of Omui were to me.

Despite the poverty, the danger, the misery, and the hopelessness, everyone treated me with such kindness.

They were the people who truly needed to be cherished. They battled monsters to keep the entire kingdom safe.

We didn't even comprehend that the town of Omui protected Nallogi. I had forgotten that truth. I was blind, deaf, and dumb to the indignities they suffered.

But I couldn't allow my friends, my family, and my loved ones to suffer either. I wanted to protect them, even if they deserved to burn.

All I could do was finish my report, so I wrote down all I saw, all I heard, and all I thought. It was complete.

It was sure to be my final report, but it was also the first report where I reported the whole truth—all that I had experienced with my own faculties.

Haruka taught me that. He could've killed me, but instead he taught me and scolded me. Although I was his enemy, he treated me with kindness.

Although I was his enemy, he gave me delicious sweets and he tried to console me when I cried. He gave me so much.

He gave beautiful clothing and rings to me and the Poster Girl. Expensive rings that had skill effects. More than anything, I valued the friendship I developed with the Poster Girl. I was happy for everything Haruka gave to me. Seeing those beautiful treasures, I resolved to do what I had to do.

I couldn't give Haruka anything in return. But no matter how small a part I played, I was going to finally repay my debt to the people of Omui!

Was there a better way to phrase it?

"THANK YOU SO MUCH. I appreciate all your help. I will do what I can. Truly, thank you." Bowing her head, Stalker Girl ran off.

"Will she be okay?" Miss A asked.

Definitely not. Stalker Girl had the eyes of someone resolved in the face of death.

Kids like her shouldn't have to feel like that. It was wrong. The Poster Girl, having befriended Stalker Girl, couldn't hide the tears welling up in her eyes.

I hugged the Poster Girl and said, "Everything's going to be okay, even if it's not right now. Things will work themselves out in the end."

Nothing was fine, but we had to keep up the pretense that it was. The girls nodded in agreement.

Haruka-kun wasn't here to see her off, and neither was Angelica.

So be it! Even if things sucked right now, everything was fine! It had to be!

A horrible, ghastly tragedy awaited us all, but I felt absolutely fine.

I felt fine because the two most monstrous denizens of this world weren't here. *You know why? They're coming for you, Mr. Tragedy.*

"Yeah, I don't even know how bad things are going to get," said Vice Rep A, "but I do know that they'll make everything not just okay, but amazing!"

"Yeah, yeah, we can't do anything but wait. They'll definitely fix this!"

I patted the Poster Girl's head while the other girls consoled her and armed themselves. Everyone seemed completely sincere as they spoke.

Ending up in this fantasy world was a tragedy for us all. We were summoned here out of the blue, and we faced new setbacks every single day. Everything around us was a disaster. We couldn't escape them, and couldn't ignore them.

But now, though we worried, we still had faith. We trusted that Haruka-kun would beat the crap out of any tragedies that threatened us.

He took the absolute smiter of all misfortunes along with him. Things were *definitely* going to work out. When we went to the Ultimate Dungeon, we could only see an insurmountable horde of monsters, felt only never-ending despair—but those two smashed all their problems to bits.

"Everyone ready?" I asked.

"Ready!" they chorused.

Those perpetrators of chaos trampled the sea of monsters underfoot, and obliterated our insurmountable nightmares. Now, they were out for another round.

"If we don't hurry up, they'll finish before we even get there."

"Yeah. With those two, I'm not sure if we even have a chance?"

I knew that a terrible fate awaited Stalker Girl.

From the resolute look in her eyes, I knew that she headed toward her doom with eyes wide open. *Mr. Tragedy is just as doomed. I almost felt sorry for it.*

The All-Time Greatest Destroyer of Tragedies and the Ultimate Vanquisher of Disasters were on their way. The results were so inevitable that we could've declared disaster dead on arrival.

That was why, despite all the threats that loomed on the horizon, we didn't give in to despair.

"It's going to be fine," I said. "She met Haruka-kun. Anyone who meets him finds happiness. So quit worrying, everything's going to be all right."

The Poster Girl nodded, dewy-eyed.

The tragic fate that awaited Stalker Girl would not come to pass. Any chance of a tragic fate vanished the moment she met Haruka-kun.

Whether her fate was painful, cruel, difficult, or hopeless, it couldn't survive contact with Haruka-kun. Inevitably, her inevitable fate was doomed. Because the Master Tragedy Slayers were going to beat the crap out of it.

An indestructible fate was about to learn what happened when an unstoppable ego crashed into it. It would learn the meaning of suffering. The terrifying future was about to experience true terror.

Run while you can, Fate, because someone who's been destroying unfortunate fates ever since he came to this world is heading your way, and he isn't alone.

No matter how inevitable our fate was, he would mangle it until it was evitable. Fate should just give up now, because I knew that Haruka-kun never would.

In a world this laden with despair and disaster, Haruka-kun repulsed all misfortune around him and attracted only joy, like a magnet. Misery was an endangered species around him, and fate would soon follow.

He would make despair itself go extinct, no problem. It almost seemed suspicious that misfortune still existed here—the townsfolk of Omui now filled their days with laughter!

Resistance was futile. Haruka-kun would keep on fighting until only bliss remained.

I knew that he would never let a girl with that look in her eyes go to her death. We all used to look like that, but he made us feel happy and hopeful again.

Sorry, Fate, but you're out of luck, I thought. He wasn't going to give up until everyone was happy. *In fact, it might be quicker if you just changed your occupation from tragedy to comedy.*

Haruka-kun mercilessly stamped out all the tragedies of the frontier. And now, with his accomplice, he was going to do the same to Nallogi. I knew it. Whenever we were on the verge of death, he always came through.

He was never gallant or cool. After all, he was no hero.

But he didn't use intimidation and terror to get his way. He wasn't grimdark.

He didn't use evil methods to fight evil. He wasn't an antihero, that was for sure.

He was arrogant. He was proud. He was selfish. There was nothing virtuous about him. He simply destroyed any obstacles that crossed his path, and one of the things that annoyed him was the thought of other people crying, despairing, suffering, and dying. Misfortune and tragedy were simply pests to exterminate. He didn't need reason or logic.

To him, destiny was just a rock in his path that he kicked out of the way. And then bludgeoned to bits.

Yup. Something in his way? He'd force it to laugh. Unhappiness and tragedy and misery were nuisances. He simply eliminated anything and everything that ticked him off.

For its own good, Misfortune should really consider becoming Good Fortune. If it didn't, Haruka-kun would simply get annoyed and obliterate it.

Reform, become something positive, or else the most terrifying people in this world will destroy you.

He would make everything all right, soon.

Even though things should go smoothly, I don't think they've ever gone smoothly.

J̲UST A LITTLE LONGER, and I could bring this matter to a close. I had to fix this myself.

I told my clan everything. I expressed my innermost feelings, reported all that I saw, and provided my careful interpretations—for the first time, I was completely honest.

Even if our entire clan escaped to Omui, the people of the frontier had no reason to trust us. Defecting like that, without warning, would have been far too suspicious. But that didn't matter. They could use us as pawns to be sacrificed on the battlefield for all I cared. At least then, we would die fighting for Omui.

My ancestors had to have been disappointed in what we became, but if we died for Omui's sake, I felt that they would forgive us. That's why our clan took one last job:

345

we informed Duke Omui of the movements, plots, and strategies of the Nallogi armed forces. That alone was enough. That was our true mission, the last we would ever perform.

Haruka was right. I had been taught well in the ways of war. If Omui wanted to win, they needed to attack—otherwise, no matter how mighty their soldiers were, the simple geography of the region would be their downfall.

If Duke Omui was willing to sacrifice his own people to draw the Nallogi army into the frontier, he could prevail, but he would never do that. He would fight to the last breath to protect his people. The Dukes of Omui had done the same for many generations—sacrificing themselves to protect their people.

Long ago, an ancient ruler of Omui protected my ancestors. In those days, we couldn't fight, and we would have died if not for the sacrifices made on the frontier.

Our clan repaid that debt with betrayal. Our final act would at last settle the balance.

In the coming war between Omui and Nallogi, the decisive battle would be fought along the long, narrow mountain road that connected our two regions. The road was only twenty-five yards at its widest. In places, it was barely ten.

It was impossible to advance rapidly through this pass. A large force would overextend itself and be forced to stop. Whoever controlled the surrounding cliffs could rain boulders and flaming arrows down on the enemy.

The cliff tops could not be reached from Omui's side, but they could be reached from Nallogi's side.

Omui's only option was to blockade the mountain pass...but the frontier entrance to the mountain pass was very wide, and their army would be stretched thin. It would not take long for Nallogi, with its greater numbers, to break the blockade and rout Omui. Duke Omui wanted to protect all his people, whereas Nallogi only needed to break through at a single point. This war was completely asymmetrical.

To avoid this scenario, Duke Omui had to invade Nallogi first. Such an attack would endanger the citizens of Nallogi, but it was Omui's only hope for victory.

The only way to win was a fast and overwhelming surprise attack that annihilated Nallogi completely. And they would have been justified, as revenge for the sins of Nallogi.

Haruka could have easily ended the war by himself. Just like he said, all he needed to do was pelt Nallogi with flaming meteors until it was destroyed.

From high in the mountains, he could easily rain fire down upon us. If Lord Nallogi sent the army after him, they would never be able to catch him. Our city would burn to the ground. Cut off from retreat and supply lines, the Nallogi military would be defeated with ease.

If Haruka set his mind to it, there was no stopping him. You'd need someone as strong as his classmates to even stand a chance.

Even so, I wanted to prevent as many deaths as possible. That's why I had to reveal to Duke Omui the positions where Nallogi forces were deployed, and the details of the traps and ambushes they had set.

Our clan would assume full responsibility. It couldn't possibly make up for all the harm we had caused, but it was all we could do. It was our clan's final mission.

I had tied up all loose ends. The people of my clan were on the move. Now, I had to inform the authorities of the city. Soon, my job would be done.

"I have returned with the report on the mysterious boy who appeared in Omui," I announced.

I gave Lord Nallogi my report. It was all over.

I wished that I could've seen Haruka one last time, but it was not to be so. *All the same, thank you, Haruka.*

White-hot rage—Lord Nallogi's hands shook as he read the report, his face a mask of fury.

"What is this?! Explain yourself at once!"

I cowered, rooted in place by his eyes full of hatred and anger. But this was my choice!

"It is exactly as I described in my report," I responded. "If you harm that town, Nallogi will be destroyed—and House Nallogi with it. There is nothing else to report. The only way to guarantee the safety of this city is to prostrate yourself before that boy and beg for mercy and forgiveness. The only route is to surrender to Omui, swear fealty, and become a vassal state. My clan is already en route to Omui as we speak, and they will inform the Duke of all the secret passages, hidden tunnels, and remote hideouts of Nallogi, as well as detailed descriptions of the city's defenses, our military capabilities and organizational structure, our special forces, and even our covert operatives. They will also inform Omui of the hidden mountain passages, the locations of our secret bases, and how they are equipped. I have taken the liberty of warning the residents of Nallogi that their lives will be in danger if they do not evacuate. There is no hope of winning against that monstrous boy, because he is no monster. He is the kindest, strongest person I have ever met. This concludes my report."

Now there was nothing more to be done.

As the daughter of Chief Shino, I did everything I could.

Now Nallogi couldn't invade Omui so easily. If they

attacked now, the losses would be beyond belief, and if the invasion managed to fail, Nallogi would be destroyed instead.

During that time, people could escape the city of Nallogi. I did my job properly. *Thank you, Haruka.*

"How dare you?! A craven spy like you—I'll kill you where you stand!"

His gleaming sword swung toward me. Soldiers closed in on all sides, leaving me no way out. But I would not run; I would stand my ground. I knew that I was beyond rescue.

My job complete, all things came to an end.

Going to Omui, meeting so many kind people there—it filled my heart with joy. The Poster Girl became a true friend.

I had eaten the most delicious sweets I had ever tasted. I ate so much incredible food and met so many sweet girls.

And, of course, I met Haruka. He gave me those sweets and comforted me when I wept.

I felt true happiness there and that was enough for me.

Even now, with tears blurring my vision, I could see the ring glittering on my hand.

I wished that I could see him once more. But if I did, I would probably break down in tears. And if he saw me weep, he would pat me gently on the head again, right?

That was my only regret, but having met him, I could die with a smile. *So...thank you, thank you, Haruka.*

All I could see was that sword. In a moment, I would be cut down.

The tip of the sword was inches from my brow.

Why am I still alive?

"Uh, long time no see? I mean, you were stalking me just last night, but length is relative! Anyway, why is there a sword, like, an inch away from your forehead? Is this a hobby of yours? Oh, are you using it to pop a zit? You shouldn't do that, y'know? They heal better if you leave them alone, y'know?"

Why was Haruka here? How did he catch the sword between his fingers? Why was he standing on top of Lord Nallogi's prone body?

And above all, why couldn't I stop crying? He gave me a pat on my head.

I thought I would never again feel his hand on my head. This shouldn't have been possible. Yet, here he was, gently patting me while standing directly on top of Lord Nallogi.

"Y-y-y-you bastard!" he wailed. "How dare you treat me like—g-grokhh!"

Haruka continued to pat my head while he stomped all over Lord Nallogi.

Yep. He was back.

DAY 48
MIDNIGHT

We have over twenty witnesses affirming how effective
Commander Armor's workout plan was.

NALLOGI
CITY

AS WE RAN, I warned my companion. While I didn't have any concerns about our strength in battle, I did have concerns about us going overboard, especially Miss Armor Rep over here.

"Don't kill anyone, okay? We're here to save them and help them evacuate, which means no killing, got it? If anyone attacks us, it's enough to just force them out of the city, y'know?"

Miss Armor Rep nodded her head briskly, but I wasn't sure if she understood my meaning. Stalker Girl left sooner than I expected.

"No, don't just nod. Tell me that you won't kill them, okay?"

She nodded.

I thought it would be a bad idea to act without letting anyone know first, so I met with Mr. Meridad. Stalker Girl apparently left while I was still in talks with the old man, so we had to follow in a hurry. I had never left the frontier before, so I didn't know where I was going, exactly. Since Miss Armor Rep insisted on following me, I couldn't fly, either.

"This is the mountain pass, huh? It's pretty long. That other city is supposed to be past here, right? At this hour, nothing in the city will be open yet, so we can just rush through, no need to dilly-dally. Once we're through the pass, I'm going to try flying, so just hop on my back, all right?"

This was a seriously long road, and we still hadn't caught up with her. We hadn't even spotted Stalker Girl yet. Did that mean she already reached the city?

This was bad. Everyone was going to blame me if anything happened to her! If she got hurt, I wouldn't only get lectured, the Class Rep would take away my allowance!

Besides, the Poster Girl would probably never speak to me again if anything happened to her friend. And she would probably kick me out of the inn for all my unpaid bills!

At last, I could sense Stalker Girl as the city gates came into sight.

"She's over there. Does that mean she's in the castle? Searching the castle sounds like a hassle. Worst-case scenario, if we didn't make it in time, I figured that I could just blow up the castle...but that plan's a non-starter now, isn't it?"

It wasn't much of a castle, too shoddy to be a tourist attraction. They probably didn't have any maps or visitor guides. Looking at it now, finding the little stalker might be pretty easy, actually. It was all showy and ostentatious on the outside, but from the looks of it, it was just a McMansion fancied up to resemble a castle.

Sure, it was a lot prettier than the frontier manor, but that was because the duke's residence was built for defense. This residence was sprawling and ornate, but the walls looked pretty thin, there were too many windows, and all the ridiculous ornamentation on the exterior made for easy climbing.

Jupiter Eye's Clairvoyance ability confirmed my observations. We reached the city gates. *No way we're gonna make it in time like this,* I thought.

"Okay, hold on tight. It's going to be a bumpy ride," I said.

Miss Armor Rep nodded and clambered on to my back, wrapping her arms around my shoulders.

I can't believe it; I'm actually giving a girl a piggy-back ride! Well, she was wearing armor, so it wasn't as fun, but it was still my first time! It just felt like I was carrying a sack of armor on my back, though. All that armor meant I couldn't feel her pressed against me.

"Don't move a muscle! Do your best to stay completely motionless!"

The Ring of the Golem Crafter was such a good find, and I could finally put it into use. It wouldn't be too late to save the people here after all.

Before, my only way of dealing with the world was mass-slaughter. However, now I could actually protect people. Even after my ultimatum, there was now a real possibility of preventing undue bloodshed. I didn't even need to kill the lord, never mind the townsfolk. *Wow, I can't believe I came up with a plan that didn't involve razing the entire region!* Well thank God I took the time to inform Mr. Meridad and the townspeople about what was happening.

"Even though my eyes see all, I was blind to the obvious," I muttered to myself. I was the one who was supposed to pull ridiculous schemes! I figured she was just a mere spy, but I was sorely mistaken.

I was surrounded by idiots, and I was always the biggest idiot of all. Why didn't I consider this possibility? I finally had a chance to use the Ring of the Golem Crafter, and I nearly lost it.

I was so excited at the prospect of being able to protect people, I misjudged the situation completely. Worried about the grave danger both regions were in, I didn't realize that the poor, innocent girl marched toward her own death. I was an absolute fool.

I had to reach her in time, nothing else mattered. No matter the cost, I would succeed. My plans were thorough—I knew her coordinates from her ring. *Lucky I didn't sell that one,* I thought.

Failure was not an option. I carefully held Miss Armor Rep behind me with some magic power. No matter how unlikely, if it was possible, I could succeed. My epic luck better pull through for me. *Now—*

"Teleport!"

I would reach Stalker Girl. Flying wasn't fast enough. My first long-distance teleport, with no dress rehearsal. *I just hope I don't end up inside a wall!*

"Oh shit! That was close! That was so close! Dude, watch where you point that sword! You could cut someone wide open with that thing! If I teleported an inch to my left, you would've chopped my head off! Why does this world keep throwing dangerous shit in my path?!"

It would've hurt so much! *Swords are dangerous!*

Oh, I reflexively caught the sword point with my

fingers, mere inches away from Stalker Girl's face. What was she doing?

"Uh, long time no see? I mean, you were stalking me just last night, but length is relative! Anyway, why is there a sword, like, an inch away from your forehead? Is this a hobby of yours? Oh, are you using it to pop a zit? You shouldn't do that, y'know? They heal better if you leave them alone, y'know?"

Fantasy worlds, man. Their skincare knowledge was seriously lacking if teenage girls tried to pop their zits with swords.

Pimples occured when pores were clogged with sebum, the common name for the inflammatory substance produced by sebaceous glands and bacteria trapped in the pores, and those bacteria could become trapped for various reasons. Popping pimples only made the problem worse. I would personally recommend washing your face and applying a hot towel to it for a few minutes, seriously. Besides, using a sword to pop pimples was totally unhygienic. And extremely dangerous.

I had no idea what was going on, but Stalker Girl was crying, so I patted her head. Most problems could be solved with sweets and head-pats, right? It was my secret technique for avoiding a lecture! Though it never seemed to work for me, it should work in principle, y'know?

"G-grokhh!"

Huh? What was that sound? If I wasn't mistaken, 'G-grokhh' was the telltale call of the orc. I hadn't seen any orcs in a while! Speaking of which, what was this soft and flabby thing under my feet?

"Huh? Why is an orc pretending to be the floor? Is this a trap? Shouldn't my Trap Ring warn me about this sort of thing? I never even got to use the damn thing, and now I find out that it doesn't even work! That dungeon is sure to get some consumer complaints and product recalls at this rate! Well, if it still existed and the boss didn't just walk out on her job one day, you know what I mean?"

That ring was defective junk after all. This orc under my feet was really squishy and nasty, too.

"Who are you calling an orc, you knave? Remove your feet at—G-grokhh!"

A talking orc? How could this be?! This was a way bigger deal than a defective Trap Ring! Even that smart-ass goblin emperor couldn't talk! This proved that orcs were top-tier monsters. They may have looked stupid, but if they could speak, that made them pretty smart for monsters. Although the meatheads were even dumber than goblins, yet they managed something that resembled human speech, so this didn't necessarily prove intelligence.

"Um, the person you're standing on and calling an orc is Lord Nallogi," Stalker Girl said. "I don't believe the duke is an orc, though I have yet to investigate the matter, so I can't say that definitively."

"Who the hell's Nallogi? I won't be able to remember his name anyway. Can't I just call him Orc N? A proper investigation is absolutely necessary! If he's an orc, we can't just let him loose in a town! That would be danger-ous! Though this one seems pretty weak, y'know?"

If the townspeople all wielded clubs like those of a cer-tain city, that orc would be in far greater danger. But for a regular city, an orc was bad news. The gatekeepers weren't doing their jobs at all! We didn't pass through the gate, so I couldn't be sure they were at fault, but even so.

For a normal town, a rampaging orc would be a major emergency, but for that bloodthirsty town, the walls were meant to keep the monsters safe from the townsfolk, not the other way around. That club-thirsty town was terrifying!

Someone dressed like a servant said, "Pardon me, sir, but that person you insist on referring to as an orc is the lord of this domain."

"No way! How the hell did an orc become a lord?! This orc looks far too stupid to manage a kingdom! It's probably even stupider than it looks. Now a kobold, that could work, but you can't expect an orc to know how to rule, can you?!"

At least kobolds were clever!

"Kobolds are sort of smart. They're like dogs, so you could probably train them to do all sorts of tricks! I recommend a regime change, y'know?"

Honestly, I wasn't sure that a kobold would even take the job of duke. It probably depended on the working conditions.

"Silence, cur! Enough of this nonsense! How dare you address a noble lord as if he were a lowly orc! How dare you mock my appearance! Guards! Kill the interloper! Tear him to shreds!"

"Huh?"

Who was he trying to talk to? If he was trying to give orders to the guards, they certainly weren't listening. None of them were even conscious anymore.

"Miss Armor Rep, I did say you couldn't kill them, but look at them! Miss Armor Rep's hazing is worse than torture; honestly, I feel bad for them. Look, I've experienced it myself, so no one knows better than me. It's a special hell that goes by the name of 'training.' Y'know?"

When she trained people, she broke their spirit and rebuilt them from the ground up. The guards couldn't even stand, so they desperately tried to crawl away instead.

I sympathized. *It sucks, doesn't it?* Even hell was too nice a place for her training regimen. Those were just warmups, too. She hadn't even gotten started yet.

Since I told Miss Armor Rep not to kill anyone, she decided to half-kill them, instead? I wasn't sure if it was a good idea to train our enemies, but it certainly looked like they were traumatized for life. They were technically alive, but they looked dead inside.

"How should I deal with this orc? My plan was to leave the duke here unharmed, but if it's an orc, maybe I should harm it. I mean, it's just an orc. Besides, this one is especially revolting. It's so soft and flabby, y'know? Should I put it out of its misery?"

"F-frokhh!"

I didn't even take out my stick yet!

Oh, the orc seemed to have fainted. A fainthearted orc? Well, if orcs could be dukes, I saw no reason why they couldn't be timid. But I'd expected, I don't know, a little more oomph from a monster. Maybe it needed some training, too? *We'll get you nice and lean and ready for action. Miss Armor Rep won't go easy on you. She doesn't go easy on anyone; she wouldn't even go easy on Billy Windsor!*

DAY 49
EARLY
MORNING

There's no law saying I can't improve the road on my way back.

INTERLUDE:
OUTSIDE
OMUI CITY

JAGGED MOUNTAINS crowded together at the frontier. The pass that wended its way through them was little more than a narrow crevice. The way forward was barely visible, but we knew what lay ahead.

"Mobilize all troops!" I roared. "Maintain formations! You only have to stall the enemy! Hold your positions!"

This pass led to Omui's sole neighbor, the traitorous city of Nallogi. That boy went into what could only be called enemy territory now. And I allowed him to go alone.

Haruka could destroy their city and demolish their castle with ease. But we couldn't let him unleash his wrath on the duke or the people of Nallogi. If he did, the whole might of the kingdom would turn on our city.

Even were he the king himself, I would've forbidden that boy from crossing that line. Nonetheless, we now hovered on the brink of war. I would never surrender in battle, no matter the odds. Despite this, I could produce no answer to the boy's words.

The previous evening, he met with me and said, "If you go to war, people will die, right? Like, the people in town and in the villages? I mean, if you only care about winning, it wouldn't take many sacrifices, but with your army, you don't have a chance of protecting your people *and* winning, know what I mean?"

If they besieged our city, we would need a powerful garrison to repel the invaders, but if they raided our villages and hamlets, I would need to send soldiers to their defense. We would be spread too thin.

But to try to avoid this war without bringing harm to the Lord of Nallogi or his people—to do this alone—was a suicide mission. What use was his strength if he couldn't fight them?

"Yeah, I think the situation has progressed faster than expected, y'know? So, I'll just go fetch the little stalker, and you folks can figure something out in the meantime, right? Hopefully?"

With those parting words, he left. I had no idea what he was talking about, but it was clear that the threat to the frontier remained.

He went on a rescue mission where he could not fight.

He would have to bring her back here safe and sound, while under attack by relentless pursuers.

Yet, he walked out of our meeting as if he was going to a picnic. I knew that I couldn't stop him. After all, he only bothered to inform me, the Duke of Omui, out of a sense of obligation. I couldn't help him, but I knew not to interfere.

Though he had decided upon his course of action before coming here, he acceded to my sole request—to spare the people of Nallogi. I did not just fail to aid him; I practically bound his hands.

I pulled my aide aside and lowered my voice, "I cannot stand the waiting, and I am boiling over with rage—perhaps we could charge them? Perhaps we could even send all our forces into the pass, unleash a valiant battle cry, and wipe out all our foes!"

"You can't break your word! You swore that you would not make the first move!"

There was nothing I could do to help. I swore to that lad, on my honor, that I would not enter the pass. It was just a little suggestion.

The thought of the Savior of Omui behind enemy lines, unable to fight, ate away at me. I felt like I could not stand idly by and do nothing.

Yet that was all we could do— as clouds of dust kicked up in the rocky wasteland swirled around us. For some reason, he made me promise to stay well back, and I could not break a vow made to our greatest benefactor.

Frustrated and impatient, we remained at the entrance to the mountain pass. He managed to return from the ancient Ultimate Dungeon, so returning from Nallogi was akin to returning from a pleasurable jaunt. I could only gaze out at the rocky crags and wait for that boy as he attempted a rescue mission deep within enemy territory with his hands tied behind his back.

"Perhaps we could dispatch our entire army to perform some aggressive reconnaissance—"

"You can't, milord! How can an entire army conduct reconnaissance?! That's no different from a full-on invasion! It is out of the question!"

"Ach, you saw through my clever ruse!"

We dawdled for a time, until a messenger appeared, racing toward us. *Has the enemy moved?*

"Refugees from Nallogi are coming this way, carrying all of their worldly belongings!" the messenger announced. "How shall we respond, my lord?"

"Perfect! Prepare for a daring char—"

The aide interrupted, "Find a representative and bring them here. Make haste!"

"—Right, precisely what I meant to say."

Something extraordinary must have occurred to cause the folk of Nallogi to flee their city. Did the boy break his promise not to attack? No, if he had attacked, there would have been no survivors. We would have to ask the refugees to find out what had happened.

"Get them to safety! Attend to any injured, and prepare carts for the transport of the sick and elderly," I said. "What action has the enemy army taken?"

"None, milord! The people of Nallogi are coming, but they are not moved by the enemy army! They are the movers, not the army! There is movement but no action!"

The report was somewhat incoherent. Such a report would normally deserve a strong rebuke, but when witnessing incomprehensible events, I could not ask that they try to comprehend them.

At the far end of this mountain pass, there was the lad who specialized in making incomprehensible things happen. Any report concerning the actions taken by such a lad would, by necessity, sound like the ravings of a lunatic.

When the great monster stampede occurred, I also received an utterly incomprehensible and impossible-to-understand report, to put it mildly.

"Captain, I leave this to you. Just report back whatever you can."

The only way I could understand such indescribable events would be to witness them with my own eyes. If the boy had achieved his mission and was returning safely, I couldn't continue to dilly-dally and cool my heels any longer—I wouldn't be satisfied until I rendezvoused with him and put this matter to rest.

My retinue and I spurred our horses onward, toward the front. Something was happening there—something of great import!

I addressed a soldier at the front. "There are movements—who is moving? Inform me only of the things you understand, promptly!"

"We are currently securing the safety of the citizens of Nallogi while maintaining our blockade and confirming the details of the present situation, milord. As of now, the situation is too incomprehensible!"

Even at the vanguard of our encampment, nothing made sense. At the very least, I hoped that the boy was responsible for all this tumult. I climbed to the top of a watchtower to see what was happening with my own eyes.

And I saw. *Hmm, incomprehensible indeed.*

If I had to describe my observations, I would say that the mountain pass that connected us to Nallogi had vanished. Yes, this was beyond my comprehension.

In its place, there appeared to be the yawning mouth of a giant cavern. Since the people of Nallogi seemed to emerge from this cavern, it must have been...a tunnel?

But monsters led and protected the refugees emerging from the tunnel—golems. If there were Stone Golems, that meant this tunnel was a dungeon. As if to confirm my suspicions, I witnessed new golems emerge from the tunnel, where they...helped the refugees evacuate? This was spectacularly incomprehensible, indeed.

"Send carts for the sick and elderly!" I commanded, "but don't interfere with the golems!"

"Yes, my lord!"

With my magical telescope, I peered into the tunnel depths. I saw an army of stone soldiers holding back the Nallogi army, protecting the refugees and giving them an avenue of escape.

The golems at the front formed a shield wall out of massive stone shields, while those behind wielded long stone spears in a dense formation, stabbing through the gaps between the front-line golems to keep the Nallogi army at bay. Breaking through the phalanx of golems would be impossible. This dungeon was protected by the mightiest stone warriors. Other Stone Golems protected the refugees as they fled.

Beyond all reason. I wouldn't dare ask anyone to

explain what I saw. I couldn't explain it even after seeing it with my own eyes.

The enemy army didn't move, but there was certainly movement. And that movement didn't involve the enemy army, so the messenger hadn't been wrong. He had given me the correct information, but the information was nonsense. Simply put, something inexplicable was happening.

Even stranger, these dungeon monsters acted on their own. There was no law in the kingdom that prohibited the use of monsters in battle. Therefore, I saw no issue with this outcome.

"Distribute any necessary medicines, prioritize the injured!"

"Yes, my lord! At the moment, there are no injured!"

Our people rushed forth to meet the refugees, but it seemed that they weren't needed. The boy had probably prepared everything in advance, though he only said that he would leave and return... This was the same lad who emerged from the Ultimate Dungeon as it collapsed in on itself and said that he had merely fallen in the dungeon and climbed back up.

"A report, sir! We have arranged for a meeting with a representative chosen by the refugees. Would you like to see him, my lord?"

"Yes, bring him here."

There was nothing more to learn by standing and staring, so perhaps listening to someone who could rationally explain these matters would help.

On the way to the front, I ran into a gang of youths, all with black hair and matching eyes who looked upon the strange sights before them, then pointed and laughed.

It looked like the boy's friends had come to help, but they could not help but laugh at this bizarre, inconceivable tableau. The moment their dark eyes saw what was happening, they understood who was responsible, and laughed uproariously. That meant that the boy was safe. Otherwise, they wouldn't be able to laugh.

LONER LIFE
◆ IN ANOTHER WORLD ◆

DAY 49
EARLY
MORNING

I held an important conference because I didn't have enough
information, and now they're mad at me.

A TUNNEL?

FINALLY, I got the last group of refugees through the tunnel to the frontier. I winced at the bright light— was it now morning?

Speaking of which, I don't remember the last time I had any proper sleep. This time, I didn't even get to engage in any private activities with Miss Armor Rep! I had a big request for her when I returned to town. At least one.

"Outside," said Miss Armor Rep. "Behind us, army... none."

The Stone Golems served as our rear guard, so there was no cause for concern. I kept them in the unbeatable phalanx formation—shields in front and spears in back. I could also make more whenever I wanted, so the enemy had absolutely no hope of breaking through.

The sounds of battle had grown quiet. If they didn't even try to break a phalanx formation in the middle of a retreat, then it couldn't really be called a battle. Arrows were useless against creatures made of stone, after all.

I made, controlled, and commanded these golems with the Ring of the Golem Crafter, so they were essentially puppets made of rocks. They weren't true monsters as they lacked a core, and they didn't die even when broken into pieces. They were simple automata.

"So, when they're smashed to bits, they just freeze in place and collapse into a pile of rubble. Even so, it doesn't look like the army has dealt any damage to the golems yet. The golems are only falling back because I ordered them not to kill anyone. The enemy's a bunch of pushovers!"

As lifeless puppets, they were essentially immortal. Since they weren't technically alive, they couldn't actually die. Without orders, they were simply stone statues. Besides, if they did get demolished, I could line them up into a makeshift barricade with ease.

So of course, there was no damage. Even if there was, they were just a bunch of rocks, anyway.

I could make as many as I wanted so long as I had enough magic power. Only a total idiot would even attempt to fight them.

Even now, the Stalker Girl followed me. She stuffed an entire jam roll into her mouth, and her eyes became dewy with delight.

"So sweet, so delicious...so sweetilicious!"

Sweetilicious, huh?

"You did a good job back there, Miss Armor Rep! Will those guards be okay? I mean in a physical sense, y'know? Mentally speaking, they're definitely broken. They were a bunch of old guys anyway, so as long as you didn't hurt them too bad... Actually, y'know what, who cares about a bunch of middle-aged losers?!"

Miss Armor Rep nodded.

Did that mean they were okay? *If she made the guards train any harder, they would've lost their minds,* I thought.

At least, Mr. Meridad couldn't complain about the results.

"Let's see, we didn't attack the city, the soldiers are physically alive, and I didn't lay a finger on Duke Orc, so I did everything perfectly! I did nothing wrong! No one could accuse me of anything! I'm as innocent as can be!"

Why did Miss Armor Rep and Stalker Girl both glare at me when I said that? That was some serious glare crossfire. They were focus-firing full fusillades of flat looks at me.

Stalker Girl said, "Sure, you literally didn't lay a single finger on him. But you walked all over him, stomped on him, trampled him, kicked him while he was down, made him faint from fear, and left him lying on the ground. I'm pretty sure I made him pee his pants, too."

Well, he was a filthy orc!

"I'll have you know that I made sure to use my feet for all my stomping and trampling! There's no way I would put my hands anywhere near someone so gross, y'know? Besides, I didn't even do it on purpose. He was already lying on the floor? When I took a step, I happened to stomp on an orc, y'know? See, I did nothing wrong! There is always only one innocent! Me! In the name of— what was Grandpa's name again?"

Having proven my innocence, I concluded my closing statement. Why was I still caught in the glare crossfire?

Sure, I left that filthy orc lying unconscious on the ground. I didn't need him for anything, and I certainly didn't want to touch him. I didn't lay a hand on him, so why was everyone nitpicking and complaining? Was it my sex appeal again? I couldn't think of a single alternative explanation. None.

Anyway, I built this long tunnel. I went with the tunnel design because I didn't want to get attacked from above. I didn't even use the Ring of the Dungeon Master to build it, so it wasn't an actual dungeon, so no one could possibly have a reason to yell at me. I wasn't going to tell the enemy army that it wasn't a real dungeon, though. *Let them freak out about a dungeon suddenly emerging in the mountains.*

The fake dungeon was perfect for scaring off those idiots and keeping them out. If I moved too far away, the golems would revert to statues again. That meant I would have to either seal them away behind a wall, or turn them into actual monsters by implanting spellstones into their bodies. I would decide later, when we had time to discuss the matter properly.

After all, the aftermath wasn't my problem to deal with. That was Mr. Meridad's job. I'm sure his people would do their best. *Good luck?*

I wondered what the kingdom would do now that they'd lost their supply of spellstones. The frontier was practically self-sufficient at this point. The wheat and potato harvests meant that the frontier had ample stockpiles of provisions should the worst come to pass. On top of that, I stumbled onto a mother lode of salt in one of the mountain caves, and Villager A's salt reserve never seemed to run out. Metal wasn't a problem either—these mountains were shot through with veins of ore, just waiting to be found. It would've been annoying to deal with them now, so I left them, but at least they were there.

"This tunnel is too long, the other end is so far away, I'm exhausted! Ugh, this sucks!"

As we walked, I remodeled the tunnel into a twisting and branching labyrinth to confuse any who tried to follow. For all intents and purposes, I was cutting the frontier off from the rest of the kingdom. Without trade, we would have to deal with deficits of sugar, textiles, and livestock, but those weren't essentials, so we'd get by just fine for a while. I'd already stockpiled as many of those goods as I could.

Well, if push came to shove, I could always fly over and buy whatever I needed. We would figure something out. The kingdom's economy would collapse long before the frontier. They had no other sources of spellstones. Meanwhile, instead of helping the frontier, the kingdom denied reinforcements and aid, kept the price of spell-stones artificially low, and skimmed as much wealth as they could. We didn't owe them anything.

While I was at it, I made some renovations to the rocky crags surrounding the tunnel. The mountains themselves would become the fortress wall of the fron-tier, with the impassable dungeon-tunnel serving as a castle gate. The frontier's defenses were now impreg-nable, garrisoned with an army of golems—and if that still wasn't enough of a deterrent, I could always turn the tunnel into a true dungeon with the Ring of the Dungeon Master. Given how few soldiers lived on the frontier, using the Ring of the Golem Crafter was the best possible defense.

"Things should be peaceful for a while," I said. "The frontier has never known true peace before, so even if it's only for a short while, this time is important. The town will prosper so long as the economy grows. This isolation can't last forever, but the duke can worry about diplomatic relations, y'know? Just to be clear, don't blame me if anything goes wrong."

The golems had their limitations—they could only follow simple orders. However, there wasn't anything complex about a heavy phalanx, and that was more than adequate. I could make as many as I needed to, so they were a pretty solid army. Plus I could always build a castle at the tunnel mouth if I really wanted peace of mind, safety, tranquility, et cetera.

"Don't you think the kingdom will see this as a rebellion?" asked Stalker Girl. "That would make you an enemy of the kingdom."

I realized then that Stalker Girl was not merely a garden-variety stalker, but a clever stalker trained in the ways of war, economics, and espionage. Not only that, but she was the daughter of the chief of a clan of stalkers—perhaps I should call her Lady Stalker Girl. Currently, she was munching on some french fries. She insisted that they were "salty-licious." She didn't exactly seem like the sharpest tool in the shed.

"Well, it's not like anyone can get through the tunnel now, so we can hardly rebel. If they want to deal with us, they can just come here themselves. Besides, it's the kingdom's fault for letting the neighboring region become so corrupt. And the kingdom has been hostile toward the frontier, right? It might be better to declare independence anyway, right?"

Under the current circumstances, the kingdom lost its advantages, so any negotiations would heavily favor the frontier. Since they couldn't actually enter the frontier anymore, the frontier could decide whether they even wanted to negotiate.

"I'm afraid the kingdom won't let the frontier go without a fight."

"Well, if they didn't want us to declare independence, they shouldn't have exploited us so much. Now that they can't threaten us with an army or cut off our food supply, they'll have to negotiate with us on equal footing. It's all up to the local duke, now. Also, I wish to reiterate that I deny all accusations! I never laid a hand on Duke Orc, which means that no laws were broken. I'm an innocent and upstanding schoolboy, y'know?"

The frontier would probably be all right on its own

now. I had no idea if that was true, though. I mean, I wasn't even a citizen here. No one even told me the name of this place. Or did they? Maybe Meri-something did? Well...Mr. Meripop's people could probably handle it, I guess.

"Goddamn, that was a long trip," I said. "Damn it, I make it all the way through my newly constructed tunnel and the first thing I have to see are a bunch of ugly, old soldiers? Should I scorch their heads?"

It was so bright! I guess the sun had come up a while ago? I was still running a sleep deficit, and a teenage boy sexy-time deficit, too!

"The Class Rep...and everyone," Miss Armor Rep said. "They're waving."

Looking around, I saw the soldiers helping the refugees. Everything was under control.

My classmates were there, too. They were waving at us, so I went over to them. Those idiot meat-nerds were pointing and laughing—I really wanted to burn their hair off.

But I couldn't, because it would be too hard to explain to old Mr. Meridad if I got caught. The people of this world had a lot of difficulty understanding what I told them. Were my words not getting translated correctly? I had to assume they weren't.

The Class Rep ran over to us and said, "It's good to see you again, Haruka-kun! You brought Stalker-chan with you, too! I'm so glad you're safe. Not that we were worried—we knew you'd be fine. But welcome back."

"Th-thank you... I'm back... th-thank you..."

Stalker Girl's eyes filled with tears as the girls patted her on the head. The meat-nerds also wept as they ran around trying to dodge my Hair Whorl attacks. *What an annoying lot.*

"So, we're back, know what I mean? We ran into Stalker Girl and she followed us back. When I found her, an orc was trying some unhygienic sword-based pimple-popping on her, so she started crying and we took her with us. That's basically what happened. Anyway, I have a serious matter to discuss... What do you guys want for breakfast? I don't have anything prepared, and barbecue doesn't seem like a breakfast food, y'know?"

"Are you kidding me?! Barbecue is your serious topic?!"

They got so annoyed with me when I tried to tell them all about the importance of breakfast. *It really is important!* Experts agreed that breakfast was the most important meal of the day!

We ate our barbecue noisily, chatting about this and that. After conferring with the nerds, I built two

Command Golems. I wasn't sure about the name, but I built two of them.

The Command Golems were designed to manufacture and manage the Stone Golems. They had almost no ability to fight, so I didn't really see the point of them.

"That's a golem?" a nerd asked.

"Yup."

"But it's a mountain."

"Yeah?"

"What the heck does the word 'golem' mean to you?"

To create the golems, I embedded level 90 spellstones into the two mountains that flanked the pass. That meant that the cores couldn't be destroyed without some serious digging.

For added security, they could knock interlopers off the mountains using an Earth Needle attack. They specialized in leadership, construction, and repair. Not only that, but because of their Regeneration, no one could excavate tunnels through them—they just repaired themselves. I figured that was sufficient border control.

Now, it was time to go home and sleep. Miss Armor Rep and I would sleep so hard that we wouldn't have any time to sleep! We're going to sleep so long and hard!

LONER LIFE
◆IN ANOTHER WORLD◆

DAY 49
MORNING

People here don't understand time management.

INTERLUDE:
THE WHITE
LOSER INN

AS SOON AS WE GOT BACK to the inn, Haruka-kun said he wasn't getting enough sleep and immediately went to his room. He wore a serene smile on his face, but he had to really concentrate just to use magic. He kept pushing himself so hard—and he was starting to make less sense than usual.

And anyway, he wasn't fooling anyone. Angelica joined him in his room, so I knew they wouldn't get a wink of sleep. No matter how much time he spent in bed, he had no intention of fixing his rotten sleep habits!

"Welcome back, welcome back."

"Helloooahh..." The word slurred into a yawn before Haruka-kun could finish it.

We were in the dining hall. Stalker Girl and the Poster Girl had a tearful reunion. They couldn't even speak;

385

they just hugged each other and cried tears of joy. They looked so happy—they must have thought they would never see each other again.

Once they knew Haruka-kun better, they wouldn't have those worries anymore, because he always kicked tragedy to the curb and stomped all over despair. Haruka-kun didn't let those things fester. He just eliminated them immediately.

He destroyed all tragedy in his midst out of pure selfishness. It was history as soon as it reared its ugly head, simply because he found it irritating.

Tragedy annoyed him, so he utterly destroyed tragedy. That's why the two could meet again. But they'd learn sooner or later.

I wasn't sure what happened on the far side of that dungeon-tunnel. But he must've created that thing to prevent misery, misfortune, and despair from reaching the frontier. He told us it wasn't a real dungeon, but it was plenty dangerous. I doubted if even our group could pass through it and survive.

"It's, like, total overkill!" Shimazaki-san said.

"Haruka-kun and Oda's group are even more terrifying when they join forces."

"Yeah, he puts in way too much effort."

It wasn't an especially tough dungeon, but it was pretty much impossible to get through.

"When Oda-kun, expert on fantasy worlds, and Haruka-kun, the grandmaster of pissing people off, work together..."

"We need to separate them ASAP!" I shouted.

A pseudo-dungeon—in order to get through, you'd have to fight your way past a literally endless supply of golems. Even if you did, Haruka-kun said he set up other traps. Yeah, we wouldn't stand a chance if we went.

They were nasty traps, too, ones that went beyond my wildest nightmares. I only caught a glimpse of this, but he even painted forced-perspective illusions all over the dimly lit dungeon. It's such a devious abuse of trick art!

"Did you see that he also painted an illusory pitfall on the ground! The worst part is that the floor on the other side of the illusion is a real pitfall!"

"That kind of stuff will twist your heart before it twists your ankle!"

Anyone would fall for that kind of trick. Since it was just an optical illusion, it couldn't be detected by abilities that found traps because it was just a painting. Anyone who jumped over the illusion would fall into a real pit. Skills weren't enough to overcome these obstacles, and if you rushed down the wrong corridor, you would just crash into a wall with a tunnel painted on and fall into another pit. The illusions were that convincing.

"The corridors that looked straight are actually curved, and the corridors that looked curved are actually straight."

"The corridors, like, have slight slopes and misleading differences in height, so it's totes impossible not to get lost, right?"

"Haruka-kun said that the Command Golems constantly change the layout of the maze, right?"

"Even Angelica looked impressed when he said that."

"He's far more devious than the former dungeon emperor!"

No matter how strong, without Area Analyze, folks would fall for a trap eventually. This was especially so, given that people from this world had likely never seen an optical illusion before. A full party of level 100+ adventurers with the rare skill, Area Analyze, might have had a chance, but probably not. Even if someone did, they'd have to face that final, impossible challenge. Knowing all the details, I still felt like I couldn't make it.

"Though the guys looked like they were having fun."

They were dying with laughter as they shouted, "Ninja Warrior Elimination Challenge!" and pointed at various traps. It truly was a combination of the two most difficult reality shows. This labyrinth was so cruel that it horrified even a dungeon emperor.

"At least now, I guess, we'll have peace."

You could call it peace, but I thought of it as shutting down the threat of war with the threat of overwhelming force. He turned the surrounding mountains into golems, enslaved them, and entrusted them with the Ring of the Golem Crafter. So, the Command Golems could make unlimited Stone Golems, and the Command Golems themselves were essentially indestructible.

And because of Servitude's experience sharing, the Command Golems continuously received a massive flow of experience points and magic power. And then they got to take advantage of all Haruka-kun's abilities as well. If you really wanted to get to Omui, you'd probably be better off going all the way around the world and through the monster forest located on the other side of the city.

So while there was technically a path to Omui, it seemed clear that no one would ever make it here. Only someone as twisted as Haruka-kun could survive that twisted, trap-infested pseudo-dungeon. And I doubted there was anyone as screwed up as Haruka-kun, so we were safe. If there was someone else like him, this world would have fallen into ruin a long time ago.

The girls complained that they were exhausted.

"There really was no reason to worry about him."

The poster girl and Stalker Girl still held each other

with tears in their eyes. Their interlaced fingers twinkled with a matching pair of glittering friendship rings.

The duke requested Haruka-kun's presence as soon as he woke up, but I doubted he would any time soon. He would've had to be asleep, and from the sounds of aggressive, enthusiastic "sleeping," I don't think he'd had the time!

Everyone fell silent. By this point, we had all reached the max level of Presence Detection, and some of us even got their skill promoted to Presence Sensing. Just glancing in the direction of his room gave us *detailed* information. We were the ones not getting enough sleep!

Nonetheless, we all soon fell asleep. We were exhausted, having followed those two all the way to the neighboring domain out of concern. But unlike them, we were going to have a long, peaceful night's rest! That was the plan, anyway.

My eyes fluttered open as I woke from my nap. Going down to the dining hall, I found a few people already down there having some sort of discussion—did something happen?

"I'm telling you, I want to hang up a series of ropes that you swing on and jump between to get across a pit. Only, some of the ropes aren't fastened, so when you grab them, you fall. Awesome, right?"

"It would be so humiliating if there was a slide that sent you all the way back to the entrance. Your spirit would be totally broken three times over!"

"Wouldn't that be enough, then? Finding an exit in a room full of secret doors, only to run into a wall and realize it's fake is already enough to break your spirit!"

"That fake door trick sure is evil. Some are paintings and some are traps, so you'd never be able to escape!"

"And your feet keep stumbling on things, slipping, and falling... He's truly heartless!"

Sounded like everyone was talking about the pseudo-dungeon. Now they were coming up with and discussing their own trap ideas.

"Good morning," I said. "You all realize that you don't want to go in there, right? Many of the traps are designed to break your gear. Some of them can even make your rations spoil! It's a waste of equipment. The girls should be especially cautious, because there are traps that will melt your clothes along with your equipment. Even if you survived, you might end up trapped inside."

"Gross!" the girls shouted.

"Let's go, bros!" said Kakizaki-kun. "We gotta check it out!"

The dungeon was crafty, diabolical, and horny—a perfect reflection of its creator.

An evil person designed that dungeon, so of course it was an evil place. It'd break your spirit before it broke your sword. It'd erode your sanity and break down your morals, too.

Anyone who managed to escape would come out a totally different person. It would turn even the kindest person into a complete misanthrope. After all, if the person who made that dungeon was a human, what did they say about humanity?

More students gradually woke up, joined the conversation, and tossed their own trap ideas into the pot.

"And that's the nastiest part!"

"No way, dude, it's gotta be that one!"

"But what about—"

"That, that, that, and that!"

For some reason everyone liked the dungeon, but no one would dare go there.

A popular attraction with no tourists. Everyone just wanted to come up with their own trap ideas. *If you keep thinking like that, you'll transform into Haruka-kun!*

"Good moooorning," he sang. "Good afternoon? I'm awake! I need to sleep! But I'm also hungry, y'know?"

The villain finally woke up, but he still looked exhausted.

The reason never changed. *There is always only one culprit! Him!*

"Good morning, Haruka-kun," I said. "The duke's aide came with a summons for you, but you were still asleep. He looked even more exhausted than you."

Duke Omui was a good man—a wise and benevolent ruler beloved by his people. However, all his soldiers and his subjects were worried about him. For generations, the lords of Omui fought to protect their people, and often perished fighting the monsters of the forest.

The same story played out down the generations. Thus, the people lamented the state their duke was in, their worry born from devotion. This was truly a kind place. The messenger looked like he was really struggling, though.

"Food comes first! The first item on my agenda! I'm starving, y'know? I've already decided on the menu! I found these fruits that taste like tomatoes, so I'm going to make omurice, got it? I mean, I'll be using mystery eggs and meat from mystery fowl, but that's the plan."

The dining hall erupted into pandemonium. Everyone was yelling and stamping their feet, chanting, "Omurice! Omurice! Omurice..."

How did this chant get started? Where did all this energy come from? I decided to join in, though. It was omurice, after all! *Omurice! Omurice!*

The commotion woke the rest of our class up and everyone started to line up. Weary eyes were now wide open. Angelica had never had omurice before, so she looked around curiously. Soon, she would understand. She would know why we made such a fuss over omurice.

"Okay, it's done! All you can eat, y'know? Bon appetit, or whatever!"

There was a moment of silence followed by the thunderous roar of, "Let's eat!"

Within seconds, the omurice chant was replaced with the sounds of nostalgic sobs around mouthfuls of egg. *This tastes so good!* We felt like we were home again.

"A-amazing!"

"Of course it is! It's omurice!"

"I can't believe I'm actually eating omurice."

"I'm so happy!"

"Haruka, seconds please!"

"Me, too!"

Tears streamed down our cheeks as we devoured platefuls of omurice. Omurice was not merely delicious—it was the taste of home.

Now blissfully full, we basked in the lingering aftertaste of omurice. Angelica, the poster girl, and Stalker Girl radiated joy, having tasted omurice for the first time.

But a lecture was still in order.

"Explain yourself!" the girls all shouted, pointing at the culprit.

Stalker Girl was literally a hair's breadth away from getting stabbed. She had actually lost a few strands of hair, that's how close it was. Haruka-kun got there in the nick of time, but before he reached her, he had stopped to buy tomatoes on the way.

Indeed, that was why he almost didn't make it. He found a village that grew tomato-like plants. The criminal had earned this lecture.

"No, it's fine. I knew I was going to make it in time, y'know? If flying wasn't fast enough, I'd just flash over, know what I mean? Just a quick flash, and I was there. I even saved her zits! Because I knew I couldn't make it, I could reach her in the nick of time, so I had plenty of time! I'm not sure if saving her acne's something I should be proud about, but y'know? Since the flash gave me time, it paid off in the end, right? We had omurice with tomato-like ketchup! How could you accuse omurice?!"

Lecture time. The poster girl was furious—I could see a vein throbbing in her forehead. She was so incensed that she started flapping both of her hands around. She apparently had an angry mysterious dance, too.

"Were you going to make it or not?!"

"Omurice is innocent. *You're* the guilty one!"

We chanted, "Omurice: delicious! Haruka: guilty!"

So then—he teleported. He used the prohibited magic of teleportation—of course we needed to lecture him! He could have died! Teleport was a dangerous spell that he refused to use under any circumstances. Who knew what could have happened! He refused to use Teleport even when he was trapped in the Ultimate Dungeon!

Even when he was training, he never teleported further than five feet, and that took all his concentration in a place with no obstacles. Yet, this time, he teleported *inside* the castle! Why was he always so reckless?

Halfway there, he realized that he couldn't make it unless he used Teleport. He had given Stalker Girl a spellstone ring, so he could track the coordinates of that ring. Since he was going to end up teleporting in any case, that meant he could take his sweet time to buy some quasi-tomatoes.

The culprit claimed that he was only exercising basic time management skills. He showed no remorse! That only meant I would scold him more! If he didn't understand the consequences of his actions, then we need only unleash the furious dance of the poster girl upon him once again!

Seriously, what is up with that dance? She was crying and wildly gesticulating her arms in some sort of bizarre dance. She was so angry, she danced at Haruka-kun. That was how concerned she was for the safety of Stalker Girl.

Look how much you made her cry, Haruka-kun. Are you reflecting on your actions now?

LONER LIFE
◆IN ANOTHER WORLD◆

Maybe I ought to make a "now hiring" pamphlet for a sexy female spy.

"LOOK AT THE REPORT! It says he sliced through heaven and earth, annihilated man-eating fiends, destroyed demons and sorcerers, and treated the masses as dirt beneath his feet."

"Well, knowing him, it was more likely that he deceived both heaven and earth, obliterated his free time, kicked reason to the curb, and disdained all common sense."

They were saying some pretty hurtful things about me. They claimed that the hero who conquered the Ultimate Dungeon was a slacker who liked to waste his time. That made no sense!

"That's not right," said Vice Rep B. "I would say he carved through floors and ceilings, sent monsters plummeting to their deaths, tricked the dungeon emperor, and clambered up so many flights of stairs. That's what actually happened."

H-hang on, there was no trickery involved! My reputation was garbage! I only enthralled her, I didn't trick her, I swear!

"According to the report from the capital, he is a giant man with gentle eyes. Who told them *that*?"

"They must've misheard. He's more like a giant pain in the ass with the eyes of a pervert."

"Or maybe a giant pervert with guilty eyes? Remember that time he went all crazy eyes, and it caused an incident at the guild hall? That must be how the rumor started!"

Why did there have to be so many about my eyes? *What's wrong with saying I have gentle eyes?* Someone was crying here, and it was me!

"Listen to this part: apparently there's a rumor of an Arch Sorcerer dressed in black known as the Croquette Apostle."

"I can't believe we finally found something true in this report. The Croquette Apostle is legit, at least."

"Huh? Wait, the logo of that food cart, The Black-Hooded Croquette, is supposed to be Haruka-kun?!"

"I heard about this! It was something like...there was this poor village, right? So, anyway, they were so poor, and no one would help them until this sorcerer in a black hood showed up, saved the day, and taught them how to make delicious croquettes! The guy who runs that croquette cart told me all about it—it was a real sob story.

Apparently, the people in town pray to this black mage every morning and every night. Doesn't seem to bring them any benefit, though."

If that's the case, then his piety has been rewarded! Sardine heads are rich in calcium, which makes their croquettes extremely beneficial! It totally brought them a benefit!

"I don't think the figurehead of their religion benefits anyone. It's more like he's at the center of every disaster!"

"Praying to him might work if only the approaching disasters were scared of *him*!"

We were supposed to be investigating the information gathered by Stalker Girl's clan, but this just turned into a competition to see who could roast me the hardest! They should study these reports, not workshop their list of disses!

Yeah, this was supposed to be a meeting on the results of her investigation, but instead it had turned into a straight-up roast? *I'll just pretend like none of this is happening and burn those idiot nerds later!*

"Look, it says that he struck fear into the heart of a dungeon emperor with but a single glance. That's actually not too far off, right?"

"Oh, yeah, he totally made the dungeon emperor tremble and cry, right? Angelica said it was the scariest experience of her life. That's actually pretty accurate!"

That's it, the dungeon emperor is getting her punishment tonight! Oh, yes, I'll punish her with this and that... I'll find a suitable punishment for every inch of her body! I'll work harder than ever before!

"'A lucky boy that fell into the dungeon only to find treasure.' It sounds like a fairy tale, but that's actually the most accurate part here?"

"Yeah, although the reality wasn't anything like a fairy tale!"

They continued to read Stalker Girl's report, and they continued to crush my ego. *Yeah, this is bullying!*

Apparently, Stalker Girl's clan were originally meant to be spies working for the people of the frontier, but when the neighboring region betrayed the frontier, her family was held hostage and forced to work for the traitors instead.

In the end, that's why her entire clan had rebelled and helped evacuate the people of that city to the frontier. Her whole clan was stupidly willing to die, but Mr. Meridad gave them an earful about their risky behavior, so it all worked out.

She said, "My clan begged Duke Meropapa Sim Omui for a chance to atone for our betrayal by sacrificing ourselves on the front lines, but he wouldn't hear of it.

Raising his voice, he said, 'What possible sin can there be in protecting your family and your people? If it is a sin, it is one that the whole duchy of Omui bears as well. It is a crime that stains my hands as well. However, if you had abandoned your family and come to the frontier expecting help, I would have cut you down where you stood. Here on the frontier, we take pride in protecting our loved ones.' He didn't punish us. Instead, he called us traitors, praised us for a job well done, and asked if we would serve Omui from now on. My entire clan wept after his speech."

Even Stalker Girl broke down crying by the end of her telling. Who was this "Duke Omoi" she described? I had never met anyone here capable of such stirring words. Anyone who could say something like that must be a real pain in the ass to deal with.

"I'm just relieved that no assassins relying on this report would ever be able to find or recognize Haruka-kun," the Class Rep said.

"So long as he doesn't wander around with his hood up and croquettes in his hands, no one will recognize him. Just the comment about gentle eyes is enough to throw anyone off the scent."

"The other reports are even worse—they say he wears jet-black armor and wields a massive two-handed sword, or that he has long blond hair and piercing, almond-shaped eyes. One of them even describes him as a silent and thoughtful man covered in scars. They're all completely wrong."

"Don't assassins typically attack in the middle of the night, when normal people are asleep? Just think how much danger the assassins would be in if they broke in while Haruka-kun and Angelica were...preoccupied!"

"In *so* many ways!"

"The assassin might get kidnapped!"

"He'd definitely regret interrupting!"

Hey! If my assassin were a sexy female spy, she'd be more than welcome to join! Should I put a sign outside the inn with directions to my room?

What could I say, no teenage boy could resist the allure of a sexy spy. Not that I had any experience with that. Maybe I should post some 'now hiring' flyers around town to recruit a femme fatale. *How do I keep getting more side gigs?*

"Finally, though this is unconfirmed, it seems that the royal family is after the treasure of the dungeon king from the Ultimate Dungeon," Stalker Girl said. "We need to watch out for thieves, as well."

"Ah, why bother?" the girls all sighed.

What would thieves want with me? *Please don't tell*

me they want to steal Miss Armor Rep?! She wore all the greatest treasures of her dungeon already, not to mention being the dungeon emperor herself! She was an invincible deathtrap for any fools who would dare to kidnap her. They would be better off finding and conquering a dungeon themselves—it would be much faster and much, *much* easier.

"In addition, there are reports that first-rate adventurers and talented mercenaries are headed in this direction," Stalker Girl said. "We're not sure if their destination is the frontier, but we have multiple confirmed sightings."

"Oh no, the Most Extreme Pseudo-dungeon Elimination Challengers have appeared!"

"They have no idea what they're getting into!"

"Those poor fools..."

They would never make it through. Even if they did, their equipment would get destroyed. It was a foolproof trap dungeon, far too much for the average mercenary. Adventurers were headed here, too?

"The adventurers might do better than the mercenaries," said Shield Girl. "They could get pretty far, maybe even set a distance record!"

"I don't think they'd have much fun if all they have to show for their trouble is a new record," the Class Rep said. "Knowing that getting through the whole dungeon is impossible, I only feel more sorry for them. They'll end up losing their equipment!"

It was better to keep them alive, if only so that they could spread word of the dangers.

"It has to be that way, though. The dungeon is a way more effective deterrent if it keeps them alive but destroys their equipment, y'know? They can't fight without weapons, and when they go back where they came from, they can warn others that the dungeon destroys weapons and armor. Eventually, no one will want to enter. And if new adventurers are hired anyway, the next batch would have to get paid enough to afford even high-tier equipment, and their benefactors will eventually go bankrupt! It's genius!" I said.

Losing weapons would be a massive blow to any army, and while it would only be a minor nuisance at first for adventurers, they wouldn't tolerate having their equipment destroyed over and over without someone else footing the bill.

My classmates even gave me a thick report of trap concepts for the pseudo-dungeon. For some reason, a whole section was devoted to sexy traps.

Must've been from the nerds, I thought, and decided to discuss the matter with them at length. One of them was a sticky trap that dissolved clothing and unleashed a tentacled monster when it was triggered. It was a heart-breaking work of staggering genius! This was truly worthy of discussion.

Besides, changing the traps out once in a while would be a great way to demoralize adventurers and make them give up. Losing their hard-earned equipment was probably enough, but I shouldn't be overconfident. My next major concern was sourcing some tentacle monsters.

Since no one could come to the frontier, we could focus on internal affairs. As long as we had peace, we could focus on conquering more dungeons and improving the local economy. The population wouldn't increase overnight, but we did get all those refugees, and the frontier was rich with spellstones, so there was plenty of room for industrial growth.

Until recently, poverty and labor shortages made it impossible for true commercial enterprise to develop on the frontier. In the current climate, the division of labor of a modern economy should begin to develop on its own, and if development was going too slow, I could just speed things up by by distributing a few magic tools of my own making.

Once goods and money began to circulate, the future of the town and the surrounding hamlets and villages would finally be secured. I would finally be able to quit my many unpaid side jobs! I could turn my attention to the one and only thing teenage boys truly cared about!

We would begin raiding another dungeon tomorrow. They were a threat to safety and progress, after all. Besides, there was always the possibility that I'd find something as useful as the Ring of the Golem Crafter. *I'm sure to find my sex appeal in one of these dungeons, too!* It had to be *somewhere* in this world, right? It had to be, right?

We spent the rest of the night exchanging intel on nearby dungeons, debating party composition, and working out dungeon strategies.

So far, the only conquered dungeon was the golem one the student council and I dealt with. The other groups had plateaued around the 40th floor. It was probably tough to get past that point with only a single party. We discussed various problems with individual skills, and their drawbacks, strengths, and weaknesses.

Finally, we discussed formations and settled on party assignments over dinner. It was well past midnight, so I served something that suited the hour: french fries with ketchup.

"How dare you feed girls fried food right before bedtime!" the girls shouted.

They somehow managed to admonish me while stuffing their faces with fries. How was that my fault? Whatever, I made some cash.

Now it was seriously late at night, so we concluded the meeting, and everyone went back to their rooms.

As for me, it was time for my side hustle, and it was time for round 2! That's right, the decisive second round in a battle where no teen boy would ever accept defeat!

Maybe a nice, long bath followed by the main event: the Nude Battle of the Bedroom. *Activate woodpecker thrusting mode—the thrilling late-night adventures of high school boys!*

◆ AFTERWORD ◆

To some of you, nice to meet you, but to the vast majority, welcome back—after much delay and fuss, at last, Volume 3! (Phew.)

This volume took me a long time to complete. So thank you very much for picking it up.

My noble managing editor, Y-san, always sends me the notice and schedule regarding the next volume of this series. But this was the first time that I looked at the schedule and went, "Are you kidding me?!"

In the end, I caused everyone a fair bit of trouble. Thank you, booota-sama, for the wonderful drawings. And thank you, Saku Enomaru-sama, for your marvelous illustrations as well. I hope we can continue to work together. You're in for a rough ride, but I can assure you that it's all completely Y-san's fault (obviously!).

411

Some of you may think I bully my editor, but I swear to you: for the first two volumes, they took such a razor to my draft that by the time they were done with it, they had leftover pages! "I went a bit overboard, so you can write an afterword," they said, with an innocent smile on their face! Who's the bully now?

And I do believe they owe me a few more apologies regarding this volume, too—*ahem, ahem!* Never mind! I would like to thank them and everyone else from the bottom of my heart—Managing Editor Y-sama, who is always helping me out, and Ouraidou-sama, whom I've caused more than enough trouble. Not to mention Bibi-sama, who assisted with the manga adaptation of the series and whom I haven't had the pleasure of meeting in person due to distance, and Saku Enomaru-sama—thank you again for your wonderful drawings.

I also offer my deep appreciation to everyone who has bought paperback copies of my books as well as those who have been reading online.

It's common knowledge online at this point that my novels rank #1 in the world for most frequent typos. So I constantly get a lot of typo notifications from people all over the internet. It's a real luxury getting to choose which typo to address on any given day. But seriously, thanks for letting me know! (Phew.)

Now that I have a typo-checking function installed, I don't suffer from the same problem. But before I had it, Yuki-sama actually made a "Typo-Squasher" website for adjusting all my errors. Thank you, Yuki-sama. You seriously saved me, especially with this volume.

Also, I'd like to thank everyone for giving their impressions and feedback. All the comments I received were really useful. They widened my perspective—and gave me a ton of great joke ideas. Thank you, thank you, thank you!

Even though I had never written anything before this series—I avoided sending texts and emails, that's how little I wrote, much less a novel—I succumbed to temptation and posted my novel online under the assumption that no one would read it anyway. I can hardly believe how much support and feedback I've received. When I realized that people were actually reading it (and trust me, I still don't understand why), I got help from so many different people, and I was eventually able to make the series a success. I couldn't thank you all more.

Thank you also to Overlap-sama. My novel had become a topic online by the time I was on the third volume, so I was excited when I received an email from what I assumed to be suspicious fraudsters offering to publish my novel in bookstores. Well, it turns out they were very real. Except for Y-san, who of course was a fraudster all along. (I jest, I jest.)

As the story progresses and the promises and the progress pile up, I still sometimes can't believe that it's all real.

So that's why I've ruined my whole story by making the gallant indomitable princess-saving hero a contrary, bashful, and deceptive liar. Well, I figure people who have gotten to the third volume probably understand what I'm doing here, but I'd like to apologize to all of you as well. That's just who my protagonist is.

Natsume Soseki is famous for translating the English sentence, "I love you," into "The moon is beautiful, isn't it?" in Japanese. But I think he has a point. When I read international fantasy novels, there are a ton of scenes that I just can't see flying with a Japanese audience. That's how I've ended up with this kind of hot-blooded protagonist. And, of course, I mean "hot-blooded" in the worst possible way: an extremely shy, stubborn person who can't tell the truth even if he wants to, and always seems to be a background character even in his most heroic moments. He's the strongest weakling there is.

I started to think it would be nice to write a character like that—someone so ridiculous, so unreasonable, so disastrous and deceptive and roundabout—and the heroines alongside him, who have reluctantly accepted him as he is. But the more I wrote his character, the more ridiculous it became, and the more I started getting deceived and pulled around by him myself. But now, at last, I've finished the third volume.

I once again offer heartfelt thanks to everyone who helped make this book a reality, and to everyone who reads it.

Now, to those of you who are wondering why this afterword is so long.

You are correct. Because this time, the scoundrel (Y) went overboard with the edits and left a whole *five* extra pages at the end! "Go crazy on the afterword," they said. I don't think it's typical to roast your editor for the whole internet to see, but...what can I say. They bullied me first.

That's just how it goes, and I hope you don't mind coming along for the ride.